BETTE

"Lyn Cote weaves a powerful story of love, secrets, betrayal, and passion during the tumultuous years of World War II. Her unique blend of storytelling and dynamic characters brings this era of history to life."

—DiAnn Mills, author of *When the Lion Roars*

"Lyn Cote lured me into realistic, gripping, and sometimes heart-wrenching encounters with an era that has left an indelible mark on both history and human hearts. BETTE is truly unforgettable."

—Kathy Herman, author of the Baxter series and *A Shred of Evidence*

"Lyn Cote's craftsmanship shines in BETTE. Her beautiful plotting includes textured settings that jet you around the world into the lives of characters so real we think we know them. Add a heroine we can all admire, and once again the ladies of Ivy Manor grab hold of your heart and hang on."

—Lois Richer, author of *Shadowed Secrets*

CHLOE

"Will steal your heart . . . With her customary high-quality plotting, Lyn Cote has brought to life [a] long overlooked period of United States history. Appealing characterizations exemplify the pathos, despair, and courage of post–WWI America."

—Irene Brand, award-winning author of *Where Morning Dawns* and *The Hills Are Calling*

more . . .

"Like finding the missing piece of a favorite puzzle . . . What a treasure! A fresh presentation of a world I didn't know. I loved this page-turner!"

—Patt Marr, award-winning author of *Angel in Disguise*

"[A] rich journey . . . Meticulous historical detail and vivid characters . . . a treat for the reader."

—Marta Perry, author of *Her Only Hero*

"A romance of epic proportions, absorbing and satisfying, that never lets you forget how the Father takes you just as you are and that His love can bring you home from the farthest journey. Cote has written a winner. You will remember this heroine long after the final page is turned."

—Deborah Bedford, author of
A Morning Like This and *If I Had You*

"A heart-warming tale . . . A compelling story driven by equally compelling characters"

—Valerie Hansen, author of *Samantha's Gift*

"Lyn Cote hooked me from the very beginning, then expertly reeled me across the pages . . . Pages full of romance, suspense, heartbreak, forgiveness, acceptance, and, ultimately, a satisfying ending."

—Slvia Bambola, author of
Waters of Marah and *Return to Appleton*

"Lyn Cote's return to historical fiction is a delight! CHLOE is lyrically written, enhancing a plot that's teeming with zigs and zags. Compelling characters take up on a journey toward happiness reached only by plumbing the depths of despair. This one's a keeper!"

—Lois Richer, author of *Shadowed Secrets*

The Women of Ivy Manor
Book Two

Bette

A Novel

LYN COTE

WARNER
Faith ®

NEW YORK BOSTON NASHVILLE

Copyright © 2005 by Lyn Cote

Warner Faith
Time Warner Book Group
1271 Avenue of the Americas, New York, NY 10020
Visit our Web site at www.warnerfaith.com

Printed in the United States of America
First Warner Faith printing: September 2005
10 9 8 7 6 5 4 3 2 1

Library of Congress Cataloging-in-Publication Data
Cote, Lyn.
   Bette / Lyn Cote.
      p. cm. — (The women of Ivy Manor ; bk. 2)
   Summary: "A woman coming of age during World War II becomes
involved in anti-Nazi espionage"—Provided by publisher.
   ISBN 0-446-69435-5
   1. Young women—Fiction. 2. Women spies—Fiction. 3. Anti-Nazi
movement—Fiction. 4. World War, 1939-1945—Fiction. I. Title.
PS3553.O76378B48 2005
813'.54—dc22   2005010471

To my father, Robert E. May,
who served in North Africa, Italy, and France,
and who received the Silver Star and the Purple Heart,
among other commendations.

To my father-in-law, Orville "Jim" Cote, who served
on the USS Bunker Hill.

To my uncle Henry Brennan, an army medic
who spent the war interned
in a Japanese POW camp in the Philippines and
who was commended officially
for saving the lives of many of his fellow prisoners.

To my uncle William J. Baker,
who survived the Battle of the Bulge.

And to my uncle Aladdin Jaremus,
and my husband's uncle Richard Cote,
who also bravely served their country.

He hideth my soul in the cleft of a rock
that shadows a dry thirsty land.
He hideth my life in the depths of His love
and covers me there with His hand.

—Fanny Crosby

Part One

CHAPTER ONE

Tidewater, Maryland, April 1936

*B*ette Leigh screamed herself awake. She jerked up in her bed. A feeble glow outside her window pierced the predawn gray. Her heart pounded hard and fast. She fought for air. *What-what happened?*

A blast exploded outside.

Gretel's scream joined hers. *"Was ist los?"*

Bette heard the sound of bare feet pelting down the hardwood hallway and then down the steps. Her mother's voice called out to her stepfather, "Roarke, wait! Get your gun first!"

Bette tossed back the covers and nearly landed on Gretel in the trundle bed below her. "Come on!" She grabbed her friend's hand and dragged her from their bedroom. Her mother, Chloe, was before them, racing down the stairs to the foyer. "Mother!" Bette screeched, afraid her mother might run outside into danger.

"Wait!" Chloe held up both hands to stop them. Bette

and Gretel halted near the middle of the staircase, both winded and panting.

Roarke hurried from the rear of the house, his rifle in his good hand. "All of you stay in here till I see what's out there." He threw open the door. Cold damp air rushed in and they all saw it at once.

A cross burned on their wide front lawn.

Bette gasped so sharply her tongue slammed against the back of her mouth, nearly making her gag.

"What is it?" Gretel repeated in a hollow voice.

Shock and fear shimmered through Bette. She tightened her grip on Gretel's hand. "It's the Klan," she whispered.

At this, Gretel pressed herself close to Bette as if seeking refuge. "Why? Oh, why?"

Roarke stalked outside.

"No, Roarke, they might—" Chloe's voice was overwhelmed by a blast from her husband's rifle.

"Come out, you lousy cowards!" he roared. "Show yourselves and face me like men!"

Silent night was the only response.

"Cowards!" he shouted. He stalked to the cross and, using the butt of his rifle, knocked it to the ground. It sizzled in the early morning dew. Bette knew she'd never forget the sound, a hissing like a poisonous snake. A snake poised to strike them.

He turned back to the house. "They shot out the parlor window." He marched onto the white-pillared porch and ripped off a paper nailed to the doorframe.

Chloe joined him in the open doorway. "What is it?"

He shoved it into her hands. "Garbage."

Mad to find out what the paper said, Bette tugged Gretel

down the steps. She peered over her mother's shoulder and glimpsed the brief note. In large, clumsy capitals, it read: "Get rid of the Jew Girl."

"What do you think about what happened last night at Bette Leigh's?"

Bette froze where she stood behind the partition in the chemistry lab of the Croftown High School. She recognized the malicious voice as that belonging to a fellow senior named Mary.

Girlish snickering. "It's about time." It was Mary's chum, Ruth; the two led a nasty clique of girls at school.

"My daddy," Mary continued with scorn, "says someone had to set the McCaslins straight. That Jew girl should have stayed in Germany where she belongs."

The partition hid Bette from their view, letting them feel free to spew their venom. What was worse was that Bette wasn't alone. She and the handsome new transfer student, Curtis Sinclair, had been asked to wash up the glass instruments after the final chemistry class. Even worse, Gretel—the target of all this ridicule—sat hunched on a lab stool beside them, hearing everything. Her expression showed that each word pierced her like thorns.

Despite the situation, Bette felt the hair on the back of her neck prickle with an awareness of Curt. Ever since he'd first arrived at the school, she had been fascinated with him; he was different than any other boy here, and she'd found herself daydreaming about him more than once. And now she stood side by side with this young man, unseen, but able to hear every horrible word spoken about her best friend. She wondered what he was thinking.

"Well, my mother said this all started when Miss Chloe ran off and married that doughboy like she did." Ruth sounded self-righteous. "She said Miss Chloe come back from New York City with plenty of strange ideas."

Bette's hands trembled as she washed the glass tubes in the small sink. Though she tried to make no noise, they clinked softly. The enforced quiet maddened her. She wanted to explode around the partition and confront them. But Gretel looked ready to faint. Would putting a stop to this gossip session help Gretel or make things worse for her?

This morning, someone—maybe a son of one of the cross-burners—had painted a swastika on Gretel's locker. Gretel had withdrawn further at this. Bette wanted to shake someone, scream her outrage. Instead, she held her peace—for Gretel's sake. *Let them leave,* she thought now. *Don't let them know that we heard their poison.*

"A Jew girl, staying at Ivy Manor," Mary snapped. "Daddy says Miss Chloe's ancestors are spinning in their graves."

"Well, the whole family is strange. Adopting kids from an orphanage," Ruth said. "No decent family does that."

"Well, Jamie McCaslin may be an orphan, but he'll inherit half a bank, and half a bank is good enough for me," Mary said slyly. "And he's dreamy."

Brisk footsteps ended the talk. "Why are you two girls loitering here?" the chemistry teacher's deep voice demanded.

"I wanted to ask you a question about the homework, sir," Mary replied in a butter-will-melt-in-my-mouth tone. She was nothing if not quick on her feet.

"Just a moment." The teacher raised his voice. "Miss Mc-Caslin and Mr. Sinclair, are you still back there?"

Bette couldn't find her voice. She rinsed the last slippery tube and handed it to Curt to dry. Now they had to walk out there and face them. Dry-mouthed, she reached out for Gretel and urged her off the lab stool. She couldn't find words to comfort her friend.

Curt looked at the two of them as he efficiently dried the last vial. "We've just finished, sir," he replied.

Bette envied him his calmness. She wiped her hands on the white cloth beside the little sink and turned to pick up her textbooks. She felt as though all her joints had rusted.

Then Curt touched her arm. Electricity shot through her. No young man had ever touched her like that—so respectful yet so intimate. "Shall we go?" He motioned her and Gretel to go first.

Her chin went up. *I'm a Carlyle of Ivy Manor, and a Mc-Caslin by adoption.* Her mother had taught her this litany when she was a child and came home crying from grade school taunts. Of course, she usually couldn't help adding, *But why can't my family be like other families?*

Curt kept his hand just under her elbow, causing her to buzz with a special awareness of him. He nodded, encouraging her.

With Gretel right behind her, Bette stepped out from behind the partition. She did not want to face Mary and Ruth, but her mother had always told her, "Honey, look them straight in the eye. That'll make them mad as fire."

So she stared into her classmates' eyes—two girls who'd tormented her all her childhood, even though their families weren't perfect either. Seeing their expressions, she knew they were embarrassed Curt had overheard their gossip and that somehow they would try to make her pay for their indiscretion.

"Thank you, Miss McCaslin, Mr. Sinclair." The teacher smiled.

She merely nodded at the teacher's thank-you. And, her spine as stiff as a broom handle, she led Gretel out into the hall. Curt stayed right with them, his hand on her arm. The gesture was both tender and devastating. She spared him a quick look as they made their way down the hall. Curt Sinclair was her opposite. Only a few inches taller than Bette, he had blond hair to her black, blue eyes to her gray. And he dressed sharp. She didn't. She wondered, what did he think of what he'd heard? Did he merely think chivalry called for him to protect them?

The three of them stopped at the end of the corridor and only then did he let go of her arm. Gretel stayed right beside Bette, saying nothing. Clutching her books to her chest as a shield, Bette looked down at her scuffed Oxfords. *Please don't say anything about the gossip. Please don't.*

"Do you need a ride home?" Curt asked politely. "My father loaned me his car today." He smiled and Bette noticed that his blond hair was parted on the side and combed back smoothly like Humphrey Bogart.

"We always walk to the bank and ride home with my stepfather." Momentarily entranced, she detected traces of golden beard on his cleft chin. She thought of running a finger over it and experienced a rush of sensation that shook her. For a second, all she could think of was Curt and his nearness. Then the horror of the past few minutes and the early morning attack surged back. She shook with it.

"I think it would be best if I drove you to the bank today," Curt said.

So he had heard about the cross. Bette wondered what he thought about it. But didn't his gallant actions give his opinion?

"*Danke*," Gretel murmured, swishing her long dark braids over the shoulders of her plain navy-blue dress. "*Danke.*"

Bette managed to nod before Curt hustled them down the staircase, whistling. The sound did things to the back of her neck. The three of them were passing the glass-encased bulletin board next to the principal's office when Bette caught sight of something pinned there and nearly stopped in her tracks. *No!*

Later on, Bette sat at the kitchen table at Ivy Manor and set her worn Oxford shoe on a flattened cereal box. Her mind buzzed with ideas of what to do about the notice she'd seen on the bulletin board. But she made herself carefully trace the outline of the shoe's sole onto the cardboard. Gretel sat across from her doing the same to Bette's other shoe. Bette's mother and the housekeeper, Jerusha, were chatting at the stove about someone's new baby as if last night hadn't happened. The radio could be heard from the parlor, playing "I'm Going to Sit Right Down and Write Myself a Letter."

The image of the flaming cross kept popping into Bette's mind, along with the nasty words she'd overheard at school, like a bad taste in her mouth. She wanted to take her mother aside and pour out the awful, hateful gossip and then curl up in her lap. But that was what she'd done as a child.

I'm nearly a woman now. I'm eighteen and I'll graduate

high school in a month. I will only hurt Gretel and Mother if I repeat the garbage I heard. That's what her stepfather always called gossip—garbage. What should she say to Gretel? Not a word about the chemistry lab had been spoken between them. And what could she do about the new notice on the bulletin board? Mary could be viciously jealous and this would make Bette a prime target.

A knock came at the back door. Even that caused a spurt of fear. But Bette stood up as calmly as she could manage and answered it. One of their sharecroppers stood with his sweat-stained hat in his dark hands.

"Is Miz Chloe home, please?"

"Certainly. Please step in. Mother?" Bette walked back to the table.

Her mother went to greet the man. "Samuel, what can I do for you?"

Bette looked over her shoulder, watching the interaction between the bowing, ragged sharecropper and her kind, neat-as-a-pin mother. Bette both liked and disliked her mother's easy way with people. Her mother was good to everyone, whether white or black, rich or poor. Because of this, people respected her mother. But they also gossiped endlessly about her. It didn't make sense.

For a moment, Bette let herself imagine the kind of family she herself wanted in the future: a husband and four children. A small house in a small city. She would dress nicely and have the neighbor ladies over for coffee . . .

Bette heard her mother close the back door and walk up behind her. She began cutting out the cardboard inserts for her shoes. Chloe stopped and patted her on the shoulder. "New shoes for you. Very soon. Thanks for being so patient."

"It's all right, Mother. I don't mind." Bette felt guilty for imagining a life so different from her parents. They were good people. Even though her stepfather was the president of the local bank, times were still hard. So many people needed help and farm prices were below rock-bottom. No doubt Mary and Ruth's parents didn't bother themselves about whether the A.M.E. reverend's son needed costly insulin injections to live, but her mother and stepfather did.

Besides, why should I even be thinking about having my own family? I'm not beautiful like Mother. Not even pretty new shoes and a dress would make Curt Sinclair notice me. Then she recalled his light touch under her elbow and her heart pounded all over again.

Her two little brothers, Rory and Thompson burst in, slamming the back door behind them. "Mom! Mom!" the two shouted in breathless unison.

Chloe turned and bent down and, catching a body in each arm, hugged them. The boys' heads came only as high as her waist. "I was wondering when you'd decide to come home. Which one of you fell in the creek today?"

"We didn't go to the creek!" Rory, who was fair like Chloe, announced in his boyish soprano. "We went to see Mr. Granger's horses."

In the background, the news came onto the radio. A broadcaster announced in a smooth professional voice, "Today Secretary of State Cordell Hull again urged that the US aid Polish Jews. Labor chiefs join 350,000 American Jews in asking for a protest to Warsaw persecution."

Bette watched a shadow pass over Gretel's face. The news from Europe was never good if it was about Jews.

"Mr. Granger, he let us comb the horses," Thompson,

who was dark-haired, continued their conversation. "It was really swell."

"When are we going to get a horse, Mom?" Rory asked.

"Unfortunately that isn't on our current list of priorities," Chloe replied mildly. "Now, go wash your hands and tell your father supper's ready and it's time to gather in the dining room."

Rory and Thompson crowded around the sink and then pelted out into the hall, calling, "Dad! Dad!"

Soon all six of them sat around the long table. Thinking about becoming an adult and leaving home made Bette look around at her family differently tonight. Roarke, with his bent arm that had been injured in the Great War, sat at the head of the table and Chloe at the foot. Gretel and she sat opposite Rory and Thompson, who were five and six years old respectively. Bette loved them all more than words could express.

As her stepfather finished saying grace, another familiar face appeared at the kitchen doorway. "Uncle Ira!" Gretel sprang up and rushed to him.

The short, balding man opened his arms and clasped Gretel to his thin chest. *"Liebchen,"* he murmured, looking meaningfully at Bette's parents over his niece's head.

Seeing the worry there, Bette's mother spoke up. "Everyone, but Bette and Gretel slept—"

"Hey, Mr. Sachs, did you know that somebody burned a cross on our lawn last night?" Rory asked.

There was a shocked silence. Then Roarke cleared his throat. "We thought you boys slept through that."

"Everybody at school knew about it," Rory declared. "I told them that you had a gun and they better watch out."

"I hear about it also," Uncle Ira said. Gently urging Gretel back into her place, he pulled out a chair and sat beside his niece. "Good evening, Mrs. McCaslin, Mister." He nodded politely at them. Ira Sachs showing up for supper on Fridays had become a weekly ritual. Gretel stayed with Bette during the week so she could ride to school with Bette. On Fridays, Uncle Ira came for Gretel and took her home to spend the rest of the weekend with him in Baltimore. The routine had begun nearly a year ago when Gretel's family had sent her from Germany to live with Ira Sachs, her great-uncle.

They'd met because Bette's mother sold their excess eggs to Mr. Sachs, who gathered eggs and then drove them to the Washington, D.C., and Baltimore grocery stores he supplied. On one of his stops in the early summer of 1935, Chloe had seen the new girl sitting in his faded pickup truck and talked to her. She'd invited Gretel to spend time with Bette and improve her broken English before school started in the fall. It had been hard at first for Gretel to adjust to living with a Gentile family, but her uncle wasn't Orthodox so he didn't keep Kosher—as he called it—anyway. In the end, Gretel had settled in as Bette's first and only close girlfriend.

Again, Bette glanced around the table. The cross-burning was just one nasty event in a continuing conflict between the majority of people in northern Anne Arundel County and her parents. No doubt Mary and Ruth would never invite the Jewish egg man to dinner and no doubt their mothers would never take in an orphan like Thompson. Chloe had explained to her why people didn't adopt orphans. They thought that most of them were bastards, children who had been conceived in sin and who even their fathers and mothers had rejected. Chloe had called it foolish, mean-hearted prejudice. She'd used the same words to explain why people called Gretel and Mr. Sachs names.

"I'm so sorry that you had to suffer this cross business," Mr. Sachs said in his thin voice, which still held a trace of German. But he passed the bowl of mashed potatoes to Chloe as if nothing untoward had happened.

"It's just a few KKK, probably liquored up," Roarke dismissed it. "Gretel, you shouldn't let it hit you too hard. They're just ignorant men, cowards."

"Hitler would like them," Gretel put in, sounding unhappy. She stirred her greens with her fork, staring downward. Gretel's parents remained in Germany, trying to keep the long-held family business. In letter after letter, Gretel had begged her parents to join her here. But visas were hard to get.

"But they wouldn't like Hitler," Chloe said. "That's what's so . . . odd. Burning a cross is just nastiness. But they wouldn't hurt you."

Bette didn't know if she agreed with her mother. Mary and Ruth had malice enough.

"I don't want you children to be afraid. Nothing is going to happen to you," Roarke said firmly.

Bette ate and watched everyone around the table in silence. By telephone this morning, her stepfather had reported the cross-burning to the sheriff—even though identifying the culprits would probably be impossible. And, after all, they were only guilty of trespassing. People here could be hateful to Gretel, although if they did more than talk, Gretel could prefer charges against them. At least it was better than the situation in Germany, where Jews no longer had legal rights. The idea boggled Bette's mind. What did Hitler have against Jews?

Then she recalled what the bulletin notice had announced—that she and Curt would be working together. When Mary's clique heard about this change, they'd be spurred on to new heights of nastiness. She'd seen both of them "mooning" over Curt.

I'll have to call the sponsor of the dance and ask to be removed from the list. Hope sparked inside her at this thought. Dad always said that discretion was the better part of valor. Perhaps she'd be rewarded.

She and Gretel were carrying dishes to the kitchen when the front door knocker sounded. When she reentered the dining room to get another armful, she stopped and stared.

"Good evening, Bette," Curt said.

"Maybe you'd like to introduce your friend?" Chloe asked politely. All the adults were staring at her.

Shock held Bette in place. Her tongue wanted to stick to the roof of her mouth. Somehow she cleared her throat. "Mother, this is Curtis Sinclair, a new student at high school." Waves of hot embarrassment flowed through her. She went on making the introductions while Curt nodded and shook hands. He was well dressed and looked like he belonged in this dining room more than she did. Suddenly, she wished she could burn her faded dress and card-boarded Oxfords.

"Do you know how to ride a horse?" Rory blurted out.

Bette's face warmed more. How could she get Curt out of here before she was embarrassed further? Who knew what might come out of Rory's mouth next?

"Sorry, I don't," Curt admitted with a grin.

"Bette, why don't you take Mr. Sinclair," Chloe suggested, "into the parlor where you two can talk uninterrupted?"

"Mom, it's almost time for *Jack Armstrong, All-American Boy!*" Rory objected.

Chloe glanced at her wristwatch. "Jack won't be on the radio for ten more minutes."

Throwing her mother a grateful glance, she walked out the door to the hallway and opened the pocket doors into the parlor. Curt followed her and then they were alone. *What can I say if he brings up this afternoon?*

Curt looked around the formal parlor and sat down when Bette did. He hadn't expected Bette to live in a house like this. "You have a really nice place." His mouth was dry with the shock of it.

"My family's been at Ivy Manor . . . a long time."

A very long time, he agreed silently. Well, he'd come here, and he'd have to go through with it now. "Did you see the notice on the bulletin board?"

"Yes, I did." She was blushing. "I'll understand if you want me . . . I'll be glad to resign—"

"I don't want you to resign." Curt's quick answer snapped between them like a crack of lightning.

"You don't?" Bette stared at him. "Then why did you come tonight?"

Well, no going back now. "I'm glad I was moved up from member to co-chair of the graduation dance committee with you." He gazed at Bette. Her ears were dainty. Her nose was just right and sprinkled with the tiniest freckles though her complexion was elegantly white, like something out of a poem. Her gray eyes were large and luminous with honesty. She was such a sweet kid. And so pretty. And she didn't deserve the guff she got from people around here.

He cleared his throat. "I've been watching you, Bette. You're not foolish-acting like so many girls at school. The world is being taken over by communists and fascists and they act like it's nothing. I admire you for befriending Gretel."

Bette stared at him. He was right. Most kids in their class barely knew what a fascist was. But what did he mean?

"My family takes an interest in what's going on in the world. That's what I miss about living near Philadelphia. It's so reactionary here I can hardly breathe sometimes."

Reactionary? She'd have to look that up in the dictionary. "Oh?" she responded cautiously. She tried to concentrate on his words, but his thick brown eyelashes and that hint of blond beard, now more pronounced, made it hard for her to breathe.

"And I wanted to ask you to go to the dance with me."

Bette tried not to look surprised. *Dance? With you?* "I'd love that," she stammered.

"Well, I've got to go." Rising, Curt held out his hand.

Bette took it. The contact of their palms ricocheted through her. It was the first time a young man had shaken her hand. It was like shaking on an agreement.

She had a date for the senior dance.

How wonderful.

How awful.

*   *   *

Bette couldn't sleep that night. Gretel had left with her uncle without a private moment in which Bette could tell her of the dance invitation. Finally, the little boys had been put to sleep and the house was quiet. Her nerves on edge, Bette tiptoed out of her room and down the hall to her parent's bedroom. She must tell her mother. Chloe would need to know so that they could figure out how to get ready for the dance only a month away.

Even though the door wasn't closed completely, she raised her hand to knock on it. Her stepfather's strained voice halted her.

"I got a letter from Kitty today."

CHAPTER TWO

S he still sends them to the bank?" her mother asked.
"Yes, just her street and state on the return address, no name."

Bette heard the scrape of wire hangers on the closet pole.

"What did she say?" Chloe asked.

"Not much. Just enclosed a check like she always does."

A check? Bette thought. Why would Aunt Kitty send them money? Were Mother and Dad in worse financial shape than she thought?

"Oh, Roarke, what are we going to do?" Chloe sounded pained. "How can we get her to understand that we love her, need her in our lives?"

"She doesn't want to hear that. Doesn't want to hear anything from us." Roarke's voice was clipped, hurt.

Bette peered through the crack between the door and the jamb, almost too shocked to feel guilty about eavesdropping.

"Do you remember telling me that Kitty was the only one the war didn't change?" Chloe sat in her pale dressing gown in front of her vanity, smoothing cream into her hands.

"Yes, and it wasn't the war that changed my sister." In his striped pajamas, Roarke sat on the side of their quilt-covered bed.

"What did?"

"That man."

Chloe paused as though stung, and then leaned forward and kissed her husband. It was a kiss of comfort, of enduring love. It held Bette mesmerized. Would any man ever kiss her that way?

Bette stood there, her hand curled ready to tap. She was afraid to breathe, afraid of being discovered. Puzzled, she turned back toward her own room. What man were they talking about? And why did Aunt Kitty, the aunt she barely remembered, send checks? And why did that upset her parents? It didn't make sense.

The next morning, Saturday, after everyone had gone off to do whatever they had to do, Bette drew her mother into her parent's spacious bedroom. Bette had always loved entering the elegant room with its high ceiling and soothing shades of ivory and light green. The maple four-poster with sheer white draperies dominated the room.

The conversation Bette had overheard in this room chased itself 'round and 'round in her mind, but she couldn't ask her mother about Aunt Kitty. Besides, she had something else more urgent to discuss. Even though, in light of the cross-burning, she felt guilty bringing up something her mother might think trivial.

"Mother," her tense voice quavered, "Curt Sinclair asked

me to the senior dance." Saying this out loud to another living person caused her heart to jerk and then race.

"*Honey.*" Chloe took Bette's hands in hers. "He seemed like such a nice young man."

"He is." Winded without running a step, Bette gathered her courage. "I know a dress for the dance will be expensive, but—"

"Of course you'll have a new dress for the dance, Bette." Her mother shook her head. "I apologize. Time has gotten away from me. You'll need a new dress for graduation, too. And dress shoes as well as everyday shoes and silk stockings. And everything." She dropped Bette's hands and began pacing.

"Silk stockings?" Bette's mouth opened in shock. She leaned back against the foot of the high bed for support.

"Of course. You can't wear anklets and knee socks for the rest of your life." Chloe paused, looking Bette up and down. "When you graduate, you will be a woman, not a girl anymore." She looked pensive, one finger pressed against her cheek. "Don't give this another thought."

Bette felt hope inflate like a balloon inside her. "Will we go to Baltimore or Washington to shop?" She'd overheard girls at school planning such shopping trips and had thought they were beyond her parents' means.

"No, I think I have a better idea." Her mother grinned suddenly and then chuckled. "I know just what to do. Oh, she'll be thrilled when I ask her."

Bette wondered who the "she" was, but was too tongue-tied to ask. It still felt too good to be true. A new dress and silk stockings . . . Wow.

From the bureau top, Chloe lifted her ancient maple-wood sewing box and took out a frayed cloth measuring tape. "Yes, it's time for you to make your debut."

Bette knew her mother had been a debutante and had attended the debutante's ball in Annapolis. But after Bette's grandmother died two days after Bette's twelfth birthday, Chloe had decided that Bette wouldn't like that or going away to finishing school. Even so, sometimes Bette wondered—if she'd been to finishing school and been a debutante, would the girls from high school treat her the way they did?

With both hands, Chloe reached around her with the tape, measuring her bustline. "You're growing into a beautiful woman, Bette Leigh." Then she measured her waist and hips and noted the numbers down on a scrap of paper. "Your father would be so proud of you."

The mention of the father who'd died before she was born gave Bette a warm feeling. Her mother always said things like that about her father. They must have loved each other very much and Bette thought the story of their romance wonderful, almost like a movie. But looking at her mother reminded her of her own shortcomings. "I'm not beautiful like you."

Chloe turned her blue eyes onto Bette. "Honey, you are the kind of woman who will grow more beautiful with every year. You aren't *cute*. You have a subtle, classical beauty that isn't appreciated until you gain some maturity. But"—she gave Bette a roguish smile—"evidently, Mr. Sinclair has eyes in his head. He sees you better than the children you've grown up with."

Bette pondered her mother's words. She'd heard them often enough, but after the way she was treated at school, she'd had a hard time actually believing in them. But now that she thought of it, she mustn't be that bad or why would Curt have chosen her as his date? *Oh, dear, when the clique at school finds out, they'll be mad as fire.* Cold fingers of dread tingled through Bette.

"I'm afraid . . . I'm sorry that your stepfather and I make you an object of curiosity."

How did she know what I was thinking? But, then, her mother was more perceptive than most other mothers. She often seemed to understand how Bette felt.

Chloe's voice had sobered. "But your stepfather and I must live the way we think is right, the way we think God wants us to live. We decided to ride out this Depression and keep our people on the land—land their families have tilled for almost a century—not throw them off in these bad times. And Gretel needed our help. I can't be bothered with the small-town prejudices here."

Bette tried to absorb this, tried to deal with the fact that her mother was speaking to her as if they were equals.

"And because I won't go along with their prejudices, it makes people want to tell me off. But they can't. I'm a Carlyle and Roarke's family owns the bank. So what people think about me, they mutter at home and their children overhear bits and pieces. And being human, they want to use it to tear you down and, they think, build themselves up. In reality, it only makes them look smaller and meaner."

Bette thought about Curt's opinion of the attitudes here. *Reactionary?*

Chloe ran her fingers through Bette's shoulder-length hair, lifting it, letting her love touch Bette. "Not long from now, you will enter the larger world and leave all this behind you. And your experience here will make you stronger and kinder than you would have been otherwise."

Her solemn tone impressed Bette. She had never spoken to her like this before. "I'm not going far, Mother. Just secretarial school in Baltimore."

Chloe smiled and shook her head. "That's not the way life works, honey. Not at all. You'll have a wonderful life all your own. I just hope that this Depression is the worst trouble that life will throw at you. You've grown up so much, especially in the way you befriended Gretel. You have a loving heart and deserve a wonderful future." Chloe embraced her.

Bette loved hearing her mother talk like this. Still, she had a hard time believing it. But at least, she'd been asked to the senior dance by Curt Sinclair. That would be enough to remember all her life.

Chloe released her. "Now go ahead and help Jerusha plant the flower beds. I have a letter to write."

Before she went to help their housekeeper, Bette wanted to ask for more particulars about the dresses, the shoes, the silk stockings. What if her mother, or whomever she contacted, didn't know what would be appropriate? But how could she voice this doubt when her mother had been so wonderful? She decided for now she would have to trust in her mother's instincts.

With her thoughts and feelings whirling around in her head, Bette left to find Jerusha.

Chloe watched her daughter walk out of the room, her mind obviously a million miles away. She wondered if Curt Sinclair made Bette feel the way Theran Black had made her feel nearly twenty years ago. Attraction between a man and a woman could prove powerful. In 1917, Chloe had been desperately in love with Theran, until . . .

She sighed, sat down at her secretary, and pulled out a piece of her pink-tinted stationary. "Dear Minnie," she wrote with a grin.

Bette felt very grownup. Over a week had passed since Curt Sinclair had come into her life. Now on Monday night, they sat together in her stepfather's den, the pocket door open. The muffled sounds of her family down the hall in the parlor listening to *The Will Rogers' Show*, her stepfather's favorite, drifted in. "But with Congress," she heard Will Rogers' distinctive twang, "every time they make a joke, it's a law and every time they make a law, it's a joke." Radio audience laughter vied with her stepfather's.

Here, so close to Curt, she felt a world apart from the girl who would have been sitting with her family listening to the show. Bette couldn't believe how her life had changed. Last Monday morning, Curt had started walking her to her classes. She'd felt many shocked and angry gazes following their progress down the school corridors. The infamous clique of girls led by Mary had glared at her, but they had fallen strangely silent. Maybe they didn't know what to say.

Bette studied Curt, his sandy hair gleaming in the low light. Why was he interested in her?

He sat beside her at the desk where they had laid out all the information about the different aspects of the senior dance to finalize, such as the refreshment list with names of people who would donate food and drink.

The dance is almost here. When will Mother say anything about the new dresses?

"I sure wish we could afford live music," Curt said.

Staring into Curt's blue eyes, Bette was caught off-guard. "What?" Then she stared at his lips. They were perfect to her—a gentle bow on the top lip and a slightly fuller bottom lip. And that golden stubble on his chin . . . She couldn't look away.

"Live music. Wouldn't we knock everyone for a loop with a swing band?" He leaned forward.

"Swing." Bette realized that he was staring at her lips, too. Her mouth suddenly went very dry. "But we have no money for a band." She let her face drift toward Curt's.

Curt looked at her in obvious wonder and tilted his head. "You got that right," he mumbled.

Bette moved the final inch till her lips were a mere breath away from his. Her blood pounded in her veins. Would he kiss her?

"Bette."

Gretel's woebegone voice startled Bette away from Curt. Bette swung around to see her friend in the doorway. Gretel was in tears. "What's wrong?"

"I . . . I . . ." Seeing her two friends so close together, Gretel faltered. "I thought Curt is gone already. I'm sorry." She drew back to leave.

"No," Bette and Curt said almost in unison, rising together.

"We're done," Curt said. "I have to get home to do homework, too." He gathered up the papers and returned them to a folder. "I'll see myself out."

Bette was torn. Gretel obviously needed her, but she

hated to see Curt leave. At school, he'd shown his true colors, too. He'd insisted on walking her to class even with Gretel at her other side.

On his way out the door, he grasped Bette's upper arm. "I'll see you tomorrow after English?"

She nodded, more interested in the stirring effect of his touch on her than his words. Then saying good night to both of them, he was gone.

Bette wrenched her mind back to Gretel. "What is it?" Bette asked as she moved to close the door to the hallway. She turned to face her friend.

"It's Ilsa. A letter come today from Berlin"—Gretel waved it forlornly—"but I wouldn't let myself read it till I had done all my lessons." Gretel wiped her eyes with a flowered hankie.

"What's wrong with your cousin?" Ilsa was Gretel's only cousin, five years older than she.

"My parents write that her husband has divorced her. He never said one word to her." Gretel pressed the hankie to her streaming eyes. "He just handed her the divorce decree."

"How could he divorce her without her knowing what he was doing?" Bette drew nearer Gretel. This didn't make sense. Divorce created a huge scandal. How could a man hide that?

"Because she is a Jew. The Nazi judge granted him the divorce because Ilsa is Jewish. That isn't law. Her husband took all the money from their bank account for himself. He packed one bag of her clothes and put her out on the street. He shut the door of their apartment in her face." Gretel's voice quavered. "She walked all the way—over five miles—to her parents' house. She did not have a penny. But her father is already

27

fired from his civil service job because he is a Jew. How will they live with no money?" Gretel sank into the nearest chair.

Bette reached for her friend's hand. She imagined a woman who resembled Gretel standing alone on a dark, foreign street, looking back forlornly at the place where she'd lived with her husband. He'd shut the door in Ilsa's face. The pain must be soul-destroying. Bette had suffered ridicule all her life for being different, but nothing like this. They could taunt her, even burn crosses on her lawn, but no one could *do* anything to her.

"Ilsa, you know," Gretel said, "ran away and married him. She was just eighteen and crazy in love with him. Her parents were not happy. He was not Jewish, but they still talked to Ilsa. They just didn't see her often."

"Didn't he love her anymore?" Bette asked, trying to make sense of this.

"I do not think he must have loved her ever, do you?" Gretel asked, suddenly stiff with outrage. "My aunt told my mother that it is because he is married to a Jew. They were going to fire him from his job."

"He divorced her over a job?" Bette tried to believe this, but she failed. Ilsa's husband must not have loved her. Bette knew that real love hoped all things, endured all things, and never failed. In her memory, she heard her mother reciting this verse. And her mother should know—she loved Bette's stepfather and he loved her. Bette wasn't mistaken about that.

"I'd like to kill him. With my bare hands around his throat." Gretel crumpled the letter in her hands and strangled it.

Bette had never heard her friend's voice so savage, so harsh.

Chloe slid open the door. "Did Curt leave?"

Bette walked toward her, instinctively seeking her help. "Yes, I—"

"Gretel, what's wrong?" Chloe went straight to the weeping girl. Gretel poured out her story as Chloe stood with her arms wrapped around her. Then Gretel dissolved into sobs.

When Gretel could speak again, she said, "My mother says that Ilsa is going to apply for a visa out of the country. Both our families will try to get together enough funds to pay for her to come here." Gretel gave them a despairing look. "Why have they waited? So long? Too long. Now Jews can only take twenty-five percent of their money out of Germany. If we had come here all together after Hitler came to power in '33, when *Grossfater* insisted I be sent to stay with Uncle Ira, they would be safe now. I am afraid for them."

Over Gretel's head, Bette and her mother exchanged worried glances. "Perhaps I can find a way to help," Chloe murmured.

"How?" Gretel asked and Bette echoed the question silently.

Chloe shook her head. "I can't make promises, but I'll try."

Later that evening, Chloe opened the door of the pale-pink bedroom of her childhood, which Bette and Gretel now shared, and looked in. Bette was asleep on the bed and Gretel slept on the trundle bed on the floor beside it. Both girls wore prim white-cotton nightgowns and looked like the innocents they were. *Dear Lord, keep them safe. Give them strength to face whatever may come.*

Chloe closed the door silently and walked down the hall to her bedroom. Roarke met her as she entered and with his good arm drew her close. She closed her eyes as he kissed her. As she breathed in his natural fragrance, she reveled in the sweet assurance of his lips on hers. "I love you, Roarke."

"And I love you."

"We're so lucky."

After an earlier explanation of Gretel's bad news, Roarke understood what she meant. "I had never known a Jewish person as a friend until you invited Gretel into our home. Of course, I knew it would make us the topic of more gossip— taking a Jew, *and* the niece of the egg man, for heaven's sake, into our home. But I didn't care. It was right and I love the way you don't care what people say about us."

"But that prejudice is nothing to what's happening in Germany." Chloe looked up at him, clearly asking for understanding. "I'm going to write to my old friend Drake. Do you mind if I ask him if he can help Gretel's family?"

Roarke knew why Chloe was asking him. She knew that sometimes jealousy still had the power to nip him, make him speak sharply to her. *Forgive my unruly tongue, beloved.* "Go ahead with my blessing."

Chloe kissed him and he forgot everything but wanting to hold her close and show her how glad he was that she was in his life . . . for good.

Almost two weeks later on a Saturday morning deep in sunny May, boxes from New York City were delivered. One box was long and flat; the other was tall and square. The postmaster himself had made a special trip out to deliver them personally. His eyes shone with his eagerness for information. Chloe thanked him warmly, but gave him no tidbits to repeat.

Then Jerusha helped Bette carry them upstairs to her parents' large bedroom. Gretel, who was spending a rare weekend with them because her great-uncle had to go out of town on business, hovered around Bette. Bette was relieved that last weekend Gretel's uncle had taken her to Baltimore and bought her a new graduation outfit. So Bette didn't have to feel guilty. Chloe came in, beaming.

"Mother," Bette asked, peering at the mailing labels, "who is Mrs. Frank Dawson?"

Chloe and Jerusha exchanged glances. Chloe nodded to Jerusha.

"Mrs. Frank Dawson is my daughter's married name," Jerusha said, pride making her dark face glow.

Bette knew their housekeeper had a married daughter in New York but it had never occurred to her that Jerusha's daughter was the one who would choose her new clothing. Worry sliced Bette's lungs. How would a stranger in New York City know what kind of dress she'd need for a dance in Croftown?

Then Chloe cut the strings, lifted off the lid of the long flat box, and pushed back the white tissue paper. Bette's gasp was only one of many.

"Go ahead, honey," her mother urged. "It's your dress. You lift it out."

First rubbing her moist palms on the front of her skirt, Bette grasped the delicate dress by its shoulders and drew it from the white tissue. The dress was an unusual shade of blue-violet silk Georgette with a white-lace shawl collar, a peplum waist, and a gracefully flared skirt that ended just inches above her ankles. She'd never worn such a dress before. It was just like something Myrna Loy would wear as Mrs. Nick Charles in *The Thin Man*.

"I knew Minnie would know just what you should wear. I told her to think very young ingénue," Chloe crowed with satisfaction.

"My, it's fine." Jerusha beamed.

"What else is in the box?" Gretel asked, peering over Bette's shoulder.

Bette managed to drag her eyes back to the box. Inside were intimate items, everything she needed to go under the dress. "Wow," she breathed.

"*Ja,*" Gretel agreed. "Vow."

"Honey, do you want to try it on or open the big box first?"

Like on Christmas morning, Bette wanted simultaneously to savor every moment and do everything at once. She took in a deep breath. "Let's unwrap everything and lay it out on the bed."

When this had been accomplished, Bette stared at two pairs of shoes, three pairs of silk stockings, two pairs of gloves, undergarments, two dresses, and a small gift-wrapped box. One pair of shoes obviously went with the party dress. They were *peau de soie* high heels and had been dyed to match. The other pair were low-heeled light-brown pumps similar to what her mother wore, not Oxfords like the girls at school.

Bette slipped the party shoes on and peered down at them. They were women's shoes, not girl's shoes. They looked funny with anklets instead of stockings. She glanced up.

Chloe nodded and smiled.

"They fit perfectly," Bette said in wonder.

"I sent Minnie a cutout of your Sunday shoes, so she'd get the right size. How do you like your graduation dress?"

This dress was a navy-blue-and-white dotted Swiss shirtwaist with a matching belt. Its skirt ended mid-calf, a bit longer than a girl's dress. And there was a little wisp of a navy-blue hat with a net veil and matching gloves. The ensemble altogether looked very grownup, somewhat intimidating. The sense that in two short weeks—after the senior dance and after graduation—she would be changed trembled inside her. A humbling and frightening feeling. She had difficulty swallowing.

"Everything's just perfect." Holding the dotted dress to her, Bette whirled around like a little girl.

"You must write Minnie a thank-you note," Chloe said.

"Minnie tell me," Jerusha added, "she happy to go shoppin' for a girl for a change. She and Frank only got the one boy."

"Your daughter has very good style, ma'am," Gretel voiced the majority opinion.

The first song of the evening, "I'm in the Mood for Love," played on the school's new electric Orthophonic phonograph. Curt led Bette to the polished high school gym floor. The gym was draped with yellow and white crepe paper, the school colors, and most of the overhead lights had been left unlighted. The gym had never looked better. Tonight, Bette hoped to begin her new grownup life—if her old rivals would let her. But if looks could kill, Mary's and Ruth's would have done Bette in upon arrival. Well, Cinderella wouldn't be the same without the evil stepsisters.

Tonight, Bette felt exactly like Cinderella at the ball. The grownup way Curt looked in his dark suit with his white carnation boutonnière swept away her ability to speak. He put his hand around to the small of her back and held her other hand out and they began the fox trot. For the past two weeks in the parlor with the furniture pushed against the wall, she and her stepfather had been dancing, practicing until she and Gretel could dance with assurance.

Under the watchful eye of the chaperones, Curt kept a respectful distance. She took a deep breath and began to follow Curt's lead. She would treasure forever this moment. She would treasure forever the looks on the nasty girls' faces as she'd walked in tonight on Curt's arm in her evening dress. She noticed that Ruth's and Mary's eyes followed her every move. Her only regret was that Gretel had gone home with her uncle as usual last night. But Gretel didn't need a date for graduation. They'd still share that.

"I hate to repeat myself," Curt whispered in her ear, "but this dress makes you look as beautiful as I knew you were. Now these other rubes are wondering why they didn't see it before."

One of the chaperones caught his eye with a stern frown and he pulled his head away from Bette's. He chuckled only for her as if saying, "Aren't they old-fashioned?"

The dance ended and Curt took her to the white cloth-draped refreshment table adorned with fresh daisies and black-eyed Susans and got her a cup of punch. Bette felt people staring at her. She lifted her chin and smiled at Curt. One sip and she saw Deep Rose lipstick on her glass punch cup, something else new for her. Her mother had warned her to touch up her lipstick throughout the evening.

The class president strolled up and asked her to dance. Her mother had impressed upon her not to let Curt have every dance. The next song, "The Way You Look Tonight," began and Bette let the class president lead her to the floor.

"I heard that the box this dress came in had Saks Fifth Avenue on it," he said as they began to dance. "My mom couldn't stop gabbing about it."

Bette shrugged. The speed of gossip once again astounded her. He tried to pull her a bit closer and a nearby chaperone clucked her tongue. Her partner grinned and gave Bette a wink. The dance continued. As the final note sounded, he said, "Don't let Curt think he'll have you all to himself."

With these heady words echoing in her mind, Bette walked from the floor and went straight to the ladies' room on one side of the gym. She needed to get away from everyone for a moment. Another dance started behind her, "Cheek to Cheek." She doubted, however, that any couple would be allowed to dance that way here tonight.

The decoration committee had done their best to liven up the bilious green-tiled institutional bathroom, without much success. But Bette appreciated the pink and white tissue paper carnations over the mirrors and the box of tissues on an embroidered scarf-covered table by the sinks.

She opened her black beaded evening bag, a gift from her step-grandfather, and drew out her shiny gold compact and lipstick, graduation gifts from her stepfather. She touched up her powder and then opened the lipstick tube and leaned closer to the mirror.

The door slapped open. Mary and Ruth walked in with a few other girls. Bette concentrated on her lips in the mirror.

"I bet you think you're something tonight with that dress someone had to send you," Mary snapped.

Ignoring a shiver of alarm, Bette acted as if she hadn't heard the words. My, how gossip flourished. Though she and Chloe had never said one word, everyone in the county—not just the class president's mother—must know that she'd received her new clothing from New York City. And her mother had warned her to expect retaliation from the clique for coming to the dance wearing the most fashionable dress. "I don't know why women can be so catty," Chloe had said. "But anything they say to you, others said to me. Ignore them."

"Yes, everyone knows your family's so busy wasting money," Ruth chimed in, "on bums and Negroes and Jews, they can't afford to do for their own."

Bette finished applying her lipstick, blotted her lips, and returned her lipstick tube to her purse. Snapping it shut, she turned and walked toward the girls. They pulled together to stop her.

CHAPTER THREE

*B*ette shook her head and gave a tiny smile. Her usual fear of these girls didn't catch her around the heart, freeze her to ice. "Don't you think this behavior is a little childish?"

Her cool nonchalance had an effect. The girls looked to one another as if to say, "What's going on?"

"Next week we graduate from school," Bette said. "This kid stuff will all be over." She shrugged. But even as she said it she wondered at her own audacity. What made her bold? Was it the dress, the shoes, the makeup? Or Curt? Maybe it was all of them and the new way her mother discussed things with her—as though she were a woman, too.

She looked at the girls she'd dreaded for years and saw their new uncertainty about her. Her change in behavior had shoved them off kilter. Shoulders back, she strode forward, enjoying the snap of her heels against the tiled floor. They gave way and let her pass through. Curt was waiting just outside the door of the gym for her. "Shall we dance?"

The chaperones had arranged everyone for a Virginia

Reel—the fellows in one line and the girls facing them. She and Curt took their places. The rollicking melody lightened the mood of the party and everyone began smiling and laughing at each other as they met in the middle to bow and curtsey. Bette couldn't take her eyes off Curt. In the low light, he radiated charisma like a steady beam. And she noticed he returned the same attention to her. Did she glow in the shadowy room to him, too?

The reel ended and a waltz began. More dances. More punch. Bette danced every dance in a whirl of music and happiness. And then it was the last tune. Without a word, Curt took her into his arms with a gentleness that left her heart throbbing. She closed her eyes, rested her head on Curt's firm shoulder, and felt Curt's heart beat under her ear. "Someone to Watch over Me" was playing. For once the chaperones didn't reprimand them for dancing so close. Maybe they sensed that it was a special moment in the lives of the young people, slowly moving through the last dance before becoming adults.

The words sang in her ear, but Bette changed the lyrics to "Curtis to watch over me." Bette didn't want the night to end. For the first time within Curt's embrace, she saw a future she hadn't expected. A wonderful future, where the past faded and where many things were possible . . .

Finally, the dance was over. Curt and Bette, as the chairmen of the dance, helped clean up and were among the last to leave; they locked the door of the school in the dark of midnight. The sounds of night were all around them—the wind rustling spring leaves overhead, car tires whining on the highway. Bette could hear Curt breathe at her side. *What now?*

Curt offered her his arm. She slipped her gloved hand around his elbow. She liked the feel of him, the firm strength in his arm. Walking beside him—hearing the click of her high heels—made her feel very feminine, womanly. A strange excitement, anticipation surged through her. A feeling she'd never felt before. Curt opened the car door for her. When she passed by him, he leaned closer and brushed his lips over her hair. Bette sat down, feeling slightly faint. Had he really kissed her hair—just like in the movies?

He drove them out of the empty parking lot. The interior of the car felt too full to her, overwhelmed by Curt's presence. She watched the headlights brighten the road ahead and clutched her purse in her lap. She wanted to say, "Stop. Don't take me home." But her parents would be waiting up for her. For a moment, she wished Curt were the kind of guy who'd take her to the local lover's lane, a place she'd only heard of. But, of course, Curt was a gentleman.

To her surprise, though, about a mile from Ivy Manor, Curt pulled the car onto the shoulder and parked near a newly tilled tobacco field. Bette smelled the fertile richness of the soil and swallowed with difficulty.

"I thought of driving to lover's lane, but not with you, Bette. You're too special."

Bette's throat tightened. She couldn't speak so she tilted her head toward Curt, inviting him to come closer. He slid near and without missing a beat gathered her into his arms. For one luscious moment, his mouth hovered over hers.

The seconds of waiting pounded in her brain. And then

he kissed her. She sighed into his mouth. With his thumb, he brushed her lower lip and then deepened the kiss. Bombarded by unknown sensations, Bette felt as if her body might fly apart. She clung to him, the one solid object in the world gone wild.

He kissed her lightly and then drew her closer, his arm around her shoulders. "I knew it would be wonderful kissing you," he murmured.

His words washed through her, melting her. She'd dreamed of falling in love and this must be it.

"I want you to know that I'm serious about you, Bette. I plan to be an English teacher. Nothing exciting." He traced her lips with one finger. "I'm going to Georgetown University. My parents will help me, but I'll have to work while I'm going to school."

Breathless, Bette took in air. "I'm going to secretarial school in Baltimore. It will only take me a year. Then my mother says she has friends in Washington and they should be able to find a job."

"I won't be able to propose to—" He paused and brushed his thumb over her lower lip again, making her body sing with excitement. "—anyone until I'm about finished."

Bette stopped breathing. Was she really hearing what he was saying or was her mind making this up, this stuff of dreams?

"I'm working my way through. It might take me five years instead of four. I know that's a long time to wait—"

She wanted to say, "I'd wait twice that long for you, Curt." But she stopped herself. For one thing, a girl just didn't say that to a fellow, and second, she didn't want to lie. She didn't want to wait five years for him, much less ten.

"That's all I should say now." Curt caressed her neck where her pulse beat. "But you'll be seeing a lot of me, Bette. As much as you'll let me."

Wherever he touched her, she tingled with awareness. She closed her eyes, turned to him, trailing her fingers through his fair hair. She stroked his golden-tanned cheeks down to his chin. His early-morning stubble prickled her fingertips and she reveled in the masculine texture of him. She wished that they could stay here like this and that she could explore . . .

Curt kissed her again. Just like in the movies. Just like Errol Flynn kissed Olivia de Haviland. Then he stopped, pulling her close and just holding her. "It's time I took you home."

She longed to protest, but he was right of course. She slid away from him and fluffed her hair with her fingers. The silence between them was complete, full of understanding and happiness. Bette smiled into the darkness and Curt drove with one hand cradling hers.

At Ivy Manor, he walked her solemnly to the door. Her parents must be waiting in the parlor. The lights were on. Her every nerve hummed with awareness of how near he was to her in every way. "Curt, thank you for a wonderful evening. I'll never forget tonight."

"Me, either." With the back of his hand, he brushed her cheek and then kissed her hand. "It won't be our last dance. They have them at college, too."

This happy thought swelled inside her, making it impossible for her to answer. Smiling, she went inside and closed the door quietly behind her.

Then she realized that her mother was speaking on the phone at the rear of the hallway, her back to Bette. "Oh,

Drake, I appreciate that so much. I don't know what you can do in Berlin for Gretel's family, but thank you. Yes. Good-bye."

Her stepfather stood in the parlor doorway. He looked over when he heard the door open. He smiled at Bette and waved for her to come to him.

In her pale satin dressing gown, Chloe hung up and turned to greet her, a smile overlaying her serious appearance. "Bette, how was the dance?"

Bette wanted to ask about the phone call, but felt funny about letting on that she'd overheard the end of her mother's phone conversation.

"Fine. I had a wonderful time." Abruptly distracted from thoughts of the dance, Bette searched their eyes. She wanted to ask them why Chloe had been on the phone so late and what this was about Gretel's family and Berlin? But her parents only asked more about the dance, obviously making an effort to change the subject, so she quickly filled them in on everything. She knew her mother would want more girlish details later when it was just the two of them.

After kissing them both good night, Bette walked soberly up the steps. Gretel's family did live in Berlin, but who was Drake? The name sounded familiar but it called up no face.

Berlin, November 1936

Drake finished a fine meal of sausage and schnitzel at his hotel restaurant and then walked outside and hailed a cab. He'd put off this errand for several days, but no longer. He'd promised Chloe. He gave the man the address and got into the battered taxi. The cabbie looked over his shoulder at Drake, frowned, and then shook his head.

"Is there a problem?" Drake had visited Germany often in the past on business and knew that most cab drivers spoke some English. So what was bothering the man?

"No, *mein Herr*, no." The cabbie put his taxi in gear and drove off in prickly silence.

After thought, Drake understood why the cabbie had hesitated. He didn't want to drive to the Jewish section. Drake watched the gray streets of Berlin pass by. More and more, Berlin depressed Drake. The first time he'd visited Berlin had been before the Great War. It had been a bustling, proud metropolis—full of cheerful smiles, colorful gardens, and light-hearted music. Then defeat and Depression had rolled over it. The marks of this still showed in the worn-down heels and frayed sleeves of its citizens.

But the biggest difference was this was now Nazi Germany. Huge swastika banners marked buildings. SS soldiers walked briskly down streets looking purposeful, official, and dangerous. They saluted each other with "*Heil* Hitler!" which made the skin on the back of Drake's neck crawl. The young German democracy had desperately needed a George Washington and they'd settled for Adolph Hitler.

They neared the Jewish part of town. Now more stores wore in their windows the signs saying *Juden*. Pedestrians wore the yellow star of David—not in pride but to be marked with shame. Along the passing streets, people walked quickly and kept their eyes lowered. He'd read about this in the *New York Times* but seeing it provoked a visceral desire to seek out Hitler and smash his smug face in.

Drake wondered how long it would be before the simmering pot called Europe rolled to a full boil. Hitler in Germany retaking the Rhineland from France. Mussolini conquering Ethiopia, of all places. Spain, rumbling with fearful, bloody civil war. Stalin purging thousands in Russia. And if the pot came to a boil, would it overflow and envelope the indifferent US?

For just a moment at this summer's Berlin Olympics, Americans had gloated when Jesse Owens, a Negro American, had won and enraged Hitler for mocking his theory of Aryan Supremacy. But it had been only a flicker. Isolationists, racists, communists, fascists—Drake wished all the "ists" here and at home would go drown themselves in the cold North Sea. The political unrest wasn't good for business and German-American diplomacy had become as tricky as dancing on a bayonet point.

The cabbie pulled to a halt. They'd reached the Berlin "ghetto." As Drake paid the cabbie, the German wouldn't look at him. Drake got out and looked around as the taxi driver roared away, glad to be free. People—all wearing the hated yellow stars—were glancing furtively at him. When he returned their regard, they looked down and hurried away, shrinking into themselves.

The yellow stars taunted him, making him recall the slurs against Jews so common at home. Why didn't any newsreels show these demeaning stars?

Getting back to business, he glanced at the address once more and then went through the door of an aging apartment building. The smell of cabbage cooking filled the stairwell as he began his ascent to the third floor. At the top of the stairs, he knocked on the first door. The conversation within ceased like a radio switched off. The door opened a crack. *"Ja?"* a man asked.

"Is this the Sachs' home? I'm Drake Lovelady. I'm a friend of the McCaslin family in the US. The family your daughter Gretel lives with."

The door opened. A thin, dark-haired man stared at him. "The McCaslins? You come from Maryland?"

Drake smiled. "I'm an old friend of Mrs. McCaslin's. She knew I was coming to Berlin on business and asked me to drop in and see how you are."

"Come in." The man stumbled backward in his haste and bobbed several times. "I am Gretel's father, Jakob."

Drake came in and closed the door behind himself. The apartment was small and very crowded with dark furniture and thin people. Gretel's father quickly introduced Drake to his wife, his father, his brother and his wife, and Ilsa, Gretel's cousin. Chloe had told him of Ilsa's divorce. This made his gaze linger on her. A very pretty girl, somehow arresting. She glanced away, her chin stubborn, proud.

Attracted in spite of himself, Drake turned back to his host. It was obvious they were just about to dine. "I'm sorry. I was hoping that you would have finished your evening meal."

"No, no," Jakob objected, looking harassed and embarrassed, "you will join us, *bitte*?"

"No, I ate at my hotel, but I would be happy to sit down with you." From under his arm, he offered an ornate, gold-ribboned box to Gretel's mother. "A gift for you."

"Chocolates!" she exclaimed, flushed with the moment. Everyone except Ilsa brightened and Drake's discomfort eased, though his eyes drifted toward the pretty girl of their own accord. "Come," said Gretel's mother. "I give you tea and we talk and eat, *ja*?"

"*Ja*," Drake agreed, smiling and turning his attention away from Ilsa.

After the meal, which consisted of boiled cabbage and dry brown bread, Drake came to the point. "I know of your troubles."

The faces that looked back at him dimmed. "Hope lost," is what they proclaimed. But none answered him, save Ilsa. "You know I was divorced? Our business is nearly broke?"

He nodded. "Mrs. McCaslin said that Gretel has been encouraging you to leave. Has any one of you been able to get a visa?"

"We don't have the *gelt*," Jakob explained, spreading his hands. "Visas are more and more . . . cost."

"I was afraid of that." Drake found himself gazing at Ilsa. She was more than pretty, he realized now, with lustrous dark hair and eyes. But it wasn't only her attractiveness that captured his notice. It was also her tenseness—she gave the impression of a taut bow ready to release its arrow. "How many of you want to leave?"

Jakob translated this for his father, who pointed to himself and shook his head. "*Alt.*"

"Father says he is too old to leave," Jakob said. "And now it's too hard to get visas. What country wants poor, middle-aged Jews? Younger friends of ours go to Kenya. Husband was banker. Now they work on a coffee plantation. We couldn't do that kind of work. And countries only want *Jungen*—young people who can work. And we can't take much with us now. How can I start again at my age?" He shrugged his shoulders in a hopeless gesture.

"Why are you asking us this anyway?" Ilsa snapped. "I'm young and I can't get out—not easily. I went to five embassies here in Berlin. Only Portugal offered to sell me a visa. You know what the visa said? That I could use it to move to any country but Portugal. No one wants Jews." She stood up, grabbed a coat, and stormed out of the apartment.

Drake's attention followed her until the door slammed behind her. He had to give her credit. She wasn't cowed—yet.

The whole family looked down at the table top. "Ilsa *ist . . .* hurt," Jakob explained.

"May I try to speak to her?" Drake rose, but waited for permission. When Ilsa had stood up, something else about her had popped into his mind. He devoutly hoped he was wrong. Jakob nodded and Drake went out and down the steps. He found Ilsa on the doorstep.

She had her arms folded in front of her. She leaned a shoulder against the peeling doorframe, facing away from the entrance. From him.

He suppressed a sudden, unexpected urge to touch her, to turn her and let her rest her head on his shoulder. She wouldn't want or accept comfort from him. But at the same time, why was she taking her anger out on him? "I came to help you, your family."

She turned to him. "Why? We are strangers."

So Ilsa was bitter enough to look a gift horse in the mouth. Like a cat licking a sore spot, she fingered the yellow star and he understood why she'd lashed out. She'd said, "No one wants Jews." How did that feel? He decided then to tell this wounded, hurting woman the truth. "I came because I once was in love with Chloe McCaslin and she asked me to help you, Gretel's family."

"You loved her?" Ilsa scoffed. "Love doesn't exist. Not for us—not for Jews."

Her sarcasm pushed him. For a moment he seriously considered shaking some sense into her. But he didn't have the right. "How much did Portugal want for a visa?" he snapped.

"Five hundred Deutschmarks." She straightened and faced him, flushed, defiant, her eyes bright in the November evening.

Drake pulled out his wallet and grabbed one of her hands. He counted the bills into her palm and folded her fingers over them. Then he put his wallet back. "Get the visa. Then come to me. I'm at the Grand Hotel. I'll be here another week on business and finishing up some diplomatic appointments."

"Why?" Ilsa held the money away from her as if it would contaminate her.

"Because Chloe asked me to get you . . . your family out of Germany if I could. From what your family said, they've given up on fleeing." Maybe it was easier to deny what was happening than face the nasty reality that they were no longer wanted in their own country and no other country wanted them either. How would he react if he were in this demeaning situation?

"I don't foresee things changing for the better here," he continued. "So you need to decide whether you're going to give up, too, or try to get out while you can."

He turned and walked away briskly. The street depressed him and he knew he'd have a long walk before he'd come to a street where taxis ran. Taxis didn't pick up Jews anymore, and Jews sat in the back of buses and streetcars—just like Jim Crow at home.

Ilsa's face lingered in his mind, making him feel things he

didn't want to feel, making him contemplate the impossible. He was a Gentile. She was a Jew who hated Gentiles — with good reason. And hadn't he adjusted to his bachelor life? He'd only ever loved Chloe and he'd lost her to a better man.

Then another unpleasant thought tugged at him — did he have the right or the obligation to tell Chloe Ilsa's secret?

Six days later, Drake stepped out of a taxi and found Ilsa standing off to the side of his hotel entrance. A jolt of pure attraction lanced through him. "Ilsa?"

Looking hunted, she met him. "I have the visa."

"Good. Come in." He took her arm, trying to reassure her of good intentions. "I'll buy you lunch and we can talk."

She shook her head. "They won't serve *Juden* in there," she taunted him.

Drake was at a loss. He flushed, his face hot.

"Come." She nodded her head toward the right. "Street vendors still sell to us. If you have *gelt*. I have none."

"Lead the way." He reached out to take her elbow, a gesture of concern.

She wrenched away. "It is best you not touch me. I'm *Jude, nicht wahr*?" Bitterness dripped from each word.

But Drake didn't blame her. The Nazi takeover in '33 had changed everything. Still, he should be glad of her fire. She wasn't giving in like her family. He'd sent them another note, again offering to help them and he'd received a polite no-thank-you in return.

So now he merely motioned her to lead on. Within two blocks, they entered *Unter den Linden,* Berlin's grand boulevard, "Under the Linden Trees." He led her to a cart selling tea in paper cups and sandwiches. The vendor wouldn't look at Ilsa or hand her the tea or sandwiches. Irritated, Drake paid him and handed one cup and sandwich to Ilsa.

She glared at him suddenly. "You realize this isn't Kosher?"

Drake stared at her. He wanted to ask her if she'd kept Kosher while married to the Gentile who'd tossed her out. But he held his temper. He could withstand her fiery darts. He even applauded her resistance to despair. "You're hungry, aren't you?" he asked at last.

"*Ja.*" She led him a few feet away to a park bench, where she ate her sandwich ravenously between gulps of hot tea. When she was done, Drake handed her his untouched sandwich. She flushed, but she took it. Staring down at her lap, she ate the second sandwich, rocking slightly against the cutting wind. "*Ich bin hungrig* always, always."

She wore a coat, but it hid nothing from him. Still he resisted pointing out the obvious reason for her constant hunger. "How long is the visa good for?" he asked, trying to keep the conversation impersonal.

"For three years."

"That long?" Passersby stared at them. An SA, a Nazi State policeman, halted across the boulevard from them and glared. It was an intimidating, malevolent stare Drake had never received from any American cop or official. It made Drake glad to have a US passport in his pocket. But Ilsa didn't and he didn't want to make her the Nazi's immediate target. Drake pulled her to her feet and discarded the paper cups in the nearby trash container.

Glancing at the SA officer, she whispered a curse and then, "Gestapo."

Drake led her away. "I'll try to find out about booking you passage—"

"I can do that. I'm just a Jew but I can arrange the rest."

He wanted to argue with her. But he decided it wouldn't do any good. The Gestapo officer remained where he was. His disapproving glare burned into Drake. But Drake shook it off. It wasn't yet against the law for Jews to talk to Gentiles. The Gestapo officer was just indulging in intimidation.

Still, Drake felt Ilsa's mounting tension within himself. He didn't like the way his gaze wanted to linger on her, the way she made the years roll off him, making him feel like he was twenty again and anything was possible. He opened his wallet. "Here is my card. If, after I leave, you need me or anything, write me or call collect. If I'm not home, my staff will take a message."

"You are very rich?" Again her tone oozed resentment.

"I'm comfortable, but I was rich in 1928." He gave a wry grin, but noticed she kept casting surreptitious, nervous glances back at the Gestapo officer. *Don't be afraid. He can't hurt you while I'm beside you.* But Drake was leaving Germany in a few days. Who would protect Ilsa then? Drake quickened their pace. *I'm just here to help out. I can't change things. None of this is my fault.* But still he felt the heavy guilt. And still, he wanted to protect this woman.

"This Chloe must be *sehr shoen* if you still want her when she's married to someone else and a mother," Ilsa pointed out suddenly with ripe sarcasm, as if daring him to get angry.

Why had she targeted Chloe? Was it jealousy or envy? "Chloe is the most beautiful woman I've ever known."

"Gretel said so in her letters. She says she is blond like

you and has blue eyes." Ilsa's tone sharpened even more. "She would make a good Aryan. Like you."

Drake stiffened at the insult. "I'm no fascist."

"And I'm no innocent. If you want me, I will go to the back entrance of the hotel. They will let me in that way. What is the number of your room?"

For a moment, he didn't understand what she was saying. Then it shocked him. "I can't believe you said that to me."

"Why not? I don't take charity. What is the number? Do you want me now or should I come back later?"

He reached out and captured her chin with an angry hand. "Don't insult me or yourself any further." He let go of her clenched jaw. "I know you're having a bad time. More than a bad time. But I didn't come to take anything from you."

"No, you are the hero of the play." She sneered at him. "You still serve your lady, Mrs. McCaslin—Chloe."

"If you met her, you'd never speak about her like that. She took Gretel in and has given her love and a home. She didn't have to. She did it because she's Chloe." He realized he was acting overly defensive—playing right into Ilsa's accusations—and made a face at himself. What this woman thought of him didn't matter. And even though he knew he wouldn't forget Ilsa Braun any time soon, they would remain strangers.

"I don't know anything of that kind of person. I am *eine Jude* in Deutschland. This is my home, but I am not wanted here. I am no longer a citizen. *Ich bin Untermenschen*, not human. I have no rights. I am nothing." She glared at him, daring him to take affront at her insults.

He had no answer for her. Frustration boiled through him. He couldn't help his blond hair and blue eyes any more than she could change her dark hair and race. He pulled out more cash and shoved it into her hand. "I don't deserve your insults. Buy yourself milk. The baby needs it now so its bones will be strong." He walked away without looking back.

CHAPTER FOUR

Washington, D.C., March 1938

*B*ette and Curt sat side by side in the impressive Presbyterian Church on New York Avenue. Bette was wearing a new black hat and gloves and had taken care that the seams of her silk stockings were straight. She always took care to look as if she fit this grand setting. Would Washington, D.C., ever cease to feel too grand for her, a little country girl?

Looking ahead, Bette recognized a few important figures—senators, congressmen, and War Department officials, some she worked for. She sat straight and proud, knowing they would see her with Curt, a handsome sophomore at Georgetown University. But more than anything, she was eager to share Gretel's exciting letter with Curt. Sharing news of Ilsa would make it feel real.

The pastor finished his sermon, which had touched on the *Anschluss*, the German takeover of Austria that very month without a shot fired. The pastor had asked for prayers for the Jews of Austria who would soon feel the Nazi heel upon them. Bette glanced around the congregation, wondering how many among them felt the same dread of Nazis.

Gretel's letters always brought news from home in Berlin and it was always bad. Bette had learned the fearful word *Eizelaktinen,* which meant random violence against Jews. Just last month, Gretel's father's store window had been smashed and he'd been dragged into the street and beaten—in front of a crowd of witnesses who'd turned and hurried away. Reading the stark words, Bette had felt shaken, as if it had happened to her own dear stepfather.

Now, amid sounds of muffled coughs and murmurs, Bette rose with everyone to sing the closing hymn. Curt's comfortable baritone joined her light soprano in the familiar words, "He hideth my soul in the cleft of a rock that shadows a dry thirsty land." But who would hide Gretel's family? "He hideth my life in the depths of his love and covers me there with his hand," she repeated this last phrase and made it a prayer for Gretel's family. But Gretel's letter had brought hope about Ilsa. Bette savored this as the benediction was pronounced.

Outside the sunshine was bright, but the breeze cool. Bette let Curt help her arms into the sleeves of her gray-wool jacket. He smiled at her and kissed her nose. "Where shall we go for lunch today?"

"You know it doesn't matter to me." She admired his eyebrows, a darker shade than his blond hair. "You decide."

"How about the Old New Orleans Restaurant?"

She nodded. They walked hand in hand down H Avenue past Lafayette Square heading for the streetcar. Overhead, the elms and sycamores along the way had bravely started to bud this week. She squeezed Curt's hand and imagined kissing his eyebrows, feeling the short soft hair under her lips. Thinking these forbidden thoughts, while they walked so circumspectly out in public made her feel naughty, outrageous.

"Are you sure you want to spend that much on lunch?" she asked. "We could just buy sandwiches and sit in the park."

"I like to show off my girl. And you're not wearing a sit-in-the-park outfit." Touching her cheek, he tucked her closer to his side. "Besides we only get to see each other on Sunday and I like to show you how much you mean to me."

The urge to point out that they could meet more often than once a week tempted Bette. But she repressed this. How could she argue with him when he complimented her and added a surreptitious kiss on her earlobe? "After lunch, I'll read you Gretel's letter," she promised. *And maybe I will kiss both your eyebrows, no matter what you say.*

"I like Gretel, but I love you," he murmured into her ear, making a shiver course down her neck.

How she loved to hear him say these things. "I love you, too," she murmured back, holding his arm tightly to her side. *So why can't we get married now, Curt?* Again, she kept her thought to herself. Why spoil the day with another disagreement about this topic? Soon, they reached the popular restaurant on Connecticut Avenue with its trademark painting of a large Negro woman wearing a long red gingham dress and red bandana tied around her head. Bette drew in the delicious aromas of fried chicken and fresh buttery corn bread.

After lunch, they rode the creaking, rattling streetcar again and then walked to the Washington Monument and sat down on one of the benches. Only a few tourists roamed the wide open space around the solitary obelisk. The cool breeze had chased most people inside, which gave them the privacy they craved. Bette wondered if the few tourists were far enough away to suit Curt's sense of propriety. Since she only got to see him once a week, she treasured their few moments of intimacy. But Curt would not kiss her until they were nearly alone. Still, she shivered with anticipation as he slipped his arm around her.

"Read me Gretel's letter," he said.

She reveled in their closeness as she opened the letter from her friend, who was working in a Jewish-owned dress shop in Brooklyn, and began reading. She soon came to the best part: " 'You'll be so happy to hear my good news. Ilsa's baby is finally well enough to travel. Ilsa was able to get passage out of Germany. When you receive this, she should be en route by train through Spain to Portugal. My family is so relieved. They were afraid that she would wait so long that her visa would lapse.' "

"I'm glad," Curt said with feeling. "I know you and Gretel have been worrying."

The tourists around the monument vanished and Bette's anticipation rose. Would Curt notice?

"Yes, it's such a relief," Bette continued as if nothing were about to happen. " 'But she won't be coming here. She hopes she can catch a ship to South America and—' "

Glancing around, Curt stopped her words with a kiss on the corner of her mouth. Bette held her breath, feeling the delicious warmth his kisses always brought her. Curt's kisses, the highlight of her Sunday afternoons.

"What else does Gretel say?" he murmured, trailing tiny kisses down the side of her neck.

"Gretel says: 'I will wait to hear from Ilsa. She will send me a telegram with the name of her ship and her destination.

When she lands, she will telegraph me again and I will go and help her get settled.' "

Keeping all her reactions to Curt muted because of the setting, Bette tried to focus on the next page. " 'I don't know how long I will stay. I'll work while she and the baby recover from the journey. I'm practicing my Spanish so I'll be ready for anything. I wish I were able to get my US citizenship but I have four more years before I can apply. I hope I won't have any trouble reentering the States on my resident visa but I'll face that if and when I must.' "

"Gretel's English has really improved." Then he turned her in his arms and kissed her full on the mouth.

Wrapping her arms around his neck, she breathed in the scent of him, memorizing the sensations rippling through her. He ended the kiss, but kept her close. "I'm worried," she murmured beside his ear. "What if Ilsa's ship gets—What if what happened to the *St. Louis* happens to her ship?"

Not long ago, the SS *St. Louis,* also from Portugal and packed with twenty thousand Jewish refugees, had been refused admittance to Central America and then the US. The ship had been forced to refuel and head back to Europe with all hands aboard. "How could America do that? Turn its back on people who need help so desperately?"

"Surely after the *Anschluss* that wouldn't happen again," Curt said. "I've heard that the US will be taking in more Jewish refugees."

Bette nodded, wishing he entered into her concern over Ilsa more than he did. But of course, he wasn't as close to Gretel as she was. And Ilsa was just a name to him.

"I hope they mean that." Sighing, Bette traced with one

finger the rim of his ear. "But all this talk about the Fifth Column . . . you know, 'secret Nazis.' I hear officers at work talking. They're afraid that some of the refugees could be Nazis in disguise, saboteurs."

Curt stroked her hair back from her face. "That Father Coughlin is the one who gets my goat. Why does anyone listen to his rabid anti-Semitism? I believe in freedom of speech, but his ranting is almost incitement to violence in my mind." He kissed her again, drawing it out, making it last.

Under the sweet assault of his lips, Bette forgot all about the problems of her time. They were too large for her to solve. The matter closest to her heart came out: "Curt, I wish we could just get married."

Ignoring her statement, he squeezed her hand even as he rose and pulled her up with him. "I have to start back. I have a lot of studying to do tonight."

"Curt, why won't you even discuss getting married? There is nothing keeping us apart but you."

"Bette," he said, steel infusing his words, "I won't marry you until I finish college and am able to support you as a husband should. It wouldn't look right. I won't have my wife supporting me."

"What does it matter if I go on working while you finish college—"

"Bette, you know the answer to this. Now don't spoil our time together."

She wanted to answer back, "I'm not spoiling our time together. Your pride and stubbornness are." But of course, she didn't. She decided to try a different tack. "Curt, I know that you're working and studying hard." She adjusted the hat on her head. "But couldn't we see each other more often? Couldn't we eat together Wednesday nights instead of just a phone call? I don't live that far from you—"

"Bette, we've been over this before." He sounded mildly peeved. "I want to be with you, too. But every hour of my week is allotted to classes, study, or work. If we married, you wouldn't see me except at breakfast and much later for a good night kiss. So what good would it be to be married?"

Bette thought that they'd have more time if they married. With her working, he wouldn't have to work and he could spend more time with her. But she wouldn't bring that up. He'd been very upset the last time she'd put it into words. She went back to her present argument. "But, why can't I see you mid-week?"

"I've told you—if I met you for dinner on Wednesday, I wouldn't be able to concentrate on my studies that night." Then he drew up her hand and kissed it. "You are a distraction. A lovely one, but still a distraction."

"I don't know if I like being called a distraction—even a lovely one," she pouted. The conflict tugged, worried her. But she shrugged it off. Her mother had explained that these types of things often came up during engagements. It was just part of beginning to work as a couple.

"Bette—" He paused, faced her, taking her shoulders in his palms. "Another two years and I should be through with school. I'll find a position as a teacher and we'll marry. I'm halfway through." He pulled her into an embrace. "And my high grades have kept my scholarship, so it won't take me five years as we'd feared. Our future is worth waiting for, Bette. At least, I think so."

Resting her head on his shoulder, she hurried to reassure

him. "Yes, you're right and by then, I'll have a down payment for a house saved."

"You don't have to do that." As always, he sounded disgruntled at this topic.

Her mother had also explained this to her; Curt's male pride was at stake. Shaking her head over the vagaries of men and their touchy pride, Bette brushed back his hair. "I know I don't, but doesn't it make good sense? Mr. Lovelady refuses to let me pay him any room or board. I buy myself new clothes all the time."

"A fact I much appreciate." Curt grinned and released her. He straightened his fedora and offered her his arm.

She took it, smiling at his compliment and filling with pride as she always did walking at his side. "I'm not saving every penny. I go to the movies and eat out as often as I wish. And I'm still saving over half my wages from the War Department. What else should that money go to but our future?"

"All right. You've got me there." He squeezed her hand in his and began leading her out of the park. "It would be nice to be able to afford a sweet little bungalow rather than renting something. I still don't really like you living rent free at Mr. Lovelady's—"

"We've been over that before, too," she scolded good-naturedly, proud that Curt wanted to take care of her. That's what every woman wanted, wasn't it? But, still, if it bothered Curt that much, he could change her living arrangements by agreeing to marry earlier than planned. So why should he complain? "Mr. Lovelady is rarely there. He says he likes the townhouse to be occupied. When he comes, he always brings along his mother as a chaperone so that the proprieties may be observed. And I like Mrs. Lovelady quite as much as I like

Mr. Lovelady. She and I always take in a concert or play together. She's such fun for an older lady."

"Well, I'd be happier if *Mrs.* Lovelady was his wife, not his mother."

"Oh, Curt." She shook his arm. "Mr. Lovelady's as old as my stepfather. Don't be silly."

He gave her a sheepish grin. "You mean everything to me, Bette."

His words made her feel small for pushing for marriage. Bette flushed with pleasure and murmured the words back to him. She couldn't think of a better way to end this conversation.

Two young people in love, they walked hand in hand to the streetcar and headed back to Georgetown. Curt walked her to the door of the red brick townhouse and kissed her good night. Glowing from his kisses, Bette didn't tell Curt that Mr. Lovelady and his mother were due in that evening. Why stir the water?

It was very late and Bette wondered if the Loveladys had been delayed until tomorrow. She wanted to tell Mr. Lovelady the good news about Ilsa. After all, he'd visited Ilsa and the rest of Gretel's family in Berlin almost two years ago. She sat upstairs in the window seat in her bedroom looking out over the jumbled skyline of Georgetown. Moonlight created a pattern of luminance and shadow. Mr. Lovelady had offered to let her redecorate the room when she'd moved in over a year ago, but she'd thought it was already lovely with its shirred white curtains, white satin counterpane, and lovely polished darkwood floor.

A copy of Steinbeck's newest novel, *Of Mice and Men,* lay open on her lap. She'd started it several times over the past week, but the story was too realistic for her taste. There was already too much cruelty going on in the world; she wanted a book that would take her away from it all, not remind her of it. Maybe she'd give in and read *Gone with the Wind* like everyone else in America.

The front door opened downstairs and voices floated up to her. She rose and went to her open door.

"We must be quiet," Mrs. Lovelady cautioned, "I'm sure Bette will be asleep by now. I've never had a train delay like that before. I'm so tired."

"It happens, Mother. Are you going straight up to bed or do you want a nightcap?"

"I'll come and have a sherry with you. I'm tired, but keyed up. A sherry would relax me."

Bette heard the sound of Mr. Lovelady hanging their coats in the front hall closet. Should she go down to greet them or not? She didn't want to intrude.

"Are you going to spend all your time running all over Washington this visit," Mrs. Lovelady asked, "or are you going to spend some time with me and Bette?"

That was a peculiar thing for Mrs. Lovelady to ask. Bette bent forward to hear better.

"Mother, Bette is practically engaged to a young college student and thinks of me as an uncle."

"Well, I still can't believe you let her mother get away from you . . ." Their voices faded as they must have gone into the front room.

Bette silently repeated the words she'd just overheard. *"I still can't believe you let her mother get away from you?"*

What had Mrs. Lovelady meant? Without letting herself think too much of consequences, Bette tiptoed down the steps and hovered in the hall, listening.

"Mother," Mr. Lovelady's voice rumbled from the parlor, "let it go. Chloe is very happy with her husband."

"I know and I wish them no harm." Mrs. Lovelady gave one of her grandiose sighs. "But what about Bette?"

"*Mother,*" Mr. Lovelady stressed with audible exasperation. "Enjoy your time with Bette but forget your romantic illusions."

Bette turned and raced silently up the steps. Breathing fast, she closed her door behind her. Mrs. Lovelady had hopes that Bette would fall in love with her son? The idea was so far from reality Bette had a hard time taking it in. She plumped down in the window seat again. Her mother had said Mr. Lovelady was an old friend. That was why he'd done Gretel the favor of visiting her family in Berlin. But had he been more to her mother? Bette recalled what people had said about her mother being a wild flapper. What had passed between her and Mr. Lovelady?

Early the next morning Bette walked stiffly into the sunny, white dining room to find Mr. Lovelady at the head of the table, hidden behind the *Herald*. "Good morning, Mr. Lovelady." She hoped the tremble she felt hadn't come out in her greeting. The words she'd overheard last night still tugged at her curiosity and conscience, made her uncertain with him.

The paper lowered. "Bette, good morning. You're looking lovely today—as usual."

She smiled, holding her lower lip with her teeth so she

wouldn't blurt out, "Did you love my mother? Why didn't you two marry?" With effort, she said in a polite, noncommittal voice, "I heard you and Mrs. Lovelady come in last night, but I was already in bed."

"Just where you belonged at that hour." He folded the newspaper and lifted his coffee cup.

She examined Drake Lovelady with new eyes. He was really quite good looking for a man his age.

He gave her one of his charming smiles. "How are things going at the War Department?"

She opened her starched cloth napkin and laid it in her lap. *Just act natural. Mother's so beautiful that probably a lot of men were in love with her.* "The usual. I type and then I file what I typed."

He chuckled. The familiar, friendly sound began to relax her. She poured herself coffee. Then she remembered what she'd wanted to tell him last night. "I received a letter from Gretel. She had news about Ilsa."

"Ilsa?" Drake gripped his cup tighter. Hearing Ilsa's name swept through him like a thunderstorm. He kept his face expressionless. But the image of the lovely young Jewess had remained starkly etched on his memory. He wished he'd succeeded in putting her out of his mind, but he'd failed completely. He'd even written her twice and wired money, but she'd never responded except with the barest acknowledgment of his gifts.

"Yes. She is on her way to Portugal by train." Bette leaned forward, her face glowing with innocent joy.

In contrast, Drake felt every one of his years and all their accumulated defeats with all their unappetizing truths. Ilsa would never even consider friendship with him. And why should she? She'd always look at him and feel obligation—and then irritation at having to be obligated to him. "Her child is well?"

"Her little girl is evidently well enough to travel." Bette sipped her orange juice.

Or perhaps Ilsa's so desperate that she's escaping while she still can. Drake stared into the murky depths of his coffee.

Since that day at *Unter den Linden* thoughts of Ilsa's offer to come to his room had lingered. They came now, un-bidden, the scene replaying in a manner different than what had actually happened: in his mind, instead of walking away, he crushed her to him and kissed her until she clung to him . . . He shook his head, sending this forbidden, foolish image away. At forty-two, he was a confirmed bachelor. And Ilsa wasn't for him. She was too young, too bitter—for good reason. And probably nothing would ever make her take a chance on another Gentile. He forced himself back to the present and swallowed his tepid coffee. "I'm glad."

"Gretel is improving her Spanish because she plans to travel to wherever Ilsa lands." Bette went on with a naive enthusiasm that irritated him like a particle of dust in his eye. It made him hope and there was no hope for him with Ilsa.

"Ilsa will need help with the baby. I'm worried though." Bette frowned. "Gretel is still not a US citizen and she may have trouble re-entering the US."

Drake reined in his sharp reaction. *This has very little to do with me. I've already done my part and I'm probably not needed anymore.* "When the time comes, let me know." He kept his voice even. "I'll contact my friends at the State Department and see what I can do."

"Thanks." Bette put down her spoon. "I'm worried. I won't breathe easy until Ilsa is safely landed in this hemisphere. What is going to happen in Europe, Mr. Lovelady? I worry . . . I worry." Bette sprinkled sugar on her cornflakes.

"That's because you are a very smart young woman." He patted her free hand, acting out his role as older friend of the family. Chloe's daughter had become lovelier as she matured over past year. Sometimes the way she turned or smiled reminded him of Chloe—when he'd met her here in 1919, nearly twenty years ago. "And you have the same caring heart as your mother." *Twenty years. Twenty.*

"I just wish I could do something."

"Bette, there is little we can do. History rolls on and over us humans—much like an SS tank." He gave the young innocent beside him a wry smile. *I can't make everything better. I can't make anything better.*

In his memory, Ilsa's drawn face and sarcastic voice spoke to him again: *"This is my home, but now Ich bin Untermenschen, not human."* And though he'd come to Berlin to help her, she'd mocked him as the "hero of the play."

I care about you, Ilsa, but you don't want me and I can do nothing more. I'm powerless against history—you knew that.

Off the Maryland Coast, July 1938

Bette couldn't believe where she was. And Mr. Lovelady's grim face set the tone as they stood at the rail of his yacht.

Not quite believing her eyes, she watched it slice through the moonlit waves of the Atlantic. This unexpected rescue mission had begun when Mr. Lovelady had come bursting into his house just as Bette was fixing herself an after-work cup of tea.

Within minutes, she'd breathlessly changed into casual slacks, blouse, and canvas shoes, called her superior at the War Department to say she'd been called away on family business and would be gone a few days. She'd scribbled a note to Curt, sealed it, stamped it, and left it out for the postman. Then Mr. Lovelady had driven her at a frightening speed through the summer sundown to Chesapeake Bay, where they'd boarded his yacht and immediately cast off.

Her emotions surged like the ocean swells below. A feeling of being caught up in a dream sharpened all her senses. The screeching gulls had quieted and then disappeared as the yacht left land far behind. Even though she'd been to Ocean City many summers and enjoyed harbor jaunts in small skiffs, she'd never been on the ocean before. Never out of the sight of shore. How would this night end? Would Mr. Lovelady's plan work?

He joined her at the rail. "The captain has finally raised the SS *Fortuna* on the shortwave radio and has gotten its coordinates. We are going to rendezvous with them in about six hours just outside the US maritime limit."

"I can't believe we're doing this." Bette's forearms rested on the railing. She leaned toward them, arching her tight back, stretching like a cat.

Mr. Lovelady stared out at the veiled Atlantic, clenching and unclenching his hands. "I just can't stand by and let what happened to the SS *St. Louis* happen to Ilsa and her child. We're getting her off that ship."

At his harsh tone, Bette's nerves tightened. The night breeze had cooled. Gooseflesh raised on her bare arms. "I've been sick ever since Ilsa's freighter was turned away from Costa Rica and then Vera Cruz." With the back of her hand, Bette rubbed her taut forehead, trying to ease the tension that gripped her. "How could they just turn them away?"

"The US is no better. The *Fortuna* is going to be allowed to dock at Roanoke. But only to refuel to head back to Portugal."

"Isn't there anything you could do through the State Department?" She turned toward him. The yacht's engine purred below them and she felt this shimmer under her feet.

"Believe me, as soon as Gretel called me in New York to tell me Ilsa's ship had been turned away at the Costa Rican port, I called everyone I could think of." Mr. Lovelady's voice shook with emotion. "And I've spent the past day going from desk to desk without luck. There is a bottleneck at the State Department. Someone named Long doesn't want Jews allowed in the US."

Bette gripped the slick railing, feeling as though she'd like to find the neck of that someone and twist it. "It's wicked."

Drake didn't bother to agree. Tonight he felt capable of murder. Maybe he could never have Ilsa in any true sense for his own, but he'd go to hell before he let her be sent back to Germany—her hell. "Ilsa's on a freighter," he said. "I can't imagine the conditions she's dealing with docking in the Gulf of

Mexico in this sweltering summer. I'm worried for her health." *I'm worried about Ilsa's mental state.*

An unbidden scene that had played over and over in his imagination for the past week sliced through him once more. He saw Ilsa holding her baby stepping off the side of a freighter and dropping—without a plea—into the dark waves below. He sensed that Ilsa was capable of this last act of defiance. A tightly coiled spring, she'd refused to give an inch those few times they'd battled in Berlin. If her ship headed back to Europe, she might not submit. The fear of this goaded him, forced him to make this attempt to save her. He could bear not having her, but he couldn't bear thinking of her dying in despair and loathing. *I'm not a praying man, Lord, but don't let her give in to the end of hope. Let me get there in time.*

"I've been dreadfully worried." Bette looked down and then back up. "But I still don't understand why you needed me to come along."

He gripped the railing, remembering Ilsa's harsh, bitter words: "Do you want me now or should I come back later?" "Ilsa has been very hurt." He chose his words with care for this young woman whom life had so far protected. She was Chloe's daughter, a caring young woman with the promise of inner steel, but he shouldn't tell her everything. "You and I can't begin to . . . understand the pain, the humiliation she's suffered. That faithless husband . . . the demeaning Nuremburg Laws . . ."

He lowered his face, staring down at the waves silvered with moonlight, seeing floating there the yellow Star of David she'd worn—degradation he couldn't imagine enduring. The salt spray sprinkled his face, leaving droplets like tears. He came up with an excuse. "I wanted you with me because you're Gretel's friend and Ilsa might question my motives for stopping the freighter out on the open sea and taking her off."

"Question your motives? Why?"

It wasn't his job to teach Bette the ways of the world. If he was reading the signs of the times accurately, she would have to face more than enough harsh realities in the coming years. "I told you—Ilsa's been through one horrible ordeal after another. I hope your presence will reassure her that I only mean her good. That help has come at last."

Bette sighed. "Gretel will be so grateful. She's wanted Ilsa to join her for so long."

And I've craved Ilsa all these months in vain. But she won't want me. And it would never work out between us— not in this world, not in this lifetime.

Even though hoping had made no sense, he'd tried but he had been unable to get her out of his mind. *Still, I won't be able to live with myself if I don't do this.* He couldn't say any more now or it would all come flowing out, sweeping away this ingénue's naïveté. "Bette, why don't you go below and try to get some sleep?"

"I can't sleep. I'll just sit out here and wait." She turned and sat in a wood lounge chair. Drake remained at the rail, unable to stop searching the vast, dim horizon for Ilsa's ill-fated freighter. Fear settled into his belly—hard and hot, pulsing like a malignant force.

Drake gripped the railing and waited out the nautical miles, bucking the Atlantic swells, tacking east-southeast for international waters. As the first gleam of dawn hovered over the vista, finally, one of his crew of two gave the shout, "The *Fortuna*'s off starboard, sir!"

Drake hurried to starboard and glimpsed the running lights of the long, low freighter. Before long, he was rowing the twenty feet to the freighter's side, Bette in the rear of the small wooden skiff. He tied up on to the metal ladder. With the skiff bobbing with every move they made, he helped Bette get started up the ladder, then scrambled up behind her. On board the gently rolling deck, they were met by a short, swarthy man in sweat-stained khakis. The deck was gritty underfoot and the smell of oil hung over them.

"Are you the captain?" Drake asked in a hushed voice, which the early morning hours seemed to demand.

"First mate. I speak English. You want one of the passengers?" In the damp, predawn charcoal gray, a crowd of shadowed shapes appeared in the mist and moved closer.

Drake folded his arms against the chill. "Yes, I want Ilsa Braun and her child."

"Me?"

It was Ilsa's voice. She was still there—alive. The relief washed through him like fresh warm water. "Ilsa, it's me, Drake Lovelady. And Bette, Gretel's friend, came with me."

Ilsa emerged from the deep gloom. She held a very small sleeping child in her arms. She looked even thinner than two years ago. Murmurs in German swelled around her. "Why have you come?" she demanded.

He heard the distrust in her voice. What did she think he would do to her that could be worse than going back to the Nazis? "To take you," he explained in a voice that said that she should have expected him, "from the ship before it docks in Virginia."

"We'll take you home with us to Washington, D.C." Bette went to Ilsa and gave her a quick hug.

"You will take me into the country illegally?" Ilsa demanded, standing stiff and unmollified. "I would be thrown in prison and then deported."

"No," Drake said, knowing Ilsa would fight him, "that won't happen. I'm going to have the captain marry us and take you into the country as my wife. You will gain US citizenship when I marry you." There, he'd said it. His voice had come out shaky. He cleared his throat and turned to the first mate. "Take us to your captain." His voice firmed. "He can legally marry us in international waters."

"No!" Ilsa exclaimed.

CHAPTER FIVE

In the dimness of approaching dawn, Drake saw Ilsa's face twist in dismay; it was a honed blade into his heart. But he'd expected this from her, hadn't he? He had to make her face the fact that she had no other choice. It was marry him or face horrors he couldn't even name. With two long strides, he was in front of her. He slipped the child from her arms and handed her to Bette. Ilsa released the child without protest. Then he leaned close to Ilsa's face and spoke low and fiercely. "I'm not taking no for an answer. You are marrying me and then we're heading back to Georgetown."

Ilsa's sunken eyes flamed at him. "I don't want to marry a Gentile, a *goy*. I don't want to marry any man." She spat at his feet. Disapproving murmurs hedged them on all sides.

"This isn't about marriage and you know it." He gripped her arms. "You know why you fled Germany." He felt the anger building in him—rage at the situation, at this woman who wouldn't give an inch. "In the *Fatherland*, you're no longer considered human and, Ilsa, it isn't against the law to kill animals."

Ilsa looked stunned; her mouth groped for words, but only a whimper came out.

I can't let you go back. I refuse. "Do you want to live or do you want to die?" He shook her arms.

Ilsa swayed, and then she nodded. "Very well. You win."

Bette hung back, as stunned as Ilsa by his words, stunned by her surroundings. She'd seen hobos begging at the back door of Ivy Manor. She'd seen sharecroppers who owned nothing but the ragged clothes on their backs. But she'd never seen degradation like this.

And it wasn't just what she glimpsed in the grayness. She'd never smelled anything like the stench that hovered over the freighter—a combination of salt water, sweat, urine, and vomit. The child in her arms reeked. She tried not to breathe through her nose, held her free hand to her side so she wouldn't cover her nose, her eyes, or turn and run away. She hadn't expected it to be like this, to see humans reduced to huddled, stinking shadows.

Mr. Lovelady turned with Ilsa, now drooping limply by the arm he clenched, and faced the first mate. "Take us to your captain."

Bette almost told him to stop gripping Ilsa so tightly, that he was hurting her, but she couldn't open her mouth. She shook inside, the horror of this scene nearly pulling her apart. Tears hovered. She forced her emotions down.

"No, I bring him." The first mate hustled away, his rubber soles slapping the deck and disappearing into the forecastle.

"Bette," Drake said, "you will be a witness. The first mate can be another." Ilsa said nothing, just stood there held up by Mr. Lovelady, barely breathing.

Bette nodded. The shadows around Ilsa shifted. Eyes gleamed in the faint light. Here and there, Bette glimpsed a pale hand or a face in profile. But the light was low and the faces were smudged with dirt and grime. Bette wanted to step back, prevent these faces from coming closer to her, wanted to close her eyes and not be here. She gripped her lower lip with her teeth to keep from crying out.

With one hand, Mr. Lovelady drew Ilsa closer to him and reaching out, gently brushed the little girl's dark, matted hair. "How is she?"

"She . . . lives." Ilsa said no more.

With the child lying against her, Bette moved to stand beside Mr. Lovelady, seeking, needing his protection. The faces drifted closer to them. As if to hold them at bay, Bette stroked the little girl's head. It felt too warm to her and the child looked more like an infant than a toddler.

Parting the shadow people, the first mate shuffled back with another older man at his side. "This is Captain Montoya."

"Captain, I want you to marry me to this woman and then I'm taking her away with me." Mr. Lovelady shook the man's hand. In the growing dawn, Bette watched him press an American bill into the captain's palm. Was it a fifty?

The captain spoke to the first mate at length in Spanish — or was it Portuguese? The first mate turned to Mr. Lovelady to translate. "The captain says he has never done this, but it is in his power. But you have to speak your own words. Then I tell him what you have said. He will write of the marriage in the ship's log."

Bette felt the soundless crowd listening and watching intently. Did they understand English? The silent gathering hovered around them now, hemming them in completely. She, Mr. Lovelady, Ilsa, the captain, and first mate stood like an island in their midst. The scene with its ghostly sentinels began to take on the aspect of a dream.

"Does the captain have any stationery or paper with the company's name on it?" Mr. Lovelady asked. "He will write that on this date he married us and you and my young friend can sign as witnesses. I'll need proof when I get back on shore."

The first mate relayed that to the captain, who nodded in agreement. Bette shivered in the chill dampness of the early morning breeze, shivered with the nearness of the company of noiseless wraiths.

Mr. Lovelady turned to Ilsa. "I don't remember all the marriage ceremony. I don't usually pay much attention. Let's just do the vows part. He held her hand. "I, Drake Lovelady, take you, Ilsa Braun, as my wedded wife. To have and to hold from this day forward in sickness and health, for richer for poorer, for better or worse, until death us do part."

Ilsa didn't move. Bette wondered if she would cooperate. Why didn't she understand what was going on? *He's trying to keep you from going back. What's wrong with you?*

"Repeat after me," Mr. Lovelady ordered, "I, Ilsa Braun, take you . . ."

Ilsa just stood there looking at him. Bette touched her bony arm. Nothing. The crowd stirred with dismay, shuffling, whispering, edging nearer. The back of Bette's neck crawled with sensation. And suddenly she wanted to scratch her arms as if her skin were crawling with vermin.

Mr. Lovelady leaned closer. "Say it."

"I, Ilsa Braun, take you, Drake Lovelady . . ."

Mr. Lovelady began again, "... as my wedded husband ..." He recited the vows again and she repeated them as if she were reading a grocery list. Then he looked at the captain. "Let's get the paperwork done."

Within minutes, Mr. Lovelady was descending the ladder to the skiff, the smudged, handwritten wedding certificate folded in his shirt pocket. Ilsa came down next. Bette with the child in one arm was the last one over the side. As she stood there on the top rung, looking toward the deck, the sun's light backlit the ghost people. They stared at her—alive yet appearing already dead. Most looked at her blankly, but a few pled silently for her to take them, too. *I can't. I can't marry anyone, hide anyone. I can't do anything.*

She lifted a hand in farewell and then let herself down the metal rungs. She stepped carefully into the rocking skiff and hunched down in the bow. Ilsa, who had settled in the stern, looked at her child in Bette's arms and murmured something soothing in German. And Mr. Lovelady sat in the middle. He rowed them away.

On board his yacht, Mr. Lovelady ordered the captain to head for Chesapeake Bay again. Ilsa took her child back. Then she collapsed into a deck lounging chair and fell asleep as if someone had hit her with a hammer. Mr. Lovelady paced the deck, which purred again with the engine's vibrations.

Leaning against the railing, Bette stood a few feet away, watching Ilsa with the child sleeping on top of her. Bette turned and looked back at the freighter, already moving away in the misty dawn. From the freighter, no one waved goodbye or called to Ilsa. They had been left to whatever fate would bring them, and Ilsa was going to America, to safety.

Guilt rose in Bette's throat. *Why is this happening? Why*

is there someone like Hitler? Why am I safe while girls like Gretel are in danger? It isn't fair! Unable to look away from the ship drawing away on the horizon, she knew she'd never forget the haunted faces in the murky dawn.

Drake had achieved his goal; he'd saved Ilsa. She and the child were here. But would she ever be his? Or would she bury herself in bitterness and hold herself away from him?

The doctor held the silent, limp child in his arms. A freshly scrubbed Ilsa in a pale summer cotton nightgown borrowed from Bette stared at the doctor and Drake from the high bed where she sat propped up on pillows. Bette had left them to buy groceries. Earlier in the backyard, Drake had burned Ilsa's clothing to kill the lice and fleas. He had showered afterward, feeling unclean, defiled.

"The child appears healthy, but malnourished," the doctor said.

"I have fed her only breast milk," Ilsa muttered, picking at a scab on her knuckle. "I was afraid the food on the ship might not be good."

"A wise decision. I don't suppose your diet has been the best, and both of you have suffered." He turned to Drake. "I'm going to administer vitamin shots to your wife and the child for a week and then she can begin to take vitamin tablets. I want her to drink lots of fresh milk and fruit juices. She should have a soft, bland diet at first until her stomach adjusts. Rich food or spices and butter will only make her sick."

Drake breathed in guarded relief. He'd feared that the child might be in danger of dying—she was so quiet, so tiny.

The doctor handed Drake the child and administered the

vitamin shots. Ilsa didn't even flinch and the child only whimpered once. "I'll be back tomorrow to check on my patients." Black bag in hand, he walked out, leaving Drake alone with Ilsa.

Drake gazed at Ilsa. Her face was clean now but still drawn and so thin, with dark smudges beneath her eyes. There was so much he wanted to say to her, but not now. "Why don't you finish that glass of milk?" He nodded toward the tray on the little bedside table.

Ilsa obeyed him without comment. He was afraid to move for fear of upsetting the child who felt so thin, almost weightless, in his arms. At eighteen months old, little Sarah weighed only fourteen pounds—about half what the doctor said she should weigh. "Do you want more toast or cheese and crackers?"

Ilsa drained the last of the milk and shook her head. "I only want to sleep. Give me Sarah, *bitte.*"

Drake awkwardly moved forward and transferred the child to Ilsa. He stood there watching her arrange the child beside her. He was wrung with pity for the little girl. And he longed to lay down beside Ilsa and hold her. Just hold her. *You're safe now, Ilsa.* "Shouldn't we have a cradle or something for her to sleep in?"

Ilsa shrugged. "I have always kept her beside me."

"I'll let you get some sleep." He turned to leave.

"Why did you do this, Drake Lovelady?" Ilsa's question stopped him.

He paused. He tried to bring up a glib explanation and found he couldn't. *I don't want this to be just a marriage in name only. But you aren't ready for the truth of how I feel, Ilsa.* "Go to sleep, Ilsa. We'll talk tomorrow."

"Does it make you feel like the hero again?" she asked, sarcasm soaking every word.

"Sleep, Ilsa." He left, closing the door gently behind him. In the hallway, he found himself wracked by waves of hot uncertainty, like a case of inverted chills. He'd gambled. He'd married her. *Please, Ilsa, give life a chance. The time for bitterness should, can come to an end now.*

A month later, Drake sat beside Ilsa with her daughter in her arms in the front seat of his Cadillac. The wind through the open car windows fanned the heat of summer over them, speeding up the evaporation, but not cooling them. Chloe had invited Drake and Ilsa to spend time at Ivy Manor. Drake had agreed to visit in hopes that somehow Chloe or the change of scenery could help him break down the wall between Ilsa and himself.

"Is summer always so hot?" Ilsa asked, holding the baby away from her.

He gripped his self control. As days had passed, Ilsa had not given an inch, remaining prickly. He'd almost come to the conclusion he should just set her up in an apartment in New York City and let her have her privacy. But he wasn't willing to give up yet. "Sometimes it's hotter." Drake tugged to loosen his tie. Then he saw Ivy Manor's chimneys in the distance. A smile lifted his mouth. Why did he think that Chloe could help him reach Ilsa? "There it is."

Within minutes, Drake was leading Ilsa up the front walk toward the front door. It flew open and Chloe with Roarke at her side came toward them with open arms. "Drake! Ilsa, welcome!"

For a few moments, everything was a happy jumble. Chloe hugged Ilsa and claimed the child, then she shook Drake's hand after Roarke had finished greeting him.

"We're so glad you've brought your bride to meet us." Chloe turned to Ilsa again and took her hand. "Come into the backyard. We'll sit out in the shade in the summer house and drink iced tea."

"I am happy finally to meet the beautiful Chloe," Ilsa said, casting a glance at Drake.

Chloe didn't react to Ilsa's odd remark. She just urged her along. Drake wondered whether coming here had been a good idea. But if Chloe with her warm heart, and the peace here at Ivy Manor, couldn't help Ilsa, what could?

Later that evening, the summer sunset laced rosy fingers through the surrounding trees, lush green and some bending their willow whips to the stream. Ilsa stood in the doorway of the cottage and watched the lovely Chloe walk away hand in hand with her husband. Seeing the couple holding hands and talking to each other stung something deep inside Ilsa. Had she ever been that loved, that carefree?

Memories of her first husband bobbed in her mind until the stark image of his hard expression—as he put her out into the street—blotted out everything else.

Rubbing her arms as if chilled, she turned back and faced the man with her in the little cottage. Sarah already slept in a bed in the cottage's one bedroom. For the first time since she'd become Mrs. Drake Lovelady, Ilsa was completely alone with him. In Georgetown, Bette was always down the hall and Drake had hired a full-time maid and cook. But here in this little cottage hidden away in a grove of ancient willows and elms, she and her husband were alone.

Her husband. No, the man who'd saved her life, the man

she should be grateful to. She shuddered. *I don't want to be grateful to any man.*

"Why have you brought me here?" she asked, lethally quiet.

Leaning against the doorjamb, Drake looked at her. "How do you like Bette's family?"

She ignored his question. Was he taunting her with Chloe, the woman he'd once loved? "I'll be happy when Gretel comes. Why haven't you taken me to New York, to see Gretel?"

"Are you hungry? Thirsty?"

Why was he always so good to her? Why wouldn't he tell her what he wanted from her, what he wanted in payment for rescuing her and Sarah? "No, I—"

"You didn't eat enough at dinner." He stood up straighter. "I'm going to pour you a glass of milk and make you a snack."

"I'm not hungry." Her stomach rumbled, protesting its hunger, making her a liar. She felt like spitting, hissing like a cat. *I don't want to accept anything else from you.*

"Little Sarah needs you to eat more," he said and gently took her hand and led her into the small kitchen. She sat down at the little table, only big enough for two, and watched him open the small white icebox. He shook a glass quart of milk and poured her a tall serving of the creamy-white farm-fresh liquid.

Her mouth became wet as the glass of cold milk begged her to take a sip, just a mouthful. But she couldn't. She stared at it, unable to move. After watching her a moment, Drake sighed and turned to slice a rosy peach into wedges. He placed them on a plate and set it before her.

"Why do you do things for me?" she asked, resting her

face into a hand. The weight of the debt she owed him threatened to crush her tonight. "I could do that."

"But you don't. You don't eat unless I tell you to. You don't sleep unless I tell you to go to bed. I must wake you in the mornings or you would sleep the day away."

She stared down at the perfect yellow, pink-tinged flesh of the peach. She wanted so much to lift a slice to her mouth and taste its sweetness, taste that unique flavor that only a peach possessed. She could not. She could not bring herself to lift the succulent fruit to her lips. She nearly wept with desire for its sweetness. "Help me," she whispered at last.

Drake sat down across from her and picked up a slice and slipped it into her open mouth. The peach was the most delicious she'd ever tasted; its sticky-sweet juice flowed over her tongue, her lips, down her chin. She swallowed it greedily and licked her lips. She felt ashamed eating it. Her mother and father weren't eating peaches. She felt like a traitor.

And then with a guilty look, she asked for another.

He wiped her chin with a starched linen kitchen towel and then fed her another slice. Then he took the glass of milk and held it to her lips. She drank half the glass in one long draught. It was delicious, creamy and cold, satisfying her hunger, her thirst—filling her.

She thought about this man. She wanted to ask, "Why did you marry me?" But how foolish. He'd married her to save her life. Nothing more. She wouldn't make a fool of herself. She couldn't survive another rejection, another chance of being put out into the street like an unwanted, inferior parcel. "I should be grateful," she said. She hadn't meant to say that out loud.

"I don't want your gratitude," Drake replied without any

trace of passion or anger in his voice. But he wouldn't meet her eyes.

"What do you want?" She accepted another wedge from his fingers. They brushed her lips, setting off an unexpected tingle that spread out and down over her face and neck. She'd felt dead for so long, the sensation nearly took her breath away.

"I want you to be my wife. I want Sarah to be my daughter."

She didn't believe his words, couldn't let herself believe them. She swallowed. She imagined his lips brushing the tender flesh of her neck. *No. Stop reacting to him.* "Why?"

"I don't know." He rubbed his neck as if it pained him.

"You must know." She imagined him folding back her collar and pressing kisses to her throat. *Where were these thoughts, these sensations coming from?* "Tell me. I must understand." Ilsa felt tears well up in her eyes. She clenched her hands in her lap. Why would he want her? Want her mixed-race child? Her own father had hated to look at his grandchild. She'd understood why. It had nothing to do with Sarah. It had to do with her husband, a Gentile, rejecting her, and about their having to wear yellow stars, and about everything else that Nazis had done to them just because they were Jews.

Drake didn't even ask her about Sarah's father. Didn't ask her for anything really.

"Men don't always know why they want something." Drake finally looked into her eyes as if probing her. "All I know is that I couldn't forget you. Isn't it enough that I came for you and brought you home? That I asked you to be my wife? I'm just trying to take care of you and Sarah and you attack me at every turn. What do you want from me?"

"I don't know." A lie. She wanted what every woman wanted, but fear paralyzed her. She looked past him out the open window to the green and chartreuse weeping willows outside. Again she imagined his lips touching her. *No. No.* She'd closed her mind to wanting any man's touch. She'd closed her mind to wanting love and justice, to wanting anything, to doing any more than nursing Sarah and remembering to breathe.

"Ilsa," he whispered, "what do you want?"

"For a long time," she whispered, the words rasping her throat, "I stopped feeling. You are trying to make me feel again and I don't want to." Deep inside and against her will, she felt herself, felt the desire to live stirring. And more dangerous the urge to reach out to another, to a man, to this man.

"Ilsa, I'm not trying to make you do anything. I just want you safe. I just want you here."

No. "You want me in bed," she challenged him. "Why haven't you just taken me to your bed?"

Drake didn't show any shock at her bald question. "I haven't taken you to my bed because you haven't wanted me to."

"I've offered several times to come to you." With just the tip of one finger, she touched one of the cool, wet peach slices.

"Yes, out of obligation. I want you to come to me because you want me, want Drake Lovelady, your husband."

She pulled her hand back from the tempting fruit and folded her arms around herself, chilled in the summer heat. "Why do you want me? Do you think I have something other women don't? It isn't true. I am just like every other woman."

"You are the only woman I've ever married," he said with

painstaking patience in each syllable. "*That* makes you different than every other woman."

What was he saying? What did that mean? "You only married me to keep me from going back to *Deutschland*." She leveled her eyes at him like a gun. "You only married me out of pity."

"Ilsa, I didn't marry you out of pity," Drake snapped. "Don't you realize that I was attracted to you, just attracted as a man to a woman? I would have pursued you—if your life in Germany hadn't been so mixed up. How could I?"

"What do you mean, pursued me?" She looked down at the peach. Every slice he'd fed her had felt like a kiss, his fingertips brushing her lips, feeding something deep inside her, something that had withered.

"I met you in Berlin—where you had to wear a degrading yellow star. Where you'd been rejected by your husband who'd promised to love and honor you for life. How could I just walk up to you and ask you for a date?" He muttered an oath. "I couldn't even take you into a restaurant for lunch. In that place with Gestapo agents watching us, how could I let you know what I was thinking, feeling?"

"You would have asked me on a date?" she asked, not believing he'd said this. "A *date*?" She mocked him with the word.

He stood up, shoving his chair back, knocking it over.

She cowered in front of him, nearly upsetting the glass of milk.

"Look at you." His voice sounded low in his throat. "You pull back as though I'm going to strike you. I'm no Gestapo agent, no SS trooper, no Nazi. I'm Drake Lovelady.

The man who loves you though he doesn't know why. The man who married you and wants you and Sarah."

She stared at him, understanding at last rippling through her. "You just want me?"

"Yes, is that so hard to believe?"

She closed her eyes, hiding them under cupped hands. "The way things have been in Berlin since '33. Some days I just wanted to walk to the River Spree and drop into its water and stop thinking, feeling, existing."

"I was afraid of that. I was afraid that you would drop over the side of the freighter and drown yourself and Sarah."

"You thought that?" He knew her that well? She looked at him, looked at his fair hair and blue eyes, the Aryan ideal she'd learned to despise. But Drake couldn't help his race—any more than she could.

"Yes, I was afraid you'd do yourself harm."

The final resistance to him began disintegrating. "I would have." She leaned forward, the words pouring from her. "If you hadn't come, I'd made up my mind I'd do that if we were turned back to Europe."

"I know." His voice welled up from deep inside, so dark, so taut.

She stared at him, scrutinizing his expression. He knew her that well? "Why did you care?"

"I told you I don't know. But it's you or no one."

She gazed at him, reading the truth in his eyes. What could she say to protect him from her own fear, her overwhelming bitterness? She still didn't feel capable of loving, but she was hurting him—that was clear. He didn't deserve such thanklessness.

Then it came to her. She only had to let him love her. Maybe she would never be able to love him back, but she could behave like a wife. "Then, my husband, let it be me." And she opened her arms.

CHAPTER SIX

December 1939

Alone in the cozy kitchen at Ivy Manor, Bette stared out the window at the snowflakes falling lazily. Outside, they gathered, creating a narrow white line at the edge of the lane to Ivy Manor's back door. The rich scents of Christmas baking hung in the air—cloves, nutmeg, ginger, and cinnamon. She rubbed her eyes. Hours and hours of filing and typing left her with tired eyes most weekends.

But her fatigue wasn't from that. Suspicion whispered through her mind. Wrestling with doubt and unanswered questions kept her awake nights. This silent admission opened her to an attack of ideas—a pack of wolves, all howling, snarling and trying to tear away her peace of mind. Why did she notice things? Why didn't she just mind her own business?

But it is my business.

No. She only had four days at home for the holiday and she wouldn't let worry spoil them. Curt was at his parents' home, too. Soon, he'd come to take her to cut down a Christmas tree. Bette wondered again if she were imagining things about her office at the War Department, if she should ask Curt what he thought.

Jamie McCaslin's face bobbed up at the side window, startling her. Home for the holidays from Columbia University, Jamie was her stepfather's much younger adopted brother. He lived with her step-grandfather, Mr. Thomas McCaslin, at the nearby McCaslin house. Always the clown, Jamie grinned and waved. She grimaced and motioned him inside. Within seconds, he burst through the back door, bringing with him the cold wind and his unique energy. "Hey, kid!" he greeted her. Before she could duck away, he shoved his large, cold hands against the back of her neck.

"Jamie!" she shrieked, jumping up and away from him.

His dark hair tousled from the wind, he chuckled and walked backward with his hands up as if she were threatening him. "Hey, I couldn't resist."

She shook her head at him, trying not to smile. In the years since they'd both left home, she hadn't seen much of Jamie. Being male, he never wrote her, of course, but her mother kept her current on all his activities as an engineering major and cross-country athlete at Columbia.

"Have you seen Gretel?" she said, flouncing back down.

"Yes, I've invited her to a few anti-Nazi rallies on campus." Jamie swung a kitchen chair around and then sat down facing its back. His wrists rested on its top. His eyes were grim. "At the last one, she even got up and told her story. And Drake and Ilsa have had us over for dinner a few times at their brownstone. Hey, why don't you take them up on the offer of a weekend in the big city?"

So far as their letters showed, the Loveladys appeared to be doing well. Ilsa was expecting now. But Bette's reason for staying in D.C. was simple. "I only get to see Curt on weekends."

A *ratatat* knock on the back door and Curt stepped inside. He was rubbing his hands together. "It's perfect weather for cutting a Christmas tree. You coming, too, Jamie?" Curt came to her and kissed her hello.

She beamed at him. He always kissed her hello and she loved it.

"Sure." Jamie pulled a stocking cap out of his plaid jacket pocket. "Let's get the hatchet." Jamie grinned.

Curt frowned at her. "You're wearing slacks?"

Bette looked down at her ivory sweater and tan gabardine slacks. "Yes, we're just going into the woods to cut down a tree." *Don't be stuffy, Curt.*

"And hey, it's cold out there," Jamie added.

"You're right." Curt grinned sheepishly. "It's just that I don't like to see women dressing like men. It just isn't flattering."

Bette had hoped she looked a little like Katherine Hepburn.

"But you look fine, Bette, just like you always do," Curt reassured her. "Come on." He tucked her hand into his elbow and squired her out into the chilly day.

"So how're the wedding plans coming?" Jamie teased as he followed them.

"By this time next year," Bette said, donning a scarf over her long pageboy hairstyle, "we'll be Mr. and Mrs. Curtis Sinclair."

"You will if this guy here isn't drafted by next year." Jamie gestured toward Curt.

"Drafted?" The word had begun to make her stomach clench every time she heard it. Bette didn't want to admit out loud that this had worried her, too.

"The draft's just being considered," Curt said stiffly. "We don't know if Congress will even bring it to a vote."

"Yeah." Jamie's mouth twisted into a parody of a smile. "I think it's a sure thing. Now that Britain and France have declared war on Germany for invading Poland, it's just a matter of time."

Fear piercing her like a fine needle, Bette made a face. "I work at the War Department, remember?" she scolded. "I hear quite enough of this at work every day. I don't need to hear it during Christmas." And she'd been instructed when she was hired that she was never to discuss anything she heard or saw at work to anyone outside the War Department. Would discussing her suspicions with Curt violate that trust?

"Well, not discussing the draft won't make it go away," Jamie said, looking grim.

"If it comes, it comes," Curt said, closing the door behind them. "I'm hoping we can still avoid this European war. A draft might interrupt our wedding plans."

Hearing this shocked Bette into silence. She forced herself to keep her mouth closed because of Jamie's presence. Another postponement? Curt was wishing the war in Europe wouldn't affect them? There was absolutely no way it couldn't affect them. And he was thinking the draft might postpone their wedding again? The cold made her shiver and adrenaline made her pulse race.

Talk ended as they tramped through the wooded parcel on the Carlyle estate. Bette strode arm in arm with Curt while Jamie jogged ahead, vowing to find the perfect tree before the "love birds" had a chance.

Feeling snowflakes melt on her face, Bette closed her eyes. She drew in the cold clear country air and wished that the war in Europe was not marching straight at them. That July night she'd gone with Mr. Lovelady to rescue Ilsa and little Sarah had made it forever impossible for her to ignore the signs of the times, to ignore what Nazi Germany stood for. And just this fall J. Edgar Hoover, the head of the FBI—the head of countering Nazi espionage by order of the president—had warned every American to be alert for espionage, sabotage, and subversion. His very words.

"What's wrong, Bette?" Curt asked, slipping one hand underneath her collar and massaging her neck through her sweater.

"Nothing," she lied, feeling her nape tingle at his touch. "Just tired." How could Curt even consider postponing their wedding scheduled for the coming August?

He tucked her closer to him the way he always did when he wanted to show concern. "Well, you'll soon be able to quit your job and be busy making a home for us. Just one more semester, darling. Let's not let war talk spoil our holiday together."

She nodded bravely, pushing away Jamie's unwelcome mention of the draft and Curt's troubling reaction.

"That's all I've ever wanted, Curt." She searched his eyes earnestly, wanting her words to say so much more that they did. "To be your wife, to make a home for us." So soon, she hoped she wouldn't be living in a crowded city. She'd be settling into a little bungalow somewhere, clipping recipes from the newspaper, making curtains, planning for their children. It would be wonderful, what she'd always dreamed of.

I'll deal with my suspicions when I get back to Washington. I can't let anything spoil this Christmas. She wanted to stop there, but her mind went on: *Because this might be the last Christmas before war.*

Washington, D.C., January 1940

Bette felt her heart jerking and jumping behind her breast bone. She'd asked for a longer lunch today so she could run errands. The truth was she had only one errand. She was going to visit J. Edgar Hoover's mother. And in front of her was the small frame home where the head of the FBI lived, the same home he'd been born in. Bette was trembling from head to toe as she faced the shiny black door. She took the brass knocker in hand and tapped twice. Would Mrs. Hoover be home? Did Bette want her to be home? Bette thought she might be sick.

The door opened and a white-haired, plump lady in a deep purple dress looked out.

"Mrs. Hoover?" Bette warbled.

"Yes?"

"I'm Bette Leigh McCaslin." She ignored the pounding at her temples. "We have a mutual friend, Mrs. Drake Lovelady senior."

"Why, yes, did Matilda send you?"

"No, but I need to talk to you, please." Bette inhaled deeply. "May I come in? I don't have much time. I'm on my lunch hour from the War Department."

"Come in, dear." Mrs. Hoover stepped back and led her into a small Victorian parlor crowded with photographs and knickknacks. She motioned Bette to sit down across from her. The house smelled of lavender and lemon polish. "Now what can I do for you, Miss McCaslin?"

"I'm worried about something at the War Department." The pent-up words gushed from Bette's lips. "I'm in charge of keeping up the personnel files and something strange has been happening. I thought I would explain it to you and you could see if your son thinks it's anything that I . . . that *he* should be concerned about."

"I see." Mrs. Hoover's pale eyes studied Bette thoroughly through rimless glasses. "Why did you come to me here and not just go directly to the FBI offices?"

Bette took a deep breath. "Because I didn't want anyone from my office to suspect that I've noticed anything out of the ordinary. And I knew that you'd played bridge with Mrs. Lovelady senior and I thought I could use that as an explanation for coming here."

Mrs. Hoover nodded. She didn't look like she thought Bette was crazy. "Why don't you tell me and I'll relay it to Edgar when he gets home this evening?"

Relief made Bette almost weak in the knees. "Thank you, Mrs. Hoover. This is what I've observed."

The next day after work, Bette didn't board the bus for Georgetown. Through the early dark of winter, she made her way back to the same small white-frame house. Within minutes, Mrs. Hoover, in a dark green dress, had greeted her and led her to the parlor again. "Miss McCaslin, this is my son."

The head of the FBI, almost six feet tall with wavy black hair and black eyes and a determined jaw line, stood facing her. Bette forced herself to return his firm handshake with a confidence she was far from feeling. *He must think this is worth his time or I wouldn't be here.* Or maybe he was just being polite, because of Mrs. Lovelady.

Next to Mrs. Hoover, Bette perched on the sofa, her knees tightly together. Mr. Hoover stood in front of the fire burning on the hearth. "Mother told me of your visit here yesterday. Are you quite sure you are the only one who touches those files? No higher-ups come down and help themselves?"

"No, sir." Bette knew she would have only this one chance to make her case, so she tried to sound as businesslike as he did. "It's been my experience that the higher-ups at the War Department are very keen on following procedure and I am the only one who touches the personnel files. When I assumed that position, my supervisor made it quite clear that no one was to touch the files but me." She tried to hide a little shiver that went through her.

"Also, sir, I can only release them to people who are on an authorized list and only after I receive a written and approved request. I take out the files, then personally deliver them, and pick them up to put them back when they are done. My supervisor said that the files would become disarranged if too many people had access to them."

"Makes sense." Mr. Hoover looked down into the glowing embers and then back up. "Has your supervisor ever accessed the files when you were out of the office, say sick or away?"

"No, sir, he has enough to do, he says." Her heart wouldn't

slow down. "The work just waits for me until I return and I've rarely missed work over the past three years. Also, whenever I have to leave my office—even during work hours—I lock my door."

"Why is that?" His sharp eyes seemed to be piercing her mind.

She steadied herself and went on: "I think most of the people at the department want the privacy of what's written about them in the files carefully guarded. I didn't start at the department in this job. I worked in two other areas before I was moved up to this position of trust."

"I see." He sat down in a floral chintz wingback chair opposite her and leaned forward on his elbows. "From what Mother tells me, you think someone is going through the files at night."

Again, his serious manner reassured her. "Yes, sir, at first I noticed that some files weren't put back neatly as I always do. I asked my supervisor if he'd needed any of them and he said no. That puzzled me because he and I should have the only keys to that area—except of course for the Secretary of War." She grinned then. "Or the custodian." She started again: "Then on two other occasions, I noticed that some of the files were out of order."

"So you decided to test your theory that someone was tampering with the files?" Hoover prompted.

"Yes, sir." The words were coming easier now in spite of his intent stare. "I put the little dots of paper from my paper punch into several files in different file drawers. The files fit very tightly together." She demonstrated this by pressing her palms together. "I put the dots in the same place in each file. I wrote down the names of the files and locked up and went home for Christmas."

"And when you got back, you found that some of the files had been moved," he carried on the story for her.

She nodded. "To make sure, I did this three more times in the next two weeks. Once there was no evidence that the files had been touched, but on the other two—"

"They had been." He steepled his fingers and gazed at her over their peak. "Very interesting, Miss. Is there any chance that you've kept track of the files?"

"Yes, sir." She opened her black-leather purse and pulled out a folded sheet of typing paper. "I have a list here of the name on every file that—to my knowledge—has been tampered with."

Hoover leaned over and accepted the list from her hand. "Has anything been changed on the files, do you think?"

"No, sir, I checked that, too. If something had been changed, I didn't notice."

His forehead wrinkled, Hoover studied the list. "You think this might be espionage?"

"I don't know, sir." Bette sat forward a bit farther. "But I just couldn't get it out of my mind. I had to put it before someone who knows more than I do."

Hoover eyed her. "Why not your supervisor?"

"What if he lied to me and he is the one tampering with the private files?"

Hoover nodded. "You're thinking clearly."

This heartened her. She gave him a tremulous smile. "Mr. Hoover, I took seriously your comments last fall about the Trojan horse of Nazi spying." She'd gained confidence as she finally allowed herself to voice all she'd been feeling, struggling with, to someone who looked interested. "I don't think there's any doubt that we're headed for war with Germany and maybe Italy, Japan, and Russia. I don't want any negligence of mine to put my country at further risk." Her heart pounded with her own audacity.

Hoover rose in one fluid moment. "Miss McCaslin, I want you to say nothing of this to anyone. I will look into it and discover if it is anything we need be concerned about."

"Thank you, sir." Bette recognized his dismissal and rose to shake hands. Just as she turned to follow Mrs. Hoover back to the door, she paused. "Mr. Hoover, will you please let me know if it is anything. I mean," she stammered, "you don't have to tell me anything I shouldn't know, but I'd appreciate knowing if this just wasn't my imagination."

"I will, Miss. You have my word."

Over two months later, Bette received a written invitation from Mrs. Hoover inviting her to play bridge at her home two evenings later. Bette called to accept and wondered if she were going to play bridge or if she were going to—finally, at long last—be told if her dots had added up to anything.

The evening arrived and Bette made her way from the bus stop through the early spring evening. The robins looked happy as they tugged fresh worms from the greening lawns. A little girl was roller-skating on the other side of the quiet street. The skates rhythmically jarred on each sidewalk crack, almost clacking like a freight train on distant tracks.

Mrs. Hoover opened the door for her and Bette had her answer when they entered the parlor and no card tables had been set up. Mr. Hoover and a tall blond young man in a dark suit stood waiting for her. "Miss McCaslin, may I introduce you to Ted Gaston, one of my agents."

Bette felt her pulse skip and hop as she tried to shake the young man's firm hand as if she were accustomed to meeting G-men every day.

From his place by the hearth, Mr. Hoover motioned her to sit down where she had on the last visit. Mrs. Hoover sat down beside her and opened a cloth bag and took out her needles and yarn. She began knitting a half-finished black sock. Mr. Gaston remained at Mr. Hoover's elbow. Mr. Hoover handed Bette a local newspaper opened to a page. "Did you see that story three days ago?"

Bette glanced down at the sensational story. "Yes, my neighbors were horrified."

Gaston chuckled. "I'll bet they were. A raid on a house of ill repute in Georgetown."

Mr. Hoover frowned at the young man. "I don't like to discuss this type of thing with a respectable young woman like yourself, Miss McCaslin. But you deserve to know that this raid was the result of what you started when you planted those little dots."

Bette stared at him, momentarily robbed of speech. *Me?*

"The *Abwehr* was targeting War Department officials," Hoover began, "who had important information about new weaponry."

"What's the *Abwehr*?" Bette interrupted and then blushed.

"Nazi spy agency," Gaston murmured.

"Yes," Mr. Hoover cut in, "we believe they have been planting 'sleepers'—spies awaiting orders—since 1933. The madam of this house of ill repute has relatives in Germany and is a fascist herself. After a detailed interrogation, she's admitted visiting Germany in 1935 and being recruited by the *Abwehr.*"

"She says," Gaston took over at Hoover's nod, "that the *Abwehr* bankrolled the house last year and threatened to imprison her relatives if she didn't cooperate. But we don't think she took much persuading."

"But what has this got to do with my dots?" Bette couldn't put it all together.

Hoover gave a brief grin. "We tailed the men on your list. All of them had access to critical military information and all of them were invited, lured to this very house." He pointed to the newspaper.

"Where they indulged themselves," Gaston said in a pleased but grim tone, "and also fell into debt at the roulette wheel at the . . . house. Photographs had also been taken of them in . . . compromising circumstances."

"I think that's as explicit as we need to get." Hoover shot a glance at his mother, who was concentrating on her clicking knitting needles.

"But who was invading my files?" Bette asked.

"One of their first victims managed to get an impression of your boss's key, have a duplicate made, and he was the one who was picking out victims."

Bette wanted to ask this man's name, but Mr. Hoover's expression stopped her.

"Anyway, Miss, you have done your country a great service. I have given the president a full report on this and he told me to tell you, 'Well done.'"

Bette goggled at Mr. Hoover. She felt blood rush to her

face and neck and heard a ringing in her ears. The president? She held it all in. Finally, she was able to breathe normally again. "I'm happy to have been able to serve my country."

"I was hoping you would say that. I've had you thoroughly investigated." Mr. Hoover watched her.

Bette looked at him in shock.

Mr. Hoover's eyes narrowed. "Because although I don't approve of women as spies or agents, I think you are just what the FBI needs right now for a specific investigation."

Near the Tidal Basin where the gloriously pink cherry blossoms were in full April bloom, Bette strolled beside Curt. Just another Sunday afternoon together. But it wasn't. She had to let Curt know—or rather, she had to lie to the man she loved. Mr. Hoover's words went around and around in her mind. And she'd almost blurted them out to Curt several times this day. How could she not tell him? But she'd been sworn to secrecy. This was a matter of national security. *This can't be real. It can't be happening to me.*

"You're unusually quiet today," Curt said, tugging at her hand.

She turned to him, hoping her worry over keeping secrets didn't show in her eyes. "I have some news for you."

"What kind?" He stopped and faced her.

"I've been offered a new position." She adjusted his collar, which needed no adjusting, letting her fingers stray against his neck.

"Really? A promotion?"

"Kind of." In reality, she was taking a leave of absence from the War Department. She'd given her supervisor the excuse of pressing wedding plans. And that she'd return in two weeks. She rested her palms against Curt's chest, feeling his crisp shirt under her fingertips.

"More pay?"

Bette nodded. *Yes, and perhaps danger into the bargain.*

"Well, you don't look happy. What is it, sweetheart?"

"I'm going to have to do some traveling with my new boss." She let her very real dismay over this surface in her tone. "So I'll be gone for the next two weeks."

"Traveling?" Curt frowned, putting his arms around her shoulders. "I don't know if I want you to go traveling around with some man."

"It will all be quite above board." She looked him in the eye. This was true. "He's older than my father." This was not true. She hated lying, but she didn't want Curt to worry. "You know I wouldn't go along with it if it weren't on the level, don't you?"

"Sure." He leaned forward, obviously intending to kiss her. "I just don't like the idea of your being away for that long."

"It won't be for long." Bette welcomed his lips and savored the light kiss. "And besides, this is your last semester and we'll be married in August and I'll be at home then—your wife." *And all this will be far behind me, us.*

"Maybe you should just quit. Why don't you spend the next few months at home? I could come on the weekends—"

Bette pressed two fingers to his lips, stopping his words. Her heart pounded with dismay. *Quit now? After years of typing and filing, something interesting pops up, and you want me to quit?* Not that he knew what was going on with her job.

Curt captured her hand and lifted it away from his lips. "I really don't want you traveling without me. Anything could happen."

"What do you mean?"

"It just doesn't look right." Curt frowned. "What would people at home think of you—"

"I said it's all perfectly above board." Bette heard herself snap. She took a deep breath. "Curt, this is for our country, for the War Department. I was honored to be chosen."

He studied her for several moments and then he nodded slowly. "Very well. Just this once, though. And I don't want my mother to find out. She's . . . she's very old-fashioned."

"All right. I can keep it mum if that's what you want." Tension drizzled out of her. She took a deep breath.

As though marking her as his, Curt pulled her into a tight embrace. "I can't wait until I have you all to myself." He kissed her again.

"That's all I ever have wanted." Her heart rose to her throat. "To be your wife. To be the mother of your children. That's what I'm looking forward to." She had always dreamed of a loving husband and children, at least three or four. A happy family. Just what she'd longed for as a lonely child living with her grandmother before her mother had come home and married her stepfather.

"Okay." Curt exhaled his unhappiness. "I guess this could be a good experience for you. Where will you be going?"

"North along the coast. I may be able to visit Gretel." *Or not.*

"Write me?"

"Of course, and I'll be back before you know it." *But I may never be able to tell you what I've really been doing. And you probably wouldn't believe me. I still can't believe it myself.*

CHAPTER SEVEN

A week later at the start of May, Bette sat very close to the passenger door of a new gray 1940 Chevrolet. Ted Gaston drove them with practiced ease through northeastern Maryland. She'd dressed in a three-piece navy-blue suit with matching gloves and hat and navy-and-white spectator pumps and hoped she looked the part she was playing. She checked her lipstick with her compact mirror and added another coat of True Red before snapping the compact closed and slipping it into her white purse.

"I won't bite, you know," Gaston said without looking her way. In his tan suit and fedora, he looked so professional, so handsome.

She wondered if she looked as nervous as she felt.

There were many things she wanted to say, but she didn't feel she could trust this man completely—like she trusted Curt or Drake Lovelady. The man beside her was an FBI agent and they were working together, but Ted Gaston wasn't like anyone else she'd ever met. It wasn't just his blond good looks and confidence. There was something about him that put her on alert, made her very aware of him. She never knew what he might say. Once, she'd even suspected he'd thought of trying to kiss her. He'd kept staring at her lips.

"I still can't believe this is happening," she answered. "Why did Mr. Hoover think I could do this?"

"He's got a great eye for natural talent. And he knows I'm good at breaking in new agents."

"You are?" She couldn't keep from sounding doubtful.

With a grin, he continued, "There's something I've got to teach you before we get to our first assignment."

"What's that?" She eyed him, wondering if he would say something provocative or even mildly insulting. He had that edge to him.

"You don't flirt," he said.

Of all the words that might have come out of his mouth, she'd never have imagined these. "What? *Flirt?* What has that got to do with our job of checking security at defense plants?"

He grinned at her, a wolfish grin. "Miss Bette McCaslin, you've come along for one reason, and one reason only: to flirt with the men while I see how easy it is or isn't to gain knowledge about new weaponry being designed and manufactured here on the East Coast."

Ted Gaston was unpredictable all right. "I don't think we're going to find out much." She refused to address the topic of flirting. "I can't believe that people just give away the secrets to their designs. Don't they want to protect them? I mean they patent them, don't they?"

"All we know is that the president of an aviation corporation up the coast reported some man with a pretty blond, claiming to be with an aviation journal, visited his factory while he was away. The blond flirted with the plant manager and got a free guided tour of the plant and was allowed to see the blueprints of a new aircraft, the B-24. Later, the president called the journal and found out they hadn't sent anyone to do a story on the B-24."

She turned to face him squarely. "You're kidding me." Mr. Hoover had given her just the barest minimum of details. He hadn't mentioned the actual aircraft by number.

"I am not. And what's worse, we don't know precisely who the man or the blond are. All we know is they weren't who they said they were—reporters from the aviation trade magazine."

Bette worried her lower lip. "I didn't realize people could be so stupid."

"Well, when men are confronted by a pretty, flirty blond, they often lose their good sense."

Bette stared at him, still not able to take him seriously. "But I'm not a blond."

Ted chuckled and winked at her. "A very pretty brunette will do in a pinch."

Bette's eyes widened. She wondered if she should call Mr. Hoover when they stopped and tell him Ted's comment about flirting. And winking didn't seem appropriate between agents.

"Don't you know how lovely you are?"

Bette fumed and let it show. *So this is how the next two weeks are going to be.* She didn't like men making comments about her looks. She didn't think she'd ever become inured to men who thought a young woman was just hanging around waiting for a smooth-talking man to sweet talk them.

"Flattery will get you nowhere."

"Flattery?" Ted cocked his head to watch her while

driving. "Doesn't that fiancé of yours tell you how beautiful you are? No wonder you don't flirt—you obviously don't have a clue of the effect you could have on men, will have on men. So let's get started. Now I'm going to teach you how to flirt and later, as we stop at restaurants and gas stations, I want you to practice until you get really good at it."

"You're nuts." She folded her arms. This wasn't what she'd signed up for.

"I'm the senior agent on this assignment and you'll do what I say, got that?" Ted's voice hardened. "You were chosen for this job because you're an eyeful and you are going to become an artful, flirty eyeful."

Bette bristled. "Mr. Hoover said he wanted me for this assignment because I notice things."

"Yeah, that's because he's too straitlaced to come right out and say that he wants you to become a modern Mata Hari—who notices things. But that was implied when he talked about the blond's part in the espionage. If you didn't get it, I did."

Bette looked away, recalling Mr. Hoover's measured words to her. Ted was right; the chief had implied she would be the FBI's "blond." Knowing that disappointed her slightly. And worried her. But she recalled Mr. Hoover's approval of her uncovering the espionage at the War Department. He didn't think she was stupid. But flirting? What next?

"Okay, first lesson, unbutton the top three buttons of that blouse and tuck it farther in your waistband. You're too buttoned up."

Bette glared at him.

"Now. You're doing this for your country, remember?"

She unbuttoned the top two buttons. "That's as far as I'm going."

Ted reached over and grabbed for the third button.

"Stop that!" She batted his hand away.

"You undo the third button or I will," Ted ordered. "Most girls undo the top one or two. But if you are a flirt, you have to go one more button."

Bette wrestled with herself. Finally, averting her eyes, she undid the third button. Her face flamed.

A few miles down the road, Ted pulled into a small-town gas station with one pump. "Okay, get out and do your stuff," he said in a low voice.

Bette gave him a sultry look. "Aren't you going to get the door for me?" She made her voice teasing and sugar-sweet.

Ted chuckled. "Good start," he whispered. "Sure thing," he said louder. He hopped out and around the car and opened the door for her.

She reached up and patted his cheek. "Thank you." She made her voice lower in her throat, a la Ted Gaston's coaching.

The young gas station attendant came out, rubbing greasy hands on a soiled, gas-smelling rag. "Fill her up?"

Bette gave him a big smile. "Well, hi there, handsome." She felt like she was imitating Mae West. Surely no man would fall for this act.

Suppressing a grin, Ted walked toward the restroom sign.

"Fill it up, please." Bette followed the attendant to the pumps.

"Where ya headed, lady?" he asked as he inserted the nozzle into the car's gas tank.

"North." She batted her eyes at him. "You fix the cars, too?"

"Sure do."

"I've always admired a man who's good with his hands." *More Mae West.*

The young man glowed and then his mouth slipped into a conspiratorial smile. "Who you traveling with?"

"Oh, that's my boss. He likes me to travel with him." She smiled. "He likes to dictate stuff to me while we drive along. It's boring, but it pays well."

She went on mouthing the kind of drivel Ted had taught her. Finally, Ted returned, paid for the gas, and off they went.

"How'd it go?" Ted asked.

"When I turned to follow you to the passenger's side, he had the nerve to pinch me." Bette glowered at Ted.

"Well, I guess J. Edgar is right. You are a quick study." And then he had the nerve to laugh out loud.

Three days later in New York City, Bette had the evening off. Ted had just dropped her a block away so he wouldn't be seen with her. An evening off from being flirtatious felt wonderful. She knocked on the door of the brownstone. Mr. Lovelady opened it wide.

"Bette's here!" Before she could respond, he had pulled her into a loose hug, bringing her inside and closing the door behind her. "We're so glad you called us. We would have been angry if we found out you'd come to New York City without letting us know."

Looking farther inside, Bette saw Gretel and Jamie, who'd also been invited, come into the front hall to greet her.

Ilsa came down the staircase, carrying Sarah in her arms. "Bette, welcome!" It was hard to believe that nearly a year ago, Ilsa and Sarah had been half-starved refugees. They both glowed with health now.

The brownstone was decorated in clean, modern lines and bright, clear colors. Bette felt welcome and relaxed, ready to enjoy being with family and with friends as close as family. Soon, they were all seated around the dining room table. At its head sat Mr. Lovelady, who insisted she start calling him by his first name. "You're not a little girl anymore," he explained. "And how's that exceedingly fortunate boyfriend of yours?"

"Curt's fine." It felt good to be herself again. "He graduates in early June. We're planning our wedding for August."

"Oh, you will make a beautiful bride," Ilsa said from her place at the foot of the table, "won't she, Gretel?"

"Of course." But Gretel didn't smile. In fact, she looked a bit pained.

"I'm sorry, Gretel," Ilsa said with a sigh. "I don't keep a Kosher kitchen here. But I asked the cook not to serve any pork or dairy with meat—"

"It's all right," Gretel said, sounding like it wasn't all right at all.

Bette looked around the table, confused. During her first week at Ivy Manor, Gretel had found it difficult to eat with her family. But she'd finally accepted that she'd have to adjust to the fact that not all American Jews observed the Jewish dietary laws.

Then Gretel made a sound of disgust. "I'm sorry, Ilsa. I am. It's just that I am Jewish and I refuse to apologize for being Jewish."

"I am not ashamed of being Jewish," Ilsa spoke up. "But I don't think that observing dietary laws is the only mark of a Jew. Drake has agreed that Sarah will go to Hebrew school as well as attend church with us. I go to synagogue and to church with Drake—mainly to please his mother who has been so kind to me. But our children will learn about both cultures and religions. This is America, Gretel. We don't have to cower here."

"Tell that to the American *Bund*," Gretel snapped.

Bette had heard of the *Bund*—Americans who supported Hitler. She'd always wondered why didn't they just go to Germany, then.

"This conversation may," Jamie slipped in mildly, "ruin my normally excellent appetite."

Gretel looked at him for a moment, obviously nonplussed, and then she laughed, her good humor restored. "Yes, the *Bund* should take any person's appetite away."

"Then let's not discuss it"—Jamie waved his soup spoon—"until we've finished this fine dinner, which may not be Kosher, but which smells delicious."

To go along, Bette sipped her salty beef bouillon. "Gretel, have you found a dress you'd like to wear as my bridesmaid?"

"You still want me to stand up with you and Curt?" Gretel asked, watching Bette.

"Yes, of course. You're my best friend." That Gretel would ask this shook Bette. Did Gretel think she would forsake a friend? "I've chosen my gown from a bridal magazine and Mother is having it made for me. If you can find a picture of what you want, we'll have it made for you."

"No, I will buy my own dress and I can easily find one at my shop. Street-length or evening-length?"

"Street-length. We've decided to have an afternoon wedding and a cake-and-punch reception immediately afterward at the church. Curt's parents, of course, will host a rehearsal dinner the evening before and Mother will host a wedding brunch for out-of-town guests that morning." Bette turned to Drake. "You and Ilsa will be coming, won't you?"

"It depends on whether I've had enough time to recover from this one." Ilsa patted her rounded abdomen, looking so happy that it made Bette want to cry. Ilsa appeared reborn. Bette remembered the way the other woman's face had looked a year ago—closed, lifeless. She recalled how Ilsa had at first refused to marry Drake. Now Ilsa's unmistakable love for her husband radiated from her like golden sunshine. It lit up the room. "If not, Drake and his mother will come without me."

"Everything will work out and," Drake said, "it sounds like you have everything under control. Have you and Curt decided on a honeymoon?"

Bette couldn't stop herself from blushing. "Curt hopes to have a teaching job by then, but he may not. He might have to do substitute teaching at first. So we aren't planning on a honeymoon until the following summer."

"You can always count on Curt to have everything planned out," Jamie inserted slyly.

Bette gave him an exasperated look. She liked that about Curt, didn't she? Who wanted to marry a man who didn't shoulder such responsibilities? Still, a familiar, yet vague uneasiness slid down Bette's spine. "Ilsa, when is your exact due date?" This comment drew the conversation away from herself, Curt, and Gretel.

When the evening was over, Jamie, Gretel, and Bette refused Drake's offer of rides home and insisted on taking the subway. Bette didn't want anyone to—by chance—see Ted, her "boss." So Jamie escorted them to the nearest subway stop and the three of them boarded a train together. Sitting beside Gretel and across from Jamie, Bette eyed the people on the subway. The whine and vibration of the subway train seemed to put up a barrier between them. And she wanted to talk to Gretel about the wedding but Gretel sat in grim, silent thought.

Finally, Bette touched her hand. "What's upsetting you?"

Jamie replied before Gretel could, his voice harsh. "She doesn't like it that Ilsa married Drake. Because of the Nazis, Zionist Gretel doesn't like us Gentiles anymore."

"That's not true," Gretel snapped, folding her arms. "You don't understand how I feel. The war in Europe has stopped the escape of refugees. My parents can't get out of Germany now. My last two letters have been returned to me. Jews are being sent to work camps. I hear terrible rumors." Gretel's voice cracked. "I'm frightened for my parents, for Ilsa's parents."

Haunting images from the night of Ilsa's rescue came to Bette. She reached out and took Gretel's hand in hers. "I'm sorry. You didn't tell me—"

"I couldn't write it." Gretel looked away as if trying to hide her distress.

"Is it because you somehow blame us for your parents' troubles?" Jamie barked.

"No," Gretel snapped. "Never."

Bette watched this conflict in helpless dismay.

"This war isn't our fault," Jamie said, looking away from Gretel. "And you know it. But every time I call, you're busy. You can't be busy *every* time."

Because of the subway speeding—humming and creaking—they'd all raised their voices. People around them, forced into eavesdropping, fidgeted, glancing at them and then away. Bette tried to figure out what was happening between Jamie and Gretel. She looked from one to the other.

"Jamie, you are a good person, a friend," Gretel said kindly, "and I have no desire to lead you on."

"Going to a movie, that's leading me on?" Jamie jabbed the words at her.

"Yes, it is." Gretel sat up straighter. "I don't know if I will marry or not. But if I do, it won't be to a non-Jew. I couldn't do what Ilsa has. I couldn't." She stood up and swept over to the door as they slowed to a stop. She turned back, but no smile lifted her expression. "I will find a dress, Bette." And then she left them—the screeching of the subway coming to a halt and the swish of the doors making it impossible for them to respond.

Confused, hurt, Bette looked to Jamie. When had Jamie fallen in love with Gretel? And when had her friend become so . . . She couldn't think of the right word. But Gretel was no longer the sweet, gentle friend who'd slept in her trundle bed at Ivy Manor. And what was a Zionist?

Jamie looked away, folding his arms in front of him. "Don't ask," he growled. "This is a stupid time to fall in love anyway. They're debating the draft right now. As far as I'm concerned, I'll be in uniform by the time your wedding rolls around. I just hope Curt won't be."

By the end of the week with Ted, Bette had her role practically memorized. She and Ted had visited four plants on Long

Island, New Jersey, Boston Harbor, and Mitchell Field. All manufactured weaponry or airplanes for the American military. They had one more to do and then they'd head back to report to Mr. Hoover at his home. The chief didn't want anyone but Ted to know about Bette's unofficial role in this undercover assignment. The FBI did not hire female agents. Bette would be paid, but her name would not appear on any payroll or employee list.

Ted pulled into the final plant's parking lot on the outskirts of Baltimore. He paused to give the grim industrial area a once-over. The loud grinding noises of many types of machinery filled the grimy, humid air. "Okay, I don't have to tell you what to do."

"No, you don't, honey," she drawled and fluffed the back of her shoulder-length hair.

Within a few minutes they were met by a gray-uniformed security guard at the factory entrance. Ted showed the man a fake press card that identified Ted under another name as being a reporter for an aviation trade magazine. He began the routine. "Hello, I'm here to take a tour of your facility as scheduled."

"We don't have no tour scheduled today." The broad-shouldered guard looked at a clipboard on a stand beside him.

Ted turned to Bette and snapped, "I thought you said that you called ahead."

Bette was still amazed at how quickly she could call up tears. "I'm sure I did, Mr. Gray. I just know I did."

His hands on his hips, Ted did not look convinced. "I don't have time to make another appointment," he snapped, glaring at her. "And I warned you about making mistakes, Miss Lansing."

Bette took a hankie out of her purse and dabbed at her eyes. "I know—"

"Hey," the guard said, looking at Bette with alarm, "I'll just call the plant manager down here. I don't know why you shouldn't get that tour." Giving her a sympathetic look, the guard dialed a dusty black phone on the wall behind him and talked for a few moments. Then he turned to Ted and Bette. "He'll be right down. Everything's okay."

Bette gave the man a "You're my hero" look of gratitude and nearly broke cover by chuckling when the man's face turned bright red. Men were so easy. Why hadn't anyone told her that before Ted Gaston? In spite of the dismal fact that every plant they'd visited had been woefully insecure, the week had turned out to be both revealing and exciting. At one plant they'd just walked in and started taking pictures. And for thirty minutes, no one had even asked why they were photographing equipment.

And Ted had proven a fun companion, one who had given her credit when she'd often been able to elicit more indiscreet information on site than he did. But she'd been very careful to keep her distance from him. Now that she was an accomplished flirt, she recognized Ted as a "lady-killer." But she was in love with Curt. And in no danger.

The plant manager hustled toward them. "I don't understand this. We just had a couple from *Aviation Times* here less than a week ago. A reporter and his secretary."

Ted began to speak. But with sudden inspiration, Bette cut in, "Was the secretary a blond?"

"Yes, and she was very young, I thought."

Ted's eyes met Bette's. He'd got it, too. "Do you have a

phone I can use? I need to call my editor and see what the mix-up is."

"Sure, sure." The plant manager, a Mr. Harding, waved for them to join him. "You can use my phone."

Ted whispered to Bette, "Keep him busy. I need to use the phone in private."

Bette nodded and hurried to catch up with the plant manager. "While Mr. Gray is telephoning, could you and I get something to drink? I'm so dry I'm spitting cotton."

"Of course, glad to." The manager looked down at her top three undone buttons and Bette knew that, just like all the others, she'd have no trouble with this man.

When Bette and Mr. Harding returned to the manager's office, Ted was looking grimly satisfied. "Please close the door, Mr. Harding. I need to enlist your aid."

Looking puzzled, Harding closed the door. When he turned, Ted produced his FBI badge. "My real name is Ted Gaston and this lady is Miss Bette McCaslin. We're with the FBI."

Harding goggled at them. "The FBI?"

Ted nodded. "Yes, I just talked to J. Edgar Hoover and he's still on the line. He wants to ask you for your cooperation." Ted spoke into the phone: "Chief, here's Mr. Harding." Then he handed over the phone.

Mr. Harding looked more and more poleaxed as he listened. He nodded and kept saying, "Yes, sir, of course, sir." Finally, white-faced, he handed the phone back to Ted.

Ted said good-bye to the chief and then turned to Bette. "Would you please go out to the car and bring in my briefcase from the trunk? I have the photos of our list of possible Nazi agents in it. Mr. Harding, we're hoping you will help us identify the agents who were here just days ago." Ted handed her his keys.

Bette took the ring of keys and hurried out. Would this pan out big? As her heels clicked down the concrete steps, she allowed a dash of hope. Had they hit their first real lead?

Four hours later, Harding slumped in his chair with one head in his hand. "I can't believe I let them look at the plans for the new four-engine Fighting Fortress."

Ted was glancing over his notes from the interrogation of Harding. He'd taken Harding over the tour time after time until he was satisfied that he'd gotten all he wanted from or could possibly get from the man. "I thank you, Mr. Harding. And what's more, your country thanks you."

"But I feel like a fool." Harding looked up, defeated. "Why did I do it?"

"We're not used to thinking about spies in this country," Bette replied for Ted. "You're an honest man so you think others are, too."

It suddenly hit her that this evening when she returned to D. C., an exciting interruption in her boring everyday routine would end. For the very first time in her life, she resented that there were some paths women were prohibited from following.

"Well, I'm going to be thinking different from now on." Harding straightened up and looked determined. "Security around here is going to be beefed up starting today."

Bette admitted to herself that she'd have loved being an FBI agent. But there were no G-women. *Why can't I do this instead of spending my days filing?*

Ted rose from where he'd been perched on the man's desk. "I think that is advisable. And though I can't give anything away, don't worry, I think we can find a way to keep the information you let slip from ever reaching Germany."

"You can? How?"

Ted grinned. "Can't tell you. Just believe that the FBI takes national security very seriously."

"I'm glad." Harding stood and shook Ted's hand. "You don't know how glad. Thank you for all your work."

"Thank you for all your help." Ted headed toward the door and then looked back. "Whatever sins you committed were paid for when you identified the two Nazis who toured your plant last week. We needed that . . . badly. Now, one more thing—you have to forget we were ever here. You can tell the company's president. The chief plans to call him personally. You cannot tell anyone else of our visit. Not your wife. Not anyone. This is a matter of national security."

After swearing not to divulge anything to anyone, Harding escorted them out to their car. They watched him march back toward the plant.

"I'll bet some changes will be made today," Bette observed, pushing away her turbulent feelings over the ending of this investigation—or at least, her part in it.

"Let's get back to D.C. fast. The chief wants us to meet him at his home. He's got something to discuss with you."

"Me?" Bette stopped in her tracks and stared at Ted.

CHAPTER EIGHT

June 1940

At the end of her first week at her new job, Bette sat at her polished maple desk in Senator Lundeen's office. As she typed a press release, the rapidly clicking keys cheered her. Each day, in her tailored two-piece suits, she tried to appear the perfect discreet secretary—an illusion, of course. Her days at the War Department had ended, at Mr. Hoover's request. And her job here had come at his behest—though she was the only one, other than Ted Gaston, who knew this. She still had trouble believing that a US senator could be consorting with an *Abwehr* agent right in the Capitol offices. And that the FBI would investigate a US senator. But that was her real job.

"Good morning, Miss."

Bette looked up from her typewriter and smiled perfunctorily at the well-dressed, middle-aged man standing on the thick navy carpet. "Mr. Viereck, back again so soon?" *To do your dirty work?*

"There is much to be done." The man had no humor in him. "I must do everything I can to stop America from making the mistake of becoming entangled in a second foreign war."

Then talk to Hitler. He started the second war. She gave the man another false smile. Mr. Viereck had been the first person she'd reported to Ted as a possible Nazi agent. Then she'd overheard him speaking to the *charge d'affaires* at the German Embassy in this very office on *her* phone. His brazenness had shocked Bette, but had made it certain that he had ties to Germany. The German Embassy on Massachusetts Avenue was a hotbed of espionage. Bette had wanted to see some action taken against Viereck. But, of course, his actions weren't illegal, just suspicious. What was her boss thinking of having anything to do with a man who was so obviously tied to German interests?

"Is the senator in?"

She nodded and pressed a button on the newly installed intercom at her desk. "Senator, Mr. Viereck is here." At the senator's response, she waved the man into the inner office, but she did not turn off the intercom. After the door closed, she lowered the volume on the intercom, so she could eavesdrop without anyone, who might pass by, guessing what she was doing. Though it was much less incriminating than listening at the keyhole, the eavesdropping made her pulse quicken. She couldn't afford to be caught. The FBI didn't recognize she existed—officially.

"I think I've solved our problem," she heard her boss's distinctive baritone, though only a whisper to her. "You can use Hamilton Fish's office."

"He's the head of the National Committee to Keep America Out of Foreign Wars, isn't he?" Viereck asked.

"Yes, and he's quite willing to send out reprints of my latest speeches in that cause."

"Excellent."

Bette noted Fish's name, but no doubt the FBI were aware of his sympathies. Outside the office door, a congressman and his secretary walked by. Keeping up appearances, Bette tucked a new piece of paper into the typewriter.

"And since my speeches are included in *The Congressional Record,*" the senator bragged, "you can get free reprints of them from the Government Printing Office."

"Excellent." Viereck's voice radiated with enthusiasm. "And can we use the congressman's franking privilege, too?"

Bette felt her temperature rising. So the American taxpayer would foot the cost of printing and postage for Nazi propaganda!

For the first time in her life, she wished she knew some colorful curses and that she had the nerve to voice them. The real question was, however, did the senator have a clue of whom he was dealing with? Didn't it ever occur to him that his agenda was aiding Hitler? That his speeches amounted to Nazi propaganda? She tightened the paper in the typewriter with a snap.

During their last phone call, Bette had reported to Ted that Viereck had already sent out copies of Hitler's recent speech offering peace—if England would surrender. How could anyone believe the same line Hitler had used to seize the Sudetenland?

"We have to stop Roosevelt before he drags us into this

LYN COTE

war," the senator said. "What did we get out of the first war over there?"

"Nothing but death, debt, and George M. Cohan." Both men chuckled at the popular isolationist line. "Also, Senator," Viereck continued, "I think I will be able to further our cause at the convention—"

From the corner of her eye, Bette saw movement. She switched off the intercom and bent as though picking up something on the floor. When she looked up, she smiled at the congressional aide who'd come to deliver something to the senator. Her heart raced, but she'd had the volume so low that she'd been barely able to hear it herself and the young man looked as if he'd noticed nothing. He departed and Bette was left wondering what Viereck was planning for the Republican Convention in Philadelphia in a few weeks.

Later that week, Curt and Bette walked hand in hand under the Sycamore trees of the quiet Georgetown street. Another Sunday afternoon together. In short sleeves, Curt carried the jacket to his white linen suit folded over his arm. Bette wore a casual red-and-white dotted Swiss blouse and dirndl skirt. It was too steamy for gloves or silk stockings.

For the first time ever, Bette had a hard time concentrating on Curt. Her latest meeting with Ted, still her FBI contact, kept floating around in her head. Thousands of Nazi dollars were being funneled into and through the isolationist congressmen and committees. Constituents were being flooded with Lundeen's speeches. Still, no one had broken the law. Was it always like this in a free country? Did the bad guys always use the Bill of Rights for their own nasty purposes?

"I still don't like all this traveling you're doing," he snapped, interrupting her thoughts. "I thought it was only supposed to be one trip."

His sharp words pushed Bette into irritation with him. *But he doesn't know.* And she realized that was the crux of the matter. *I'm leading a double life I can't reveal even to the man I love.* What had she gotten herself into? Is this what she really wanted?

Her mind still wouldn't switch to Curt. Photographs of Nazi agents flashed in her mind. Ted was preparing her for the GOP convention, to watch for these men and women, these spies and traitors. "Curt, it's just part of my job. I—"

"First," he interrupted again, sounding aggrieved, "you're gone for nearly two weeks in May and now a week in Philadelphia. Isn't there anyone else in the senator's office who can go to the convention?"

"The senator wants me to go." *And so does Mr. Hoover.* The purpose for Bette's attendance at the GOP Convention was twofold: her surface one, to help the senator and George Viereck continue stoking the isolationist frenzy; her hidden one, to keep tabs on Viereck and other *Abwehr* agents for the FBI. So far they'd done nothing illegal. But she was to be on the lookout for any direct payoffs or bribes. Or any new faces.

Curt drew her to a shady park bench and they sat down side by side. "Maybe we should move up our wedding date."

"No." Bette's denial came so swift and urgent that she shocked herself. *I'm in too deep, Curt. I can't back out now.*

Curt looked as startled as she felt. "Does this job mean more to you than us?"

Bette struggled to bring up words. What explanation

could she give? She couldn't tell him the truth. She had been sworn to secrecy. The biggest question was why did she want to go on with this type of work when it separated her from Curt? Was it being trusted to do something bold and important for her country? Or what? "It's hard," she spoke the truth at least, "for me to put this into words."

"Try me."

Why am I doing this? Even if I told Curt, he wouldn't believe me. Spying on people isn't like me at all. And according to Ted, that's why I'm so good at it. She searched for the real reason she wanted to do this.

Curt watched her, not touching her, frowning.

Finally the images from the freighter on the night when they rescued Ilsa poured through her mind. The pale, defeated, hopeless faces in the gray dawn never failed to move her. "I think . . . I think it has to do with Gretel and Ilsa."

"What could they possibly have to do with your trip to Philadelphia?" Curt searched her face. He looked angry with her.

Bette found herself mangling her purse straps. Everything she did that strengthened the US weakened Hitler, and Hitler had targeted Gretel's family, her race, and finally, the rest of the world. How to phrase this without giving herself away? "We can't ignore what's happening in Europe."

"But the senator you work for is a blind isolationist," Curt exclaimed in frustration. "What can working for him do to help Gretel?"

"You're right, I know." She pursed her lips, groping for words, for a plausible explanation. "I'm hoping that I might be able to do something to change his mind."

"That doesn't make sense." Curt's disgust sounded clear.

He was right. But it was the best she could come up with. "I'm worried, Curt, so worried. I don't think we can stay out of what's happening."

This changed Curt's expression, softened it. He took her hand. "On our Sundays together, you and I've always tried to ignore what was happening overseas."

Yes, we've tried to have a private life. I love this man so much. How can I help him understand what I can't tell him? Please. She nodded and squeezed his hand. The contact brought back that reassuring connection she always felt with him. "But we can't anymore." On this, they agreed. She tightened her hold on his hand. "Germany now controls Holland, Belgium, Luxembourg, and northern France. And just think how much of middle Europe Hitler grabbed before he attacked Poland. Do you think he'll stop there?"

"No." Curt's denial was flat and harsh.

No wonder their words were stirring up emotions, even anger. *We can't stop it.* She stretched her tight neck. "Now there's a bill proposing a peace-time draft. Sometimes, I sympathize with my boss's trying to keep us out of war. A draft . . . It's too close to . . ."

Looking away as if he didn't want to face her words either, Curt caressed her hands within his, his thumb stroking the sensitive flesh of her palm. "We're just two people in love. And the world's gone crazy."

They both fell silent for a time. The blazing sun beat down. Shafts of it from between the glossy green leaves overhead heated Bette's shoulders. The sound of cars motoring by, of pigeons cooing to each other and flapping their ineffectual wings, of a girl giggling nearby—just ordinary Sunday afternoon noises.

What did a bomber sound like when it soared overhead? What did buildings blowing apart sound like? Were flamethrowers silent? What about a machine gun? Did it sound like the ones in the movies? Or worse?

Bette felt sick, shaken. But she knew it was inevitable: what would come, would come. She'd made her choice already. She'd do anything to see Hitler crushed. Even keep things from the man she loved. Closing her eyes, she rested her head against Curt's firm shoulder. "We're an ocean away from what's happening, Curt. But that isn't far enough now that the Nazis have high-powered bombers and submarines. It's like being in a waking dream. We're on the beach watching a tidal wave coming straight at us. And we're frozen in horror—we can't get away from it."

Curt put his arm around her. "I'm happy I'm not marrying an ignorant woman"—his voice was rough, low—"a woman who hasn't a clue about what's happening all around her. But we must go on anyway. We are going to go on with plans to marry in August—despite the war in Europe and even with the possibility of the draft." He kissed her cheek, keeping her tight against him, as if protecting her. "It might still be voted down."

Bette nodded, but didn't believe a word he said about their wedding. World and national events could separate them at any moment. Why hadn't they married two years ago when she'd first asked him why they shouldn't? They could have had two years together before this . . .

For some reason, she suddenly thought of home, of Ivy Manor, on this summer afternoon. Her mother and stepfather would be sitting in the summer house discussing the Sunday paper, kissing when they thought no one would see them.

Bette sighed. She'd always loved the story of her mother's elopement with her father just days before he'd been shipped overseas to France. Now she glimpsed how it must have felt, the torture her mother must have endured. The runaway marriage sounded romantic twenty years later, but at the time, her mother must have suffered in a way Bette was just beginning to realize, to share.

I could lose Curt. He could die like my father did. She wanted to weep, felt the tears gathering in her throat. She forced them down. Their time together might be short and shouldn't be spoiled by tears.

She would face the present, go to Philadelphia for the FBI while continuing with her wedding plans. She would continue her double life for a while longer. But now she admitted silently that Curt and she—just as her parents had been in 1917—were unwilling passengers on the roller coaster that was 1940.

GOP Convention, Philadelphia, June 1940

"I will fight to the last ditch to foil interventionists," the senator from South Dakota shouted, pounding the podium, "the rabble rousers, the deceptionists in their high-financed campaign to start this country shooting!" Applause swallowed up the rest of the Republican delegate's words.

Amid the raucous, perspiring crowd, Bette sat still, watching, listening. Before she'd left D.C., Ted had dropped over and given her photos of more suspected *Abwehr* agents and Nazi sympathizers. She was on the lookout for them here at the GOP National Convention. Today was the day they would most probably make appearances.

Today the Republican Party was to vote on whether or not to pass legislation urging isolation from the European war. The War Debts Defense Committee, the Islands for War Debts Committee, the Make Europe Pay War Debts Committee and finally, the whole hog organization, the No Foreign Wars Committee—Bette was sick to death of them. But she kept smiling and saying, "Yes, sir," to her boss, even as she noted down his activities with Nazi sympathizers.

Right now, she wished she were almost anywhere else than sitting here between her boss and Viereck. Her gaze roamed the swirling, bunching mass of people gathered in the convention meeting hall. The men wore straw hats with red, white, and blue hatbands and buttons declaring the candidate they were supporting.

Viereck had been buzzing around the GOP Convention like the King Bee. He always had a bright smile for her, his favorite senator's secretary. She smiled, but did not flirt. So far that ploy hadn't been suggested and she didn't feel like flirting with a Nazi.

In her lap, today's newspaper sat opened to a full-page ad, paid for by Viereck and others: "Delegates to the Republican Convention and to American Mothers, Wage-earners, Farmers, and Veterans! Stop the War Machine! Stop the Warmongers! Stop the Democratic Party, which is leading us to war!" All around her, murmurs swelled at the speaker on the platform. To applause, the congressman from South Dakota finished his diatribe against becoming involved in the war in Europe and started gathering up his notes to leave the podium.

In the general commotion, another louder and even more demanding gale of strident voices rolled through the auditorium. Before Bette's eyes, people swarmed up onto the platform and forced the speaker away from the microphone. A young man stepped to the microphone. "Americans, resist Hitler!" The address system crackled with the high volume.

The general uproar escalated. "Get off the platform!" voices shouted. Viereck and Lundeen sprang to their feet and began to push forward in the crowd. Bette strained to see over the people, but everyone else had stood up, too. Finally, she got up and stood on her chair. The people who had taken over the platform began pinning yellow Stars of David to their shirts and blouses. "War is coming!" they shouted. "How can we be at peace in a world at war? Hitler wants conquest, not peace!"

Guards in uniform were pushing their way through the roiling crowd toward the platform. Police—their billy clubs in hand—hustled inside the rear double doors. The crowd parted before them. Bette leaped down from her chair and began shoving her way to the front. Someone she needed to see or something she needed to witness might take place at the clash point of the two groups and she needed to be there in order to report details to Ted for the FBI.

She elbowed her way the last few feet to the front. The press of warm bodies nearly suffocated her. She gasped, drawing in gulps of hot, humid air. She scanned the faces around her. She was rewarded when she glimpsed the face of a man whom the FBI suspected of funneling Nazi money to isolationist groups. Who else would she see?

Then . . . she saw Gretel. Bette nearly choked on her own breath. Gretel! Here? With the Star of David on her blouse, Gretel loomed above Bette on the platform. A policeman reached Gretel and gripped her by the arm. He dragged her toward the steps. Bette strained to keep her eyes on her friend. *I have to help her.*

The crowd swirled and pressed Bette right up to the stairway down from the podium. She felt like a paper boat on the tide. Her boss popped up at her side and took her arm protectively. Bette stared up at Gretel—suddenly aware that she didn't want Gretel to see her here. *How will I ever explain?*

At that moment, the shock of recognition hit Gretel. Bette saw Gretel mouth, "Bette!" and then the crowd surged, carrying Bette away from the steps. She kept her eyes on Gretel. One of the protesters began to fight a policeman. Gretel lost her footing and went down into the swarm of bodies. Would she be trampled? "Gretel!" Bette screamed, her voice swallowed up amid the chaos. The crowd pulled Bette away. Some woman behind her began screaming. Was it Gretel's voice?

Bette's heart pounded as she struggled against the tide of people—trying to go back to help her friend. "Gretel," she screamed inwardly, "Gretel!"

CHAPTER NINE

Early August 1940

Bette and her mother sat in wicker chairs that had sat on the front porch of Ivy Manor for generations of summers. Just as Bette had helped finish clearing up the breakfast dishes, the postman delivered the mail. The two of them, each with a letter in hand, had come out for some fresh air before the heat of the day. Now, they rocked slightly out of rhythm in the morning sunshine.

The day promised to be a scorcher. Perspiration already beaded Bette's brow. The local seamstress was due any time now to do the final fitting of Bette's wedding dress. Bette had come home to prepare for the wedding, which loomed before them only weeks away. She wondered why this wasn't a happy thought.

Bette held Gretel's plain white letter loosely in her hand, still unopened. An unnatural reluctance held her back from slitting open the envelope. Why? The answer came swiftly. The image of Gretel being manhandled off the stage in

Philadelphia remained stark in Bette's mind. She recalled the horrified look on her friend's face; would she ever forget it?

"I'm so glad you're home," her mother said once more. "I was afraid you'd try to work right up to the week of your wedding and there's so much to do."

Bette tried to smile. It had been wrenching to quit her job. Not her visible job at the senator's office; she couldn't get away from Lundeen and Viereck fast enough. But quitting her secret job for the FBI had cost her. Of course, Mr. Hoover had thought it only proper for her to resign on the eve of her wedding. It had been unusual enough for him to use a woman as an agent, but a married woman—no, impossible. Why was it all right for male agents to be both official and married? This inequality stung, but that wouldn't change anything.

"I can't wait any longer." Chloe waved her letter, which had come from New York, too. "I must read what Ilsa and Drake have to say about their little boy."

Bette watched her mother eagerly slit open the envelope and begin reading. Knowing that to wait any longer would invite curiosity about matters Bette didn't want to reveal, she slit open Gretel's letter. She spread the one folded sheet of stationery and read:

Dear Bette, I find that my schedule makes it impossible for me to attend your wedding. Please accept my regrets. Yours truly, Gretel.

Bette read the stilted words over and over and over. A sinking feeling gripped her as if her stomach had turned into ice and was sliding to her toes. *Gretel must have recognized*

Senator Lundeen and thinks I support his isolationism. How could she believe that of me?

Bette closed her eyes, forcing herself to keep her fierce reaction to Gretel's regrets invisible. *So much of my life in the past few months has been invisible.* But that was over now. And this knowledge only lowered her mood further. *I didn't want to quit. I don't want to sit on the sidelines. The stakes for us, for the world, are too high.*

"What does Gretel say?" Chloe asked.

Bette silently wrestled with the deep pain of Gretel's rejection. But she said in a falsely mild tone, "Gretel writes that she can't make the wedding."

"Oh, no," her mother moaned, glancing at Bette. "Why?"

"She says her schedule makes it impossible." Bette tried to strike the proper measure of dismay, not the devastation that was stabbing her.

"That just isn't like Gretel." Chloe frowned, her blue eyes troubled. "I just can't believe—"

"This isn't a normal year," Bette interrupted.

Chloe nodded, her teeth gripping her lower lip, studying her.

"What about little Jonathan?" To turn her mother's attention aside, Bette tried to infuse her tone with some true interest. Ilsa and Drake had taken a different tack toward the European war and all that it entailed. They wouldn't condemn Bette without taking the time to confront her. That's what really hurt. Gretel had tried, convicted, and sentenced Bette without a hearing.

But what could she have said anyway? *"It's just my job."* A pitiful excuse. But the truth was a secret. Bette clenched her jaw against the sharp teeth of Gretel's rejection.

"Drake says they had Jonathan circumcised by a rabbi at the hospital," Chloe continued, unaware, "and they're planning a christening in November to please Drake's mother. Ilsa says her son nurses like every meal is his last and is round and fat and happy. And Sarah is very protective and proud of her little brother."

"I'm so glad . . . so glad for Drake and Ilsa." Bette struggled to keep her mask in place.

Chloe nodded. "Yes, Drake finally found the woman for him and Ilsa is so happy. Except, of course, she's worried for her family. They've been taken from their home in Berlin and no one can or will tell Drake where they have been taken. His contacts in Germany have been useless."

Bette lowered her forehead into one hand, hiding her face from her mother. No, there was no complete happiness, no complete peace with war looming over all. Ted had divulged to her some classified information about what was happening in Europe and she couldn't repeat it to anyone, didn't want to repeat it. Jews and other dissidents were being concentrated in work camps—probably slave labor camps—in Germany and Middle Europe. That much the FBI knew. Were *these* the rumors Gretel had spoken of on the subway that night in May? *No wonder she hates me.* Bette writhed inwardly at this. Would this inner conflict lessen with time, now that she was just another civilian?

Bette watched Curt drive his father's 1935 Chevrolet up their lane and she tucked the letter back into its envelope. She fought tears. In her present mood, she realized with shock that she wasn't thrilled at seeing Curt arrive unexpectedly. *I should be thrilled.* But what lies or half truths might she have to tell him today?

In an off-white linen summer suit, Curt mounted the steps and leaned to softly kiss her hello. He greeted her mother and then sat down in the rocker beside Bette. It creaked against the white planks. "I just came to tell you that I'm leaving for a job interview in Pennsylvania this morning."

"Pennsylvania? That's not too far," her mother commented.

Curt nodded as he unbuttoned his collar button. His tan silk tie hanging around his neck, its tails dangling down like a long scarf. "I would prefer to stay in Maryland or northern Virginia, of course, but Pennsylvania has more schools."

Bette tried to look interested. *Why am I feeling this way—like I'm not connected to anyone here? Why don't I care about Curt's job-hunting?*

"Of course, I wonder why I should even bother," Curt said, unconsciously agreeing with her mood. "Every school principal points out that the draft bill may pass this month and I'd probably be one of the first drafted."

"We don't know that for sure," her mother murmured. "You and Bette will be married by then and surely they won't draft married men first."

Curt's expression hardened. "I don't want people believing that I married Bette just to evade the draft. Bette and I have already discussed the possibility that we might have to postpone . . ."

Bette lost track of what he was saying. When had they discussed actually postponing their wedding? But in direct conflict with this sentiment, his words brought Bette unexpected relief. Did she want to marry Curt this month or postpone the wedding again? She looked up and studied him. "Do you want to postpone our wedding?" she asked, trying to sound natural, completely uncertain as to whether she wanted a yes or a no.

"No, of course I don't." Curt hunched over with his elbows on his knees, staring at the white-plank floor. Not at her. "But I don't want my motives to be misconstrued either."

Baffled by her own inconsistency, Bette twisted Curt's grandmother's engagement ring on her finger. "What do you mean?"

"I don't want people to misconstrue the reason for going through with our wedding. I don't want people thinking we married just so I wouldn't be drafted."

"Curt, why would they think that?" Chloe cut in. "Everyone knows you two have been engaged and intending to marry for years."

"People around here know that. But principals in Pennsylvania that I'm applying to might not. A teacher has to be so careful of his reputation."

"I can't argue with you on that point," Chloe admitted.

Bette tried to sort through all her conflicting emotions and reactions. *I don't want the wedding put off again, but . . .* The desire to be back in Washington hunting down more Nazi spies rushed through her. *I don't want to be left out. But . . .*

"I don't know what to do," Curt admitted. And even this was indicative of the times they lived in; Curt was always certain about everything.

"I'm sure . . ." Chloe began and then halted.

Bette glanced at her. "What?"

Her mother gave her a wry, apologetic smile. "I was going to say I'm sure everything will work out, but I realized I can't say that."

"None of us can." Curt stood, his chair continuing to

rock without him. "I have to get going to arrive in time for the interview." He drew Bette up and embraced her, holding her comfortably as if they'd been married for years. "I'll call tomorrow and tell you how it went."

His touch never failed to stir Bette, but this time, she resisted it. She said her good-bye and hoped Curt didn't notice her preoccupation.

Just as Curt disappeared around the bend, the seamstress drove up their lane. Within minutes, the three women were in Chloe's bedroom upstairs. Bette stood in her slip in front of the free-standing full-length mirror as plump, perspiring Mrs. Jenkins slipped the silky white satin gown over Bette's head and shoulders. Then the woman fastened the hidden buttons under Bette's arm and stepped back.

Bette looked at her reflection. The cap-sleeved dress had a V-neck, which was tucked back on both sides with rhinestone buttons, creating the effect of curtains tied back. The bodice was close-fitting and the skirt flared out from the waist, ending at the bottom of her knee. She would wear a small white hat with a short veil. The white satin glimmered in the morning sunlight. But inside, Bette felt as shadowy as murky night.

"It looks lovely on you, dear," her mother said from the side of her bed.

Bette tried to smile, but her mouth only crimped at the corners.

The seamstress knelt in front of Bette, marking the hem line with a yardstick on a base. "I just have to hem it and it's done."

"It's lovely," Bette managed to say. Chloe agreed, but her eyes never left Bette's face. Bette stared at her reflection, avoiding her mother's scrutiny.

Finally, the seamstress had finished and hurried away with promises to return the next day with the completed dress. In front of the looking glass, Bette slipped on her light blue cotton dress again and combed her hair with her hands, turning the ends under.

Chloe came up behind her and lightly took her shoulders in hand. "Bette, honey, you don't have to go through with this wedding if you don't want to."

Her words froze Bette in place. *Am I that transparent?* "I don't want . . ." And then the dam separating the two halves of Bette's life became tissue paper and disintegrated. She burst into tears.

"What is it?" Chloe wrapped her arms around Bette. "What's wrong?"

Bette struggled to stop the flow of tears in vain. *Everything's wrong.* But she couldn't say that. "I'm worried about Curt, about the draft," she mumbled.

Her mother said no more, but from her pocket handed her a hankie embroidered with forget-me-nots. "God's still in control, Bette. Even when everything looks hopeless, there is always hope."

Bette nodded obediently, but didn't believe a word of it. Chloe was just trying to make her feel better. *I'm not going to feel better until Hitler is defeated.* And now retired from service before the war had even started, she could do nothing to help bring that about.

New York City, November 1940

Just inside the double doors of the downtown cathedral Drake kissed Bette's cheek in greeting. Bette smiled but said nothing. She'd forced herself to dress with care in a new purple outfit, but she hadn't really been in the mood for a family gathering.

She gazed around her, trying to look interested. The church must have been over a century old. It was solid stone outside and the maple woodwork and floors inside had a warm, rich patina. Small stained-glass windows let in the autumn sunshine, splashing jewel tones—reds, blues, and ambers—on the white walls. But her mind was occupied, mulling over and over her early-morning, totally unexpected, phone call from Ted Gaston. She tried to pay more attention to those around her.

Drake glanced fondly over at his wife. Ilsa stood talking to Bette's mother. Ilsa didn't look as if she could be the same woman they'd rescued from the freighter two years ago. Bette took satisfaction in seeing Ilsa so healthy and happy and she noted that Ilsa kept glancing at her husband, always with a smile.

"I'm sorry your wedding had to be put off. We all thought you'd be here on this happy occasion with Curt as your husband," Drake murmured.

"Curt didn't want anyone to think he'd married me to evade the draft," Bette repeated what Drake already knew, unable to stop herself. Part of her wanted to be angry with Curt over his decision and another part was grateful. But the whole experience had left her dissatisfied. As soon as Curt had been drafted, she'd gone back to Washington to the War Department at Mr. Hoover's behest, but without any specific instructions. She was simply to keep her eyes and ears open. Did the call from Ted mean she was needed again?

"Foolish pup," Drake commented. He looked proud enough to burst with the joy of the day. "I could have, should have, told him—grab the girl and forget everything else."

"My advice, too." Bette's stepfather, with his hat in hand, joined the conversation. "These young men don't know what we know."

Drake shook Roarke's hand. "Too true."

With Jonathan—a plump baby with round, rosy cheeks—in her arms, Ilsa turned from greeting Bette's mother. Wearing a hat that was a confection of silk flowers and net, Ilsa leaned over and kissed Bette's cheek. "We're so glad you came. It's so good to have family and friends with us." Little Sarah in a cherry red dress clung to her mother's skirt.

Bette kissed Ilsa and Jonathan and then bent down to kiss Jonathan's big sister. She wasn't surprised that Gretel was nowhere to be seen. Bette couldn't, wouldn't wound Ilsa by asking about Gretel. Gretel wouldn't be happy about this christening, though Bette thought that Ilsa was doing her best in a difficult situation. A mixed marriage couldn't be an easy one. But how could Ilsa not want to please Drake—the man who'd saved her, the man who'd adopted her daughter and loved Sarah as his own? And it was plain to see that Drake and Ilsa adored each other. Their love radiated like a physical warmth when she saw them together. "Curt would have come, but he's in Wisconsin for basic training."

"Wisconsin?" Drake echoed her. "With army bases all over the South, they have to send him to Wisconsin in November?"

Her father snorted. "Welcome to the army."

"We made it," Mrs. Lovelady senior said, sounding out of

breath. She and Drake's father hurried into the church foyer. "The traffic is awful for a Saturday."

"Everyone's Christmas shopping," Bette's mother pointed out.

Again, hugs and kisses made the circuit of the group and then they walked into the small chapel where Jonathan would be christened. The room was paneled in rich maple and one wall was a stained-glass window depicting Christ's baptism. Bette stood apart from the fount and the group around it—the Episcopal priest in his black suit and clerical collar, the proud parents, grandparents, and her parents, who were to be Jonathan's godparents.

Bette's unruly mind drifted. She hadn't been able to believe her ears this morning when Ted's voice had wished her a cheery hello over the phone. She'd actually stuttered as she asked him how he knew where she was.

"I called your home and they told me your hotel," he'd said. "I impersonated your boss at the War Department."

"Why are you calling?" Bette had clutched the receiver, pushing down the welling up of hope.

"You didn't get married," he replied. "And I need you to help me out."

"With what?"

"I'm here tailing someone and I could use a backup."

"I've never tailed anyone—"

Breaking into her reverie, Jamie in a white shirt and dark suit burst in behind her, bringing a rush of stiff, cold air with him. He was tall, handsome as always, but looked strained. "Sorry I'm late," he apologized in a low voice.

The christening went on, formal yet somehow touching,

with the baby boy gurgling and then crying when the cold water washed his head. Warm laughter and loving words flowed over and through them. Bette felt cut off from these tender emotions. Curt had left, taking with him what had remained of her true feelings, leaving her deadened. She hadn't been able to shake the thought that maybe she and Curt would never marry. The war could come crashing over them at any moment. Curt might be sent off to fight and never return. She closed her mind to these horrible possibilities.

Maybe that's why Ted's call had affected her so. She would have another chance to work against the powers that threatened her dreams of love and family. She thought of her white-satin wedding dress, carefully packed away in a box at Ivy Manor. A poignant symbol of the fate of her private life. *What exactly does Ted want?*

The christening ended and the party adjourned to Drake and Ilsa's brownstone for luncheon. The eight adults and two children sat around the dining table, eating flaky golden quiche and crunchy-sweet apple crisp and chatting about Sarah and Jonathan and Christmas plans. Bette was certain that Gretel's absence was what made Jamie look so strained even as he joked with Drake about changing diapers.

Bette scrutinized each face around the table, trying to see if she and Jamie were the only ones wounded by Gretel's absence. Of course, Ilsa must feel it. Was it her love that caused her to keep touching Drake and her children or her feeling of being cut off from the rest of her family? Certainly Drake revealed his concern and love through his tender and worried glances at his beloved Ilsa. Did Gretel have any idea how her rejection cut those who loved her? Did she care?

"I might as well announce it now while everyone's together," Jamie said in a cold voice that sliced through the happy chatter. "I've enlisted in the Navy Air Force."

"No!" Chloe exclaimed, shooting out of her chair.

"It's done." Jamie grimaced. "I don't expect anyone to be happy or to understand. But I've done it. I leave for basic training in two weeks."

Chloe burst into tears. Roarke stood up and drew her to him. The Loveladys looked on in dismay and sympathy.

"I understand," Bette whispered to Jamie. Even as she touched his hand under the tablecloth, she glanced at the clock. She needed to be home this afternoon. Ted would be calling her and setting up a meeting. Yes, she understood why Jamie had enlisted. So had she.

At Times Square, Ted in a discreet gray suit and hat hung back in the holiday weekend crowd, the perfect cover for his tailing job. He glanced at his watch, keeping in mind that sometime this afternoon he wanted to call Bette again. The November breeze was anything but gentle. His ears were nearly ice. Ahead, he tracked his two subjects: one short and rotund and wearing thick-lensed eyeglasses; the other tall, erect, and dark-haired with a slashing scar on one cheek. The two started across the intersection against the light, ignoring the surging traffic. Ted hurried so he wouldn't lose them.

It all happened too fast to do anything but shout. The tall suspect bolted ahead as though unaware of the traffic. Suddenly realizing his peril, he jumped to avoid a car racing toward him. This leap put him in the path of a cab from the other direction. A screech of brakes. A sickening thud. Startled screams. The tall man with the scarred cheek lay, crumpled and twisted, in the middle of the street. A traffic cop's whistle pierced the hubbub. A police car jammed to a halt, its red light flashing. Ted stood as stunned as the other witnesses.

Then the downed man's companion grabbed up his fallen comrade's brown briefcase and plunged into the crowd. "Hey!" someone yelled. "Hey, he's stealing the guy's bag!" But it appeared that everyone was too busy shouting and pushing to react.

"It's a Jew plot!" the short man shouted back, confusing the bystanders. He melted into the gathering crush of the gawkers before anyone could get a firm grip on him.

Ted still pushed his way through the suffocating crowd. But the excitement drew onlookers like free candy. Ted struggled on, shoving between tightly packed bodies, but the short man had vanished from Ted's line of sight. So Ted turned back to the accident victim. The first Nazi wouldn't be running very far away.

Pushing to the front, a police detective flashed his badge and began questioning the cabbie who had hit the tall man.

"A guy with him stole his briefcase," the cabbie said, shaking his head and wringing his hands.

"Yes," Ted added, able to edge his way forward, "and he had a German accent."

"Yeah," the cabbie went on, "he shouted something about Jews. I didn't catch it."

"A German accent?" The New York detective looked concerned.

An ambulance clanged in the distance. The detective near the injured man started waving his arms and shouting. More police whistles. The ambulance snaked through the crowd of onlookers to the victim.

Ted watched the second of his Nazi agents being lifted onto a stretcher and up into the ambulance. He wanted to say something to the detective, but held back. If Ted were the fallen man's companion, he would wait nearby long enough to hear where his friend was being taken so he could find out if he survived or not. If Ted showed his badge, he'd call attention to himself and blow his cover. Worse, this would announce to the Nazi suspect: "You were being followed." Ted also couldn't take just any police detective into his confidence. That would have to be handled at a higher level than he. So he hovered around the black-and-white ambulance, one of the crowd.

"Where are you taking him?" he asked the man shutting one of the ambulance doors. He hoped no one would think this an odd question for him to ask.

"St. Vincent's!" the medic replied.

The detective glanced around as if trying to see who had asked this question. Ted looked as nonchalant and uninterested as he could. The detective climbed through the remaining open door and the ambulance clanged away.

Ted scanned the crowd once more for the short, round man with the briefcase. No luck. So Ted searched for the nearest phone booth. He had to call headquarters to report this development. He glanced at his wrist watch. The urge to call Bette first welled up in him. But after he entered the nearby drugstore and pushed into a phone booth, he made himself dial the FBI number instead. *Later, Bette.*

At the Benjamin Hotel, Bette paced the floral carpet in her room. The afternoon had passed, the evening had crawled by, and now the long night yawned before her. Only a little after 10:00 p.m.; her parents in their suite were probably already sound asleep. While Bette, still in her street clothing, stared at the bedside phone, willing it to ring. Why had Ted called her this morning and then not kept his appointment to call her again?

Bette found herself raking her arms with her nails. Nerves. Just nerves. To distract herself, she sat down at the desk in her room and took up pen and hotel stationery. "Dear Curt," she penned, "the christening went well. Jamie was late, of course. He'll probably be late for his own wedding . . ." She looked at the final word she'd written. She'd meant to write "funeral." She dropped the pen and, unable to prevent it, began sobbing.

I was supposed to be Mrs. Curtis Sinclair this Thanksgiving.

Her arms ached with wanting Curt. She'd waited four long years. And then Gretel had sent her regrets and Curt had preferred to be drafted rather than let anyone think he was a coward. That was it, wasn't it? A foolish, little-boy way of thinking. At least, that was how it had struck Bette when Curt had finally made the decision. And it had hurt her even as she had been relieved in a way. In the final analysis, who cared what people thought? The war was coming anyway—anyone could see that. She'd pleaded with Curt to no avail.

We could have had a few months, maybe a year together before he had to go. Why didn't you marry me, Curt? Then everything would be as it should be. Ted wouldn't have called me if I had married. This wouldn't have started all over again. But she was too honest not to admit that she wasn't unhappy Ted had called. Why did life have to be so complicated? She sprang up, restless. Where was Ted? Was he lying somewhere hurt . . . dead? And suddenly she wasn't weeping because Curt wasn't there. She was weeping because Ted hadn't called back.

The phone rang.

She grabbed it, cutting off the second ring.

"Bette, it's me, Ted."

"Why didn't you call earlier? I've been so worried." She couldn't keep the quaver out of her tear-thickened voice. She wiped away her tears with her fingertips.

"Sorry. Really am sorry. Just . . . something really strange happened today. I'm still working on it."

"Strange? You're still in the city, aren't you?"

"Yeah, did you hear about that accident in Times Square today?"

"Yes, it was on the evening radio news." She twisted the black phone cord between her fingers.

"Well, I can't say any more over the phone, but that's what held me up from calling you—"

"Why?" Her mind raced ahead. Ted wasn't calling her just to pass the time of day.

"I take it that your parents have turned in for the night."

"Yes." She felt herself revving inside—like a car idling on high.

"Good. I'll be at your hotel in about fifteen minutes. Meet me at the side entrance. We need to talk."

CHAPTER TEN

*B*ette couldn't help feeling guilty as she crept from her room, down the quiet hotel hallway. Stealthily, she passed the elevator and went down the steps to the main floor. The empty stairwell had led her to the side of the quiet lobby. She welcomed the concealment offered there by the tall rubber plants and fig trees. She was glad her wool coat was black, not red like a flag. As she turned to go out the side entrance, she glimpsed the desk clerk raise his eyebrows. Well, let him. She was over twenty-two and free to do as she wished.

His collar turned up against the cold, Ted waited in the black shadows just beyond the lighted entrance. "Right on time," he said. "That's my girl."

She knew she should scold him for this form of welcome, but it fit her mood exactly. "When you didn't call, I was so worried. What *happened*?"

Ignoring her question, he took her arm and hurried her down the block and around the corner. "Here's my car. Get in." He opened the door for her and practically shoved her inside.

His urgency made her pulse speed up another notch. When their doors were both shut and the car in motion, she asked, "What is it? Where are we going?"

Merging with traffic, Ted stared out into the street of tall buildings illuminated by streetlamps and neon signs. "That auto accident involved two suspected *Abwehr* agents."

Bette gasped. *"Ted."*

"I watched it happen right in front of me." He stopped at a red light and waited. "I was tailing them, trying to get a bead on their activities and anyone they came in contact with and *bam!* One of them was so busy thinking or whatever, he charged right into Manhattan traffic. He got hit—then chaos, gawkers, and what's worse—his buddy got away—with a briefcase. He was yelling something about a Jew plot."

"Who was his companion?" The light changed to green.

"Don't know his name." Ted sped on. "But I do have a lead on the guy who died—"

"He died?" Ted's car was black and silent as it purred through the quieted streets. Only restaurants—pools of color and motion in the city night—still beckoned people.

"Yeah, inconvenient, huh?" Ted glanced her way and then back to the street sign above. "We can't question him now. But the NYPD did a great job. I had already contacted the chief about this when the NYPD called the FBI office here on Foley and said they thought the guy that was hit and the guy who legged it with the briefcase might be Nazis."

"Wow." Bette could almost see the whole thing playing out in her mind.

"Right. It's not often that civilians pick up on things like that. And they were quick about letting us know."

"So where does this leave us—" Bette stammered. "I mean, you?"

"*You* and I are on our way to the hotel room of the victim." Ted checked his luminous watch dial. "The police have already been through it, collecting evidence. But they thought the FBI should go through it, too. The chief knew you were here and told me—"

All of a sudden it hit her all over again—how much she loved this. After months at the War Department, she'd jumped at the chance to meet Ted. But all she asked was, "How did the chief know I was here?"

"Mrs. Lovelady had written Mrs. Hoover about the christening," Ted went on, "and mentioned you and your parents were coming up for it. But not your fiancé. Why didn't you tell me the big wedding didn't take place after all?" Ted taunted her. In the rippling light from passing streetlamps, he gave her an assessing side glance.

"No, he didn't want . . ." She fell silent, unwilling to voice Curt's decision, knowing her own confusion over it would be hard to hide. "He was drafted," she announced succinctly, "so we decided to postpone it until his year is done."

"Fool," Ted muttered. "Doesn't he know the war is a foregone conclusion at this point?"

Ted shared her opinion? This nearly opened the floodgates. Bette longed to pour out her frustration with Curt, but held back. A wife, or even a wife-to-be, didn't criticize her husband to another man. Her mother's good example had been enough to teach her that. Plus, honesty compelled her to admit to herself that she didn't want to be sidelined, unable to do anything to help her country.

"Sorry for butting in like that," Ted apologized, shifting uncomfortably behind the wheel. "We live in difficult times. I know what I would do if I were in Curt's shoes, but I'm not Curt or in his position."

Bette couldn't trust her voice. So she touched Ted's shoulder, just a gliding pat to show she appreciated his understanding.

He captured her hand as it moved away and gave it one quick squeeze before dropping it. "Now we're on our way to the hotel room to go over it."

Back to business—that was Ted. "To see what the NYPD missed?" Bette hit her stride again.

"That's my sweet little brunette flirt," Ted chortled. "I can always count on you to get it."

Again, Bette let his flippant comments ride. She knew Ted by now, knew that he liked to get a rise out of her.

Before long, they walked up the stairs of another Manhattan hotel, a little less impressive than the Benjamin. Ted led her to the door on the third floor and unlocked it. "They gave Headquarters a key," he whispered, "so we wouldn't have to show ourselves at the desk."

Bette nodded and stepped inside the darkened room. Ted locked the door behind them. Bette reached for the wall switch and Ted's hand caught hers. "Wait. Let me pull the drapes."

"Why?" she whispered as he passed her.

"Someone—the other agent or another Nazi who knows this guy died—might be watching this room from across the street, from another hotel room or maybe from the roof. With binoculars, they could see our faces clearly. I don't want to blow our covers."

Her cover—an entirely new thought. She heard the metallic sound of drapes being pulled closed on a rod and then Ted's okay for the lights. She groped around the wall by the door, found the switch, and flicked it. Light from a faded bedside lamp pooled in a circle on the floor.

Ted switched on a matching lamp by the window and then crossed to the bath and turned on those lights, too. "Now the police are done, so we don't need to worry about disturbing fingerprints or anything. But they didn't find anything incriminating as far as espionage. I don't want to leave this room until we've exhausted every possible place." He knelt down and slid under the bed.

Bette stood where she was, letting her eyes rove over the drab, worn-looking room in gray and blue. She considered the white-tiled bathroom and rejected that as a place to secrete documents or photos. No, too much steam and dampness. That left the almost bare room, just a bed lamp and a chair. She slowly surveyed it, once, twice. What was it that didn't look right?

Ted grunted as he moved around under the bed, obviously prodding and poking the underside of the springs.

Then she realized that something about the lighting in the room didn't look right. She studied the glow from the two lamps, reflected on the walls, floor, and ceiling. The two lamps were identical so they should look the same and radiate the same light. They didn't. She walked over to the bedside lamp and sat down.

"Hey, thanks," Ted complained softly from underneath her.

Bette ignored him and rotated the lamp on the night-stand. "Ah," she breathed.

"Ah?" The bed jerked. "Ow!" Ted exclaimed with pain in a hollow whisper. "That 'ah' better mean something. I just bumped my head."

"It's in the lampshade," Bette murmured.

Ted was standing beside her within seconds. "What's in the lampshade?"

"Do you see how the lamp by the draperies casts different shadows?" She gestured toward the floral print lamps.

"Not really. What are you . . ." He fell silent.

She opened her purse and from a small red-silk pouch took out tweezers. Then she bent the lamp over. The lampshade was in two layers: an inner celluloid layer that was stiff and smooth and a pleated fabric outer layer. The shade was topped by frayed, starched lace. She slipped the tweezers into a gap between the two lines of lace and drew out a rolled slip of paper. Suddenly her heart pounded.

"You little sweetheart," Ted cooed. "What did you find?" He bent to the nightstand, unrolled the paper, and spread it out under the lamp.

She leaned close to his shoulder and looked at it, too. The letters didn't make any sense. "Is it in code?"

"Yeah." He kissed the paper. "Gotcha."

She'd tried not to remember what this was like—so exhilarating, so exciting. The police had missed it. *She* had found it. "Will you be able to read it?"

"At Headquarters they'll decode it." He looked over and beamed at her. "How did you notice it?"

Trying to appear modest, Bette nodded toward the lamp-shade. "This one didn't give out as much light and when I looked closer, I noticed that some of the folds were darker. I bet the police searched the room in the daylight. They might not have turned on the lamps. Even if they did, it probably wouldn't have been as obvious in daylight."

Tilting the lamp toward her, she dipped the tweezers in again and pulled out another page. She did this three more times, finding three more pages. She then moved to the other lamp and rescued one more page. "They should have put the same number in each shade. I might have overlooked them then."

"I doubt it." Ted took the pages from her. He looked down at the five sheets of hotel stationery in his hand and then tossed the papers onto the rumpled bed. "You never miss a trick. You're unbelievable." Without warning, he pulled her to him and kissed her.

The shock of Ted's lips meeting hers took her breath away. Then he wrapped her in an embrace that pressed her against him with an intimacy she'd never experienced. She gasped for air and Ted plunged them into a second kiss. Curt had never kissed her like this—as if life and death were bound up in one kiss. She'd thought she'd been awake before this. But now she was fully alive, fully aware of every inch of the man pressed against her. *I should pull away.*

She tried to protest, but Ted's kisses rushed over her like breakers on a high sea. She felt as if she were being sucked into the tide. She kissed him back—urgent, demanding, surprising herself. She clung to his broad shoulders, digging her fingers into his wool suit jacket. His every move and touch heightened her senses. Then he nudged her back and she felt him lower her onto the bed.

Feeling the mattress give under her weight splashed

through her like plunging into ice water. "No." She jerked her head away.

She gasped for air even as he started another kiss. Her conscience reared up. "No." She pushed against him. "No."

"That's three no's." He had the nerve to chuckle. "A lesser man might take it that you don't like his kisses." Looking down at her, he gave her a slow smile filled with sensual promise. "But you do like my kisses, don't you, Bette?" He traced her chin with his index finger.

Her face flamed, but she refused to give in to embarrassment over her lack of control, refused to let Ted intimidate her. "You are very good at it," she said coolly and straightened up away from him. She was pleased to see that he hadn't expected this from her. "But I am an engaged woman."

"Yes, but just how engaged are you, Miss Bette Leigh?"

Two days after helping Ted find the hidden pages, Bette strolled nonchalantly into the elegant lobby of the Waldorf-Astoria Hotel as if she were here for pleasure—not for a mysterious appointment. She'd received an early call from Ted and had agreed to meet a third party here today at 2:00 p.m. Any third party that Ted knew must be involved in espionage some way. Could it be Mr. Hoover and Ted hadn't wanted to say that over the phone? This meeting could turn her life upside down again. The possibility thrilled her. And perplexed her. Yet she hadn't been able to refuse.

"Just how engaged are you?" Ted's outrageous question from two nights ago echoed in her mind. She'd slapped his face and pushed him away—horrified at her behavior. She'd let Ted push her down on a bed and kiss her, not once, but repeatedly. And recalling this, her treacherous lips tingled, mocking her.

What was she going to do about Ted? She didn't think he was the kind of man to take no for an answer. Or even three no's. But Curt seemed similarly stubborn. Men. Hadn't she been ready a few months before to put all this FBI work aside and become Mrs. Curtis Sinclair? Then Curt had overruled her, insisting they wait again. *If Curt had married me, I wouldn't have been with Ted.* Something quite true but that did nothing to absolve her. Now a similarly bossy phone call from Curt this morning had left her trembling with an inexplicable anger. It seemed that Curt wanted it both ways, too.

She strode through the luxurious lobby to the stairway and then up the steps. She'd dressed with care and wore a new black dress and purple hat with a black veil that covered her face, tying back at the rear of the hat. Ted had told her she was to report to a room on the second floor. In minutes, she stood before the door and knocked on it three times. A middle-aged man opened the door. His gaze flashed over her as though photographing her with his eyes. "Miss Browning?" he voiced his password.

She nodded and replied with her password, "Yes, I'm Miss Bette Browning."

He stepped back and waved her inside.

She entered, her nerves thrumming with unaccountable anger and nervous anticipation. Inside the luxurious room, Ted waited in the background. She halted in surprise. He merely nodded his greeting as if seeing her awoke nothing in him.

Saying his name with a note of polite inquiry, she ignored

the way she reacted to seeing him again. Her senses had gone crazy and that didn't please her. Angry or not, she was still engaged to Curt. "I didn't expect to see Ted today," she said lightly over her shoulder to the stranger. She was glad she'd dressed up. Today, she didn't look like a woman with whom a man could take liberties.

The stranger smiled at her. "I know. That's why you were given passwords to verify our identities at this meeting. But I was just about to leave my office when Ted appeared so I asked him to come along with me today."

Ted just happened to turn up at your office? I don't think it was just a coincidence. But Bette kept this unspoken. Had he come to taunt her? Or kiss her again? He was no better than Curt. She wouldn't be manipulated by either of them. But Ted's presence continued to swirl her emotions in directions she didn't want to pursue. Why did things keep happening that complicated her life more and more?

"Please let me introduce myself." The stranger offered her his hand. "I'm Bill Stephenson, head of British Intelligence in the US."

She shook hands, studying him surreptitiously. Mr. Stephenson wasn't as tall as she was and had an indeterminate appearance. He was the kind of person people would pass by without a thought. "British Intelligence—I don't understand. You don't sound English."

He chuckled. "I'm Canadian. Come over here and sit down at the window. What I'm going to tell you now is very secret. Very few people have been trusted with this information."

Bette stiffened as the importance of this meeting hit

home. Her earlier hasty conversation with Curt paled in this context. As did Ted's kisses. What could British Intelligence possibly want with her?

Motioning for her to take a seat, Mr. Stephenson sat in a brown leather chair beside a desk. Bette seated herself opposite him in a matching chair and Ted pulled over a straight chair, completing their tight circle. "First of all," Mr. Stephenson said, beaming at her, "I'd like to thank you for your excellent work in finding those pages in Joseph Lopez's hotel room. Ted said it only took you a few minutes to find them."

"Joseph Lopez?" she asked, concealing how this praise made her feel inside—buoyant.

"Yes, that's the name of the victim of the traffic accident," Stephenson said.

"The man Ted was tailing?" She allowed herself a glance at Ted, but then looked quickly away. This wasn't the time or place to give any thought of her foolish attraction to Ted.

"Yes. We have the key to the *Abwehr* code and we used it to decipher those pages. Believe me there was a lot packed into those five small sheets." His smile widened.

"I'm glad." She felt herself warming with more pleasure. She'd done it. Not Ted. Not the man.

"Not as glad as Prime Minister Churchill, President Roosevelt, and Mr. Hoover were."

"They know . . . ?" She blushed and lowered her eyes, self-consciously. This was almost too much to take in.

"You shouldn't act surprised, Bette," Ted inserted. "Mr. Stephenson knows that you started your career in espionage by blowing the whistle on a Nazi operation to blackmail War Department officials."

She looked at her black gloved hands folded in her lap

and said nothing. But she wished Curt Sinclair were here, listening to Ted tell the head of British Intelligence what she was capable of. Then Curt might not think she was just sitting around compliant and unimportant—less important than everyone else and what they would think of him. She finally admitted to herself that, at heart, Curt's decision to postpone their wedding had insulted her.

"Really? Quite impressive, Miss." Mr. Stephenson looked at her keenly as though weighing and measuring her. "Quite." He cleared his throat. "After FDR's reelection this month, Winston Churchill asked your president to help us set up an espionage center here in the US."

"Why here?" she asked.

"The German blitz is bombing London nightly."

"I know." The radio broadcasts from London were difficult to listen to. The scream and whistle of bombs and then the thunderous explosions—shattering, horrible.

"Well, now come more secrets: the British and US governments must be prepared for anything, especially sabotage. One week after the US election, bomb blasts rocked three East Coast war production plants. The blasts occurred at ten minute intervals—at 8:00 a.m., 8:10, and 8:20. There can be no doubt that these were the work of Nazi saboteurs."

Bette wondered why she had not read about these in the newspapers. Was the government keeping this quiet?

"And if England falls," Mr. Stephenson continued, his tone darkening, "we must be ready to continue the fight over here. I've been in conference with Mr. Hoover and we see eye to eye and intend to stand shoulder to shoulder."

"What can I do to help?" Bette couldn't stop herself.

The Canadian grinned at her. "I have a proposition to put

before you. You see, we think you would be an asset in a certain operation of ours. Interested in hearing about it?"

She nodded, not trusting her voice. Yes, she might as well serve England. Curt had called wanting her to marry him right after boot camp. *Just because now he decides he* misses *me*. Well, Curt had made his decision and now she would make hers. *I want to be in on this. I want to do what I can, show what I'm capable of.*

"What I'm going to reveal to you involves a violation of international law, but we feel that Nazi Germany is a special threat to the free world. And we think we are justified in using every means possible to defeat them. They are willing to do anything to defeat us."

"I am willing to do whatever it takes to defeat them," Bette's voice found itself and came out firm and true. She lifted her chin.

"Excellent." Mr. Stephenson patted her gloved hands in a fatherly way. "British Intelligence has set up a mail center on our island of Bermuda. There, we go through all the correspondence from the US and Canada on its way by ship to Germany, Italy, Spain, and any country under Nazi control. Our special fears right now concern more possible industrial sabotage in America. England can't afford to have the industrial power of our ally, the US, hampered in any way." The man's voice hardened.

Bette had read the papers. She knew that England stood alone against Hitler and desperately needed all the military materials the US could give.

"And it won't be hampered if we can help it," he continued. "On Bermuda, we even go through diplomatic correspondence which, of course, violates international law. Now, we want to know if you would be interested in working for us as well as the FBI—because we share all information gleaned—on Bermuda."

"Bermuda?" She repeated. Spying? On a tropical island? The two seemed incompatible. "What would I be doing exactly?"

"You would be taught how to open and then reseal mail so cleverly that no one can detect the tampering," Mr. Stephenson said. "You would learn codes, ways of making invisible ink visible, and much more. Over here in North America, neither Canada nor the US has had a need for many agents in the past so we are scrambling to gather good people to do the work. Your aptitude for noticing things that others don't makes you an excellent candidate for this assignment. Does it interest you?"

"Yes." It sounded fascinating and being asked to do such work thrilled her to her toes.

Mr. Stephenson looked at her in surprise. "Just yes?"

"I told you she's not a chatterbox," Ted put in, sounding amused.

"Obviously not." Mr. Stephenson chuckled. "When could you be ready to go to Bermuda?"

"I'd need to go home to Maryland, pack, and then I'd be ready." Her mind already spun with excuses and explanations to give to her family and friends. And Curt.

"Excellent." Mr. Stephenson rubbed his hands together. "I love American efficiency." He rose, as did Ted. Bette stood also and accepted another firm handshake from Mr. Stephenson. "I'll let Ted explain the minor details, but let me again thank you, Miss, for being willing to help us stop Hitler."

"My pleasure." Bette let Ted lead her to the door. Outside, she walked beside Ted, a bit stunned herself at her quick acceptance. Marrying Curt hadn't even crossed her mind.

"So I guess," Ted whispered in her ear, "you still want to be a spy."

His tempting nearness was overshadowed by his words. This was the first time anyone had used the word *spy* in describing her. *I'm a spy?* Said like that it sounded preposterous. "Don't be silly," she scolded in an undertone as they started down the carpeted steps.

"Wonder what your English professor would have to say if he knew."

Bette didn't respond. But now she wondered the same thing. So many times she'd wished she could tell Curt about her real work. Well, the wedding wouldn't be taking place right after boot camp like Curt had *instructed* her this morning—in the two-minute phone call the army had allowed him.

She'd write him her regrets. The wedding would have to be postponed until he was home from the draft—just as he'd insisted when he was drafted. He'd made that decision. And it would stand. Anyway, she'd have to stay in Bermuda long enough to make it worth the time and trouble taken to train her. Curt wasn't the only one who could serve his country.

"Come on," Ted taunted cheerfully. "Admit it. You'd rather be doing this than marrying your professor."

Bette gave Ted a sidelong glance. He didn't need to know the truth about her own confusion about her motivation and she'd best keep him off balance if possible. "Working in Bermuda will be a good way to spend my time while Curt's away. Curt and I plan to marry when he is done next year."

"Want to bet?" Ted grinned, leaning close and trying to kiss her cheek.

She stepped out of his reach, strangely exhilarated by their sparring. *"No,"* she said with a sassy lilt. "Because I don't want to take your money." She hailed a taxi herself and left him laughing at the curb.

CHAPTER ELEVEN

Hamilton, Bermuda, October 1941

*B*ette stepped out of the flamingo-pink, colonial-style Princess Hotel, which was the British headquarters of the mail censorship operation. As always, the balmy breezes brushed past her face and ruffled the palm fronds high over-head and the sun shone warm on her shoulders. This year's hurricane season, nearly over, had been calmer than usual. She wore a comfortable blue-cotton shirtwaist and sandals. No stockings or gloves, for this was paradise.

It was hard to think of autumn gold and red tingeing leaves at home. Maryland wasn't all that far away. The Bermuda Islands were beyond Cape Hatteras, off the North Carolina coast. Picturing the red maples and golden oaks around Ivy Manor, she came to an abrupt halt when some-thing—someone—else caught her attention.

"Ted?" She suddenly found she was having trouble draw-ing breath.

"In the flesh." Dressed in a sharp gray suit, white shirt, and blue tie, he was a sight to behold. He'd been leaning against a palm tree down the drive. Now he straightened and sauntered over to her.

It had been nearly a year since she'd seen Ted, but the passage of time had done nothing to mute her marked reaction to him. She'd have to tread lightly. It wouldn't do to let Ted know he still got to her. Would she never forget those stolen kisses in that New York hotel room?

"Here on business?" She turned her face just in time so that his welcoming kiss merely grazed her cheek. Her skin tingled at the touch of his lips.

He chuckled low in his throat. "Still playing the hard-to-get flirt, I see."

"Well, you're the one who taught me how." She started walking briskly up the steep slope around the corner of the hotel, making him fall into step with her. She would set the pace, not Ted. Her silly attraction to him would remain her secret. And she was very good at keeping secrets. "What brings you to Bermuda?"

"I had some vacation time I needed to use up," he said off-handedly, "so here I am."

Bette didn't believe that. The Ted she knew ate, slept, and dreamed the FBI. But then he was good at keeping secrets, too.

"How's your work coming along here?" Ted asked, keeping up with her. Their footsteps ground crushed seashells and gritty sand as they walked. "Like it?"

"I love it."

"I hear you're still wowing the upper echelons." He unbuttoned his jacket and folded it over his arm. "Discovering a way to make an unknown invisible ink visible—not bad. You're gaining quite an impressive reputation."

Bette snorted. "I was always good at chemistry. What do you want, Ted?"

"I don't know why you never accept compliments, never think I'm serious."

She shrugged. "What do you want, Ted?"

He took hold of the bare skin just under her short-sleeve, halting her. "To see you."

Ignoring the wave of sensation traveling up the sensitive flesh of her arm, she stared up at him and studied his expression. Was he serious or not? She couldn't tell.

She'd recalled his face countless times over the past months. She'd be at her desk reading the mail and some glimpse of Ted—his wicked blue eyes or his devil-may-care smile—would come up, superimposed over the page in front of her . . .

Suddenly she realized he was staring down at her, grinning. She'd taken too long to reply. She slipped her arm free and started off again. "Walk me to my rooming house."

He fell in beside her again.

"How are we doing in the US?" She had to keep this meeting on her terms. Ted always tried to take the upper hand. "Have you caught any Nazis lately?"

"Had an interesting assignment in New Jersey. It always gets me how Nazi agents think every American who immigrated since the Great War wants to help Hitler."

"They are single-minded." She could think of two reasons why Ted had come to Bermuda. Was he here on business, and just teasing her while he was here? Or had he really come to continue to push his attentions on her?

"Yeah, Nazis are stupid. They think German-Americans will sell out their adopted country for an autographed photo of *Der Fuehrer*." He made a sound of disgust.

"Well, that kind of cupidity only helps us. What do you want, Ted?" she prompted. Over the past year, the German advance had continued into Greece, Yugoslavia, and finally Moscow. The Nazi Army was like a voracious pack of wolves, devouring Europe.

The road had leveled out and they were walking near a spectacular sheaf of purple bougainvillea cascading over a high wrought-iron fence. Ted pulled her to a stop under the flowering veil. "I want to know why you and Curt failed to tie the knot. I heard you postponed the wedding again."

"What business is that of yours?"

"You know why."

She knew she should pull away. He was standing much too close. She stared up at him as he tugged her deeper into the shady natural shelter. The sweet scent of the flowers rushed through her senses. "Well, the one-year draft was extended by one vote—you know that. Curt's request for leave has been denied twice." The scent of Ted's lime aftershave mingled with the fragrant bougainvillea—a heady mix.

"You still don't see that marrying Curt Sinclair will be a mistake—a big one."

She pulled out of his grip. "Ted, I've been engaged to Curt for five years—"

"So you take longer than most to realize you've made a mistake."

"I'm marrying Curt." She found herself gazing at Ted's lips, remembering how they'd felt on hers. *Stop it.*

"Bette, you won't be happy being a teacher's wife. You've gotten hooked by the work we do. You aren't tame anymore."

He leaned close, his mouth hovering over hers, his voice persuasive velvet. "I understand that. *We* understand each other. Curt will never understand or appreciate all you've done, all you've accomplished. I do. Curt will never understand the woman you've become. You're not that shy young woman I met in the Hoover parlor in 1939."

"If that's true, then Curt will never be the same either." She felt the connection with this man begin re-weaving between them, a spider web of shared experience and attraction. *No.* "Curt's been in the army for nearly a year, has graduated from officer's training. Just because we've both taken different turns than we ever expected doesn't mean we still don't love each other."

"I love you," Ted announced.

The declaration took her by surprise—a sneak attack. Sucking in air, she stared at him and then turned her shoulder. "What do you want from me?"

"Give Curt back his ring. And when the war is over, we'll marry."

She should have known. Ted Gaston had gall all right. "So I'm supposed to jilt Curt, who postponed our wedding a year ago and then wait for you who knows how long?"

"No, Bermuda isn't far from Washington." Ted feathered his fingers through the hair above her nape. "We can carry on an affair and then marry when the war is won."

"An affair?" Bette saw red. She slapped Ted's face. "How dare you?" She drew her hand back to slap him again.

He caught her wrist. "It's an honest proposal."

"It's a proposition and I'm not a woman who enters into *affairs*." She tried to pull her hand from his grip.

"I know." He kissed her wrist. A shockwave of sensation rippled up through her flesh as he gave her a teasing grin. "I just wanted to get a rise out of you. Let's get a license and I'll marry you this week."

"You are impossible." She ducked out from under the bougainvillea and marched off.

Ted hurried behind her, laughing. "Come on, Bette. You're going to end up married to me, not the professor."

She halted and turned to face him. "As soon as Curt can get leave, we will marry at Ivy Manor. *You* won't be invited to the wedding." She started walking away again.

"You're making a big mistake, but very well." He hurried to catch up with her. "How about I take you out for dinner tonight?"

"Don't you ever give up?" she asked in exasperation.

"No. Besides, we both have to eat. Why not together? You know the island. You pick the place."

"Okay, fine. Just remember I'm marrying Curt. He says there's a chance he'll be able to get away around Thanksgiving or at the latest early in December."

Ted just chuckled.

Very well. He wouldn't tell her why'd he'd come. She'd have to do some digging to find the real purpose of Ted's visit.

Honolulu, Hawaii, November 1941

From the Hickman airstrip at Pearl Harbor, Jamie drove along the ocean to the white, sandy street along Waikiki

Beach. He parked near the tropical pink Royal Hawaiian Hotel, the jewel of Waikiki. As he strode toward the hotel, he let the gorgeous scene of palm trees, sunshine, bountiful orchids, and hibiscus—all blooming in reds, pinks, whites, and lavenders—make him smile. He glanced around for his friends, a few of the officers who'd made reservations to have Thanksgiving dinner here at the Royal Hawaiian's oceanside restaurant.

Entering the lobby, he halted, stunned. He'd glimpsed a face he'd never expected to see again. "Aunt Kitty!" he blurted out.

Aunt Kitty turned and stared at him without recognition. She wore a long, slim island dress in a red-and-blue floral print with several orchid leis around her neck.

He yanked off his airman's cap and smoothed his unruly black hair back. "It's me, Jamie—all grown up."

Shock, then pleasure—lit her brown eyes. She hurried toward him, her arms wide. "Jamie! Whatever are you doing here?" She threw her arms around him and hugged him tightly.

Seeing her brought up images from his memory—a summer house on the beach at Ocean City, Maryland; the orphanage; the first time he met Kitty's parents, who had adopted him, made him a McCaslin. His throat tightened with emotion. He couldn't speak.

"Well, who's this hugging my woman?" A tall, suave-looking man in his middle years came up behind Kitty. He wore white linen Oxford slacks and a casual royal-blue shirt and was smoking a cigarette.

Aunt Kitty released Jamie and turned to the man. "Derek, this is Jamie. I told you about him."

Some undercurrent passed between Aunty Kitty and this Derek. Jamie didn't like it or Derek. He sounded drunk and it wasn't even eleven o'clock yet. Still, Jamie shook the hand Derek held out. "How do you do," he said.

"You're a handsome young buck." Derek looked Jamie up and down. "You could make a mint in Hollywood. Have you ever done a screen test? Louis B. likes your type."

"Right now I'm working for Uncle Sam," Jamie turned aside Derek's words with a grin.

"Soldier, sailor, candlestick-maker?" Derek recited the words like a nursery rhyme.

"Captain in the Navy Air Force." Jamie pointed to his stripes. "I'm stationed here near Pearl."

"Impressive. Very impressive. Well, we must be going. Invited to Thanksgiving dinner with—" Derek halted and looked around the lobby. "Can't tell you," he murmured. "Very hush-hush. Don't want reporters to know they're on the island." Derek looked very self-important.

Jamie didn't have a clue what the man was talking about, but he wouldn't ask either. "Then I'll wish you Happy Thanksgiving." He turned to Aunt Kitty. "How long are you staying in Honolulu?"

Derek took Aunt Kitty's arm. "Give Kitty your phone number. If she has time, she'll give you a call. But we've tons of invitations and I have to get back to Hollywood sooner than later." Derek hurried Kitty toward the hotel entrance.

Aunt Kitty looked back at Jamie apologetically and mouthed, "Call me here. Tomorrow."

Jamie watched Derek steer Kitty outside and hail a taxi. Seeing Aunt Kitty had brought back a rush of memories. But the most poignant one—one he'd never gotten over—was of the day she'd departed, leaving him in the care of her parents at the McCaslin house in Maryland. He'd always be grateful to Kitty's parents, Miss Estelle and Mr. Thomas, for adopting him. But he'd never understood why Aunt Kitty left.

Who was this Derek, anyway? Was he the reason she never came home to visit?

Sunday, December 7, 1941

In a simple dark-wool skirt and white blouse, Bette sat in the noisy parlor at Ivy Manor. Today was the day of her wedding. She'd repeated that to herself several times, but it didn't feel real. This long-awaited event couldn't possibly be taking place on this very ordinary chilly December day, could it?

But everyone in her extended family—save Gretel and Jamie—were there around the parlor: her parents, brothers, Ilsa and Drake and their children, and Drake's parents. And everyone was chattering and laughing. Curt was over at his house with his parents and out-of-town family. She'd only shared a few moments with him yesterday when he stopped on his way to his parents' house.

And when he'd kissed her, she'd pictured Ted in her mind. That wasn't right.

But Ted was never very far from her mind, no matter how hard she tried to stop herself. She'd never been able to find a motive for Ted's visit to Bermuda. Could it really be true— had he just come to spend time with her? She also hadn't taken his proposal any more seriously than she'd taken his proposition. She couldn't imagine . . . She halted that line of thought. *I love Curt, not Ted. I'm marrying Curt.*

Outwardly, she knew she looked cool and possessed. She'd learned how to do that working with Ted. Inside, she felt only confusion. *I know what I want. I do.* Soon, she and mother would go upstairs and she'd put on her wedding dress and they'd all drive off to church for the two o'clock wedding. Most of the county would be attending the ceremony at St. John's, the Carlyle family church.

As usual, her mother was the most beautiful woman in the room. She already wore her mother-of-the-bride dress. A lavender-blue silk sheath with a high Mandarin collar and short flared jacket—nothing like the dowdy dresses other mothers wore at weddings. But then how many mothers had kept their figures as trim as her mother had?

Ilsa was looking more lovely every time Bette saw her. When Ilsa had hugged Bette on arrival, the other woman had whispered, "I hope you and Curt will find the same happiness Drake and I have. I nearly let what had happened in Germany destroy our chance for love. Don't let this war spoil your wedding. You love Curt and he loves you. That's all that matters."

Easier said than done, Bette had thought but not said.

The phone rang in the hallway. Was someone calling with last-minute regrets? Rory, her eleven-year-old brother in his first formal suit, hurried out to the hall and picked up the phone. "Bette!" Rory called. "Come on! Jamie's on the phone for you! All the way from Hawaii!"

Bette thrilled with sudden excitement. She hurried into the hall and grabbed the phone from Rory's hand. "Jamie! Where are you?" She choked back a sob.

"Still near beautiful Honolulu. It's only morning here, but I figured it was almost time for you to be heading for the church." His voice was faint and the connection was scratchy, but to Bette he sounded wonderful.

"Thanks for calling, Jamie." She swallowed tears. Where had all this emotion burst from? "I was just thinking about you." *And about Gretel.* She wouldn't say that—grind salt into Jamie's wound. "Are you okay?"

"Oh, yeah, it's rough duty here—tropical breezes, palm trees, hula girls." Jamie chuckled. "I just wanted to wish you and Curt the very best before I head to the mess for morning chow."

"Oh, Jamie, thanks. It means a lot to hear from you." She clung to the phone as if it would bring her close enough to touch Jamie.

"Well, we're still best friends, aren't we?"

"Yes, yes, always." And Bette began to weep because she knew Curt had wanted Jamie to stand up with them as she had wanted Gretel to be her maid of honor. Now Jamie was serving in the Navy so far away and who knew where Gretel was? She'd never answered letters, written, or called. Bette wiped her moist face with her hands.

Chloe came up behind Bette. She interrupted Jamie, "Here's Mother—"

A sound like a muffled explosion came over the line.

"Jamie?" Bette frowned at the phone. "Jamie?"

"What's wrong?" Chloe asked.

"The line went dead." Bette wondered about the noise she'd heard. Had it just been the telephone line? So she stood there holding the phone against her ear, waiting for the operator to come on the line. When she did, she merely said that the line had been disconnected and asked Bette to please hang up. Bette did. "I'm sorry, Mother, we were cut off."

Chloe looked pained, but nodded. Then she walked back into the parlor.

Bette waited by the phone. Surely Jamie would try to call back. But would he be able to get another long distance connection? Minutes ticked by until Chloe came into the hall and paused beside her. "Bette," she murmured, "it's time we went up to dress. It's time to go to the church."

Bette nodded and followed Chloe up the familiar staircase, hoping that Jamie would call again soon.

At the front of St. John's Episcopal, flanked by Drake in a dark suit as best man and Ilsa in lavender silk as matron of honor, Bette held Curt's icy hand and recited her vows, "For richer for poorer in sickness and health, for better for worse." *In war and in peace,* she added silently. Did Curt have the same thought? They were different now, but their love hadn't changed, had it? "Till death do us part."

As handsome as ever in his dress uniform, that of an infantry lieutenant, Curt said his vows with a solemn expression. Each important word pierced Bette like a hot dart.

Ted's laughing face came to mind. She pushed it away. *If I'm thinking of Ted, should I be marrying Curt? No, I don't love Ted. I love Curt. Why couldn't we have married last year when I was still sure we should? What's going to happen to us now? When will he leave for real war, not just more training? Lord, Mother says there's always hope, but I don't feel that. This should be a happy day. But I feel like this is a funeral, not a wedding.*

And then it was over. She and Curt were joined now till death parted them. The priest pronounced them man and wife and they turned hand in hand toward the beaming congregation. Everyone was smiling. Except for Chloe; she was weeping at Father's side. Yes, her mother would understand *all* the ramifications of what was happening here today. After all, she'd lost Bette's father in 1917.

With a beribboned cake knife held in both their hands, Bette and Curt posed by their wedding cake, a lovely white three-tiered confection, baked and decorated by Curt's mother. The wedding photographer had posed them carefully and everyone was watching, murmuring encouragement to them. Bette felt like a store mannequin. Or the celluloid bride atop the cake.

Suddenly the doors into the church hall burst wide. "They've bombed Pearl Harbor! I heard it on the radio! The Japanese have bombed Pearl Harbor!"

Bette released her hold on the knife and sagged against Curt. He dropped the knife; it clattered to the floor. She turned in his arms. This is what she'd been dreading all day—really the last three years. "Jamie called me today. I heard a loud noise over the phone and then it went dead. It must have been a bomb exploding. Oh, Curt. Jamie could be hurt." *Could be dead.* "Oh, Jamie."

CHAPTER TWELVE

After a light supper at the McCaslin house where they would spend their two-day honeymoon, Curt sent Bette up to the master bedroom. With Mr. Thomas passed away and Jamie overseas, the house stood empty with the housekeeper and her husband as caretakers. Jamie had known she wouldn't want to spend her brief honeymoon in a hotel, so he'd written that they use it till Curt's leave was up.

Now, Bette paused at the doorway of the ivory-and-beige room, which hadn't been redecorated since Jamie's grandparents had occupied it. It was lit only by two small bedside Tiffany lamps. Bette stood there, remembering the night Miss Estelle, her stepfather's mother and Jamie's adopted mother, had passed away in this room.

Probably this memory should be disturbing, but it wasn't. The room had a faded, homey quality like a comfortable old family quilt. And her memories of Miss Estelle were only good ones. Miss Estelle had been one of the wonderful people who had come into Bette's lonely childhood along with Jamie. *Jamie.* Her heart ached for him—her very first friend, as close as a brother. She'd prayed for his safety all afternoon and evening.

A fragment from a long-ago hymn sang in her mind. "He hideth my life in the depths of His love . . ." Since she had no better words of her own, she sent this plea heavenward. *Father, protect Jamie. As the bombs dropped, as he fought, please let him have been protected. Whatever has happened, hide my dear Jamie, my first friend.*

This evening, Curt had sent her up first to give her time to undress and prepare for their first night together. She sighed as she pushed away her fears. Curt always thought everything through, always planned ahead. Once she had valued this trait, but now . . . Although she knew it was forbidden, she couldn't keep herself from imagining Ted's approach to a honeymoon.

But no. She stopped herself. *I have married Curt and I will put these thoughts, temptations, out of my mind now once and for all.* She walked to the closet, opened it, and began undressing. She hung her wedding dress on a padded hanger, smoothing her hands over the satin once more, and then opened a flat pink-and-gold department-store box with a peignoir set inside, a gift from her mother. The soft white fabric shimmered in the low light. She slipped out of her undergarments and into the satin gown and robe, shivering at the touch of the cool, silky fabric sliding over her bare skin. Then she went to the window and looked out into the darkness and heard Curt mount the steps.

He entered, coming up behind her. He still wore his khaki dress uniform. Taking her arms into his hands, he kissed the nape of her neck. Then he bent his forehead onto her shoulder and squeezed her upper arms. "We're not," he murmured, "the only ones who chose today to marry, you know."

She relished the reassurance in his touch, feeling the pressure of his military insignia, bars, and ribbons against her flesh. When he was with her like this, she could forget the war, forget Ted. But she couldn't glean much meaning from his cryptic comment. "What did you say?" Her low voice matched his.

"I mean it's hard to have a wedding day that will become a historical date. We'll always remember not just our wedding day, but . . ."

"I see." She halted him abruptly, turning to face him. She and Curt and their families had spent the hours after the wedding reception at Ivy Manor listening to the radio, her worry mounting with each report. She didn't want to talk about world history, about the horrible danger hanging over all of them. But she couldn't act as if she weren't aware of the significance of the attack on Pearl Harbor. Jamie's voice over the crackling connection haunted her.

She braced herself, her hands resting on Curt's shoulders. "We've waited a long time for this night, Curt, our wedding night. I don't want anything to spoil it, but now that you brought it up, all I can think about is Jamie—whether he's alive or dead. And where this war will take you." There— she'd voiced her overwhelming fear.

"You know this means war?"

"Of course I do," she snapped, anger flaring hot and wild in her. "Ever since 1939 when Hitler invaded Poland, it's just been a matter of waiting for the sword to drop. Don't talk down to me, Curt. I'm not an ignorant girl. I'm a woman."

He stepped back from her, studying her. "I'm sorry,

Bette. I know you're a woman. A beautiful woman. And my wife." He tugged her slowly to him and then buried his face within the satin collar of her robe.

His intimate touch released long-suppressed, dormant sensations that swept away her anger. *Curt, hold me, love me.* Bette leaned into his embrace, kissing his ear and stroking his thick, blond hair. "I've wanted you for so long," she whispered.

"Not as much as I've wanted you." He pressed urgent kisses to her throat and collarbone. Then his hands moved slowly down her spine as if memorizing her form. "You're so beautiful and so desirable. I've dreamed of this night over and over again."

Floating on a tide of sensation, Bette recalled her solitary nights on Bermuda. Through her open window, she'd listened to the lap of ocean waves and thought of what it would be like to be married to Curt. "Me, too." Banishing any thought of Ted, she lifted his face with both hands and kissed his mouth. *Curt, make me forget everything but you.*

He clasped her to him, deepening the kiss. Then he drew away and led her to the bed. Gently he nudged her down. "It will just take me a moment." He walked to the closet, opened the doors, and began undressing within the semi-shelter of the closet doors.

She leaned forward, craving his nearness, wishing he would hurry. *Curt, I love you, only you.*

"Bette, I want you to quit your job censoring mail in Bermuda and move home to Ivy Manor."

Curt's words rolled over her, knocking her down like an avalanche—suffocating her. She went cold and gooseflesh popped up on her arms. "Move home to Ivy Manor?" she parroted, sitting up straighter.

"Yes, Bermuda is much too far from stateside, too close to the open Atlantic. German subs have been waylaying merchant ships all along the Eastern coast. Hitler might decide to take over Bermuda for strategic purposes and I can't think that the English have much manpower there to defend the islands. You must come back to Maryland. I want you safe."

Each of Curt's pronouncements jolted her. Bette knew all about the German depredations on merchant ships. She'd personally foiled several of these attacks by intercepting coded letters headed for the *Abwehr* with merchant marine shipping routes and dates. She felt like telling Curt this. But, of course, she'd been sworn to secrecy—had taken an oath, in fact, and couldn't reveal her work even to her husband. Her supervisor had reiterated this before she'd left Bermuda for her wedding. "Curt, we are at war."

"I know and I want you safe." He shut the closet doors and came toward her, wearing blue-and-white-striped pajamas.

She searched her mind for a way to make him understand that she must continue her work. "I'll be as safe as anyone can be in a war," she said judiciously.

"I don't want any argument about this," Curt said, looking determined. "I'm your husband and I want you here in Maryland for the duration."

Bette flamed with sudden rage. She tangled her hands into the soft, worn quilt, gripping the end of her self-control. "Perhaps I ought to call your commanding officer," she said, oozing sarcasm, "and tell him that I'm your wife and I want you here in Maryland for the duration."

Curt stared at her as if dumbstruck. "Bette, I'm a man—"

"I'm well aware of that," she snapped. "I wouldn't have married you if there had been the slightest indication that you weren't a man. But being a woman doesn't mean that I will spend this war sitting at home knitting you socks. Maybe you don't have a clue, Curt, about what this war is going to demand of all of us. But I do. I've spent the last four years in government service. I know—" She fell silent, again hampered by her vow of secrecy.

"You don't even sound like my Bette." Curt said the words in a tone of confusion, wonderment.

"People change, Curt. I'm not the sweet little girl you took to the prom. I've been to the big city." She chose her next words with extreme care. "I've been in positions of trust. I've worked with men, powerful men, who knew things the general population wasn't to know. I am a part of this war." She reached for his hands. "Please understand. I'm valued for what I can contribute to defeating Hitler, and now Tojo in Japan."

He stood apart from her. "You're my wife now. Didn't you tell me that that was all you ever wanted to be? I want you safe. I insist on this, Bette. It's my job to keep you safe. And you won't be sitting here knitting me socks. You have proved your value with the War Department work. I just want you to find something close to home where you can keep busy," he lectured on. "Maybe your stepfather will need you at the bank. His male tellers will enlist or be drafted and he'll need someone trustworthy to take over. You'll be a comfort to my parents and yours—especially with Jamie in the Pacific."

She stared at him, her lips parted in amazement. Curt wanted her—the woman who'd been praised by Winston Churchill and Franklin Delano Roosevelt for her espionage work against the *Abwehr*—to tuck her tail, come home, and be a bank teller? The idea was ludicrous. Didn't he understand their nation hung in the balance? America must defeat Nazi Germany, and whatever service she could offer would be given. Bette listened to his words and could not prevent her mind from bringing up Ted's words: *"Curt will never understand, never appreciate what you've accomplished."*

But she recognized in Curt's eyes the stubbornness in him she'd noted a few times before—like last year when he'd postponed their wedding. He wasn't obstinate very often, but on a few occasions she'd found him implacable. She wanted to say, "Curt, this is our wedding night, let's not fight." But she knew he'd persevere until she agreed to what he wanted. He would fight all night, argue away their wedding night until she gave in. *If we had more time; if I could tell him about my work. He doesn't know and I can't tell him.* "All right, Curt," she lied, her heart breaking. *Forgive me, Lord, for lying to my husband. I just can't face fighting with him when our time together is so short. Forgive me.*

"That's my girl." Curt beamed at her. "Now I—"

Before he could pronounce another edict and force her into another lie, she rose up and kissed him. *No more talk, Curt. No more.* She ran her palms over his chest and down his arms. Ted had taught her how to distract a man. And this was her husband—the man she could show her love to. The military had given her "professor" some muscles and their taut strength thrilled her. She deepened her kiss, keeping his mouth too occupied to form words. And then, knowing it would shock and please him, she began to unbutton his shirt.

He sucked in his breath. But he smoothed the robe from her shoulders and it slipped soundlessly to the faded beige carpet. "I don't want," she whispered against his cheek, "you to think of anything but me tonight. Nothing but me and you." She pushed his shirt back and bent her face to his chest. She rubbed her face into his skin, breathing in his natural fragrance. A heady scent—she knew well.

He nudged her down onto the bed again and came down with her. "I love you, Bette. No matter what happens, never forget that."

Her love for him, so long denied, slithered through her like warm butter. "I love you, Curt. I always have and I always will. Never forget that."

December 24, 1941

Chloe and Roarke stood in the doorway of Rory and Thompson's bedroom at Ivy Manor, hearing the boys' prayers. A small fire burned on the hearth in the room and the windows rattled in the winter wind. The scene warred with Chloe's emotions—her stomach roiled with worry and sorrow. "Well," she said, her voice catching her throat, "we'll let you boys get to sleep now."

"Good night, sons," Roarke said.

Chloe held Roarke's hand tightly as they walked down the darkened hall and into their bedroom. On Chloe's vanity lay two colorful, glittered Christmas cards: one from Bette, one from Jamie, and a letter from Gretel—each child gone from her. Each card had been a spear through her heart. Chloe walked over and fingered them. "Gretel's letter worries me most," she murmured.

"I know, it almost sounded like a last farewell." Roarke's voice was heavy with worry. He shrugged out of his brown corduroy robe.

Chloe opened the card and read again the brief note: *I am leaving New York now. I have work to do. I will never forget your kindness to me. May God be with you—always. Love, Gretel.* "She won't be writing again. I feel it, Roarke. We've lost her. And so has Jamie."

He came up behind her and put his good arm around her, pressing her back against his chest. Roarke stroked her hair. "Gretel broke his heart."

Chloe bent her head back and grazed Roarke's chin with a kiss. "And Bette went back to Bermuda and Curt thinks she's moving home to work at the bank with you."

"That will cause trouble. But they'll have to work it out. They're man and wife now." Roarke turned her in his arms. "I pray to God this is over before Rory and Thompson get much older. I can't believe the world has let this happen again. Didn't we learn anything from the first war in this century?"

"*We* learned much—you and I." She kissed him. "But the world evidently learned nothing." She kissed him again, seeking that solid strength he always brought her. His kisses made her forget the emptiness of losing Gretel, Bette, and Jamie to this war, the war that threatened to devour the whole world in its flames. "We're helpless," she whispered. "Only God has enough power to change this, to end it."

Roarke pulled her closer, tighter, maneuvering his bent arm around her so she rested in the cradle of his arms. Silently, she offered a prayer for her children and those of every other mother who wept and prayed tonight. When would this war end and who would survive to come home?

Part Two

CHAPTER THIRTEEN

Ivy Manor, April 1946

*H*er blood fizzing in her veins, Bette paced the front porch of Ivy Manor. The same wicker rockers that adorned the ivied porch every year, April through October, had already been placed outside for spring afternoons and evenings. The magnolia trees bloomed with their pink and white petals. The scene was so familiar that Bette merely breathed it in with the fresh scent of spring morning.

She glanced at her wristwatch once again and then straightened her belt. She'd dressed with care for this reunion. She wanted to look her best for Curt. She wore a deep purple rayon dress with a black peplum waistline, a matching Peter Pan collar, and the amethyst earrings Curt had given her as his wedding gift. She smoothed her shoulder-length page.

"You look lovely, Bette." Chloe stepped out the front door. "He'll think you're beautiful. And you are."

Bette managed a tight smile. One thing still worried her.

She tried to stop the words, but they came out anyway, "Why didn't he want me to meet his ship?"

Chloe looked serious . . . worried. "I've been meaning to talk to you and I guess this is my last chance." Chloe sat down and looked away from Bette down the lane to the road.

Bette gazed at her mother, whose expression made her almost afraid of what she'd say.

"War changes people, Bette. I don't know if it's that he's had to learn to kill people and learned what it feels like to have someone try to kill him or . . . what. He'll be Curt but he'll be different. Maybe he didn't want you to come to the ship because he just wasn't ready to see you, not ready to let go."

Bette sank into the chair beside her mother, suddenly weak at the knees. "Let go of what?" she whispered.

"I don't know. He may be mourning some of the things he did. Or mourning the death of some of his buddies—feeling guilty that he survived." Chloe took her hand. "It may not be easy, honey. It wasn't easy for your stepfather and me. It took us years to reconnect."

Her mother's hands warmed Bette's chilled one. "Wasn't that because you married *my* father before the war, not my stepfather?" *Curt and I are husband and wife—what could change that?*

"Yes, that's somewhat right. Your stepfather and I hadn't made that commitment before he went to France." She squeezed Bette's hand. "You and Curt were sweethearts for a long time before the war and you married before he left. Yes, you have that going for you. But nothing is for certain." Chloe frowned. "Roarke loved me but the war had . . . injured him."

Bette didn't think her mother was talking about her stepfather's frozen arm. She knew she was trying to help her but her words were only raising Bette's anxiety level, sharpening her nerves. Again, thoughts she'd held back flowed out, unstoppable. "Am I being jealous because I think he should have come here first—instead of going to his parents?"

"I don't know. Something must be making him unsure of how to fit back into this life. Maybe he's afraid you won't love him like you did."

"Why would he think that? I love Curt with all my heart." *Could his love have cooled toward me? No. Not Curt.* Her pulse skipped a beat. *He'd never do anything like that.*

"I don't seem to be able to find the words." Chloe pursed her lips. "You've both grown up—apart from each other. You aren't the same young girl Curt married. You've spent the war censoring mail in Bermuda. Curt's been in North Africa and then Europe. Letters can only convey so much . . ."

Bette pictured the Princess Hotel on Bermuda—a bittersweet memory. The headquarters where she'd done much more than censor mail to keep military information out of letters was just a hotel again. Everyone she'd worked with had returned to their civilian lives, taking the secrets of that place with them. She still couldn't reveal her wartime service. But yes, it had left its mark on her. She had loved her work, but would she ever take anything at face value again? "I did what needed to be done."

"Then you have that in common with Curt," Chloe murmured. "I had changed too during the first world war and that made it harder for Roarke and me to talk, to begin to become close again."

Bette recalled her lonely childhood years before her mother came home. But the overwhelming import of today overshadowed everything else. "Why are you telling me this?"

Chloe interlaced her finger with Bette's. "Love him. Just give him love, but also give him time alone. He has to have time to work things out for himself. Just love him and let him know you accept the man he's become."

Bette nodded, feeling uneasy and almost frightened. Yet excited all the same. *Curt will be here soon.* And her body warmed, anticipating being alone with him tonight.

Her stepfather, somehow both smiling and somber, joined them on the porch, putting an end to the conversation. He said nothing, but gave her a hug that emphasized his support.

Then all her waiting and wondering ended. Curt was there, driving his father's well-worn Chevy up the lane toward Ivy Manor. Because of wartime rationing, it was the same car that Curt had used to take her to the prom.

Seeing him, worry again reared inside her. Why hadn't he come to her first? *I'm his wife.* She pushed these unworthy feelings down. She couldn't allow herself to be petty at a time like this.

Curt parked the car. His father got out and helped his mother and Curt's younger sister out of the backseat, but Curt didn't stir. Bette waited on the top step, her hands clenched together. Curt's hesitation lengthened. His father turned to wave him out of the car. *Shouldn't he be running to me?* A terrible sense of wrongness squeezed Bette's heart with icy fingers. She had trouble finding her breath.

Finally, Curt eased out of the car and started toward her. Her ambivalence over his show of reluctance kept her frozen in place. He reached the bottom step and a barrier inside her melted. She rushed into his arms, tears pouring from her eyes. "Curt, oh, Curt, my darling." She threw her arms around him and felt his go around her—tight and reassuring.

"Bette," he murmured in her ear. "Bette." He kissed her and his lips set the familiar fire in her veins and she wished they were alone.

But then his father began snapping photos with his camera. Bette wiped away wet tears with fingertips and smiled when instructed to do so. A grinning Mr. Sinclair, an older version of Curt, went on taking photos of various poses. Several featured Bette wearing Curt's military hat at a rakish angle and her kissing Curt in various places—his cheek, his forehead. She Eskimo-kissed him with noses. Curt began smiling, but the foolishness must have embarrassed him because he held back somehow. But soon she was laughing instead of crying. And glad their parents shared their joy.

"Everyone," her mother invited, beaming beside the double doors, "come inside. Jerusha has been cooking all day and we're the lucky ones who get to eat it."

When Curt didn't offer his arm, Bette went ahead and tucked her hand inside his elbow and they entered Ivy Manor together. When they reached the dining room, Curt dropped her hand and seated her formally—without a word or endearment. It was as if someone had reminded him of an old grudge between them. The light in his eyes had been switched off again. Why? A sick feeling leaked through her. *What's wrong, Curt? Or is this just my imagination?*

Later in the gathering twilight, Bette stood side by side with Curt in the cottage at Ivy Manor. Something was very wrong.

After a day of celebration and feasting, his family had finally gone home. Then her mother and father had escorted them here to the cottage and now strolled away toward the big house. Plainly, Curt was upset. Was she the only one who sensed his misery? What could he possibly be sad about?

Beside her, he closed the door, pulled away from her, and then stopped in the middle of the kitchen. He just stood there like a stick figure without emotion or identity. Something forbidden crouched behind his shuttered eyes. She'd never felt so alone in all her life.

Unable to bear this one minute more, she walked into his arms without invitation. She kissed him, breathing in his scent, remembering the last time they'd been together. They'd only seen each other once during the long war. He'd come home for New Year's Eve 1943. That had been a passionate reunion, nothing like today. She waited for him to respond to her embrace. Finally, she felt his arms go around her—somehow tentative, somehow new, somehow the same. Her tension loosed a notch. She breathed again.

"I was so frightened you wouldn't make it through four years of war," she murmured. "It's almost a miracle."

"A lot of guys didn't make it."

She analyzed his gruff voice. Was her mother right? Was he feeling guilt at having survived? "I know and I'm sorry for their families, but this war wasn't our idea. We didn't have a choice."

"I know that." He jerked away from her. "Don't you think I know that?"

She could come up with nothing to say. How could she help him cross over the bridge back to her, back to their life together? Remembering her mother's advice, she ignored his remoteness and, taking his hand, led him toward the small bedroom. Surely physical intimacy would bring him closer to her. She'd show him her love was as strong, as true as ever. "I'm glad Mother suggested we stay here at first. We have more privacy and can get acquainted again."

Curt made no reply.

She wouldn't be daunted. Here alone together, she could reconnect with him, show him how she had longed for his touch. She took his arm and drew him the last few steps into the small bedroom. Feeling unnatural, exposed, she made herself go to the closet and begin undressing, trying to do it as if she'd been undressing in front of him for the past five years. Curt hung back in the doorway, staring at the bed. When he made no move to enter, she was forced to speak. "Curt, is there something wrong?"

He jerked his head as if he'd been a million miles away from her. "No. I'm just tired. That's all."

Was he telling her he was too tired for them to sleep together? Surely not. She turned from him and continued hanging up her clothing. She made herself finish and put on her nightgown. *We are married. Though this feels strange, deep down, we're the same people we were in 1941 when we married.* Still, she sensed that this was not the way it should be. His holding back was the problem, not the years apart.

In her pale satin nightgown, she bravely sauntered toward him and took his hand. "Come, Curt. You're at home now and we're finally alone." She helped him shrug off his gray-green officer's jacket and starched khaki shirt. When he was standing before her bare-chested, she ran her fingers lightly over his chest. He sucked in breath and she was relieved to see that her touch still had the power to entice him.

Then she went to the bed and folded down the covers. She perched on the bed with her legs folded under her and watched him finish undressing and donning his pajamas. When he turned, she held out her arms to him. Desire for him billowed up in her, ready to spill over. "I love you, Curt. I always will. I gave you my promise, remember?"

He nodded and took her into his arms, kissed her and then slid in beside her. She sighed as passion for him flowed through her, warm and irresistible. But why hadn't he responded with "I love you, too"? She pushed this silly thought aside. He was here, kissing her, and that was all that mattered. She deepened their kiss and let her hands rover over his back. After all, this was real life, not the movies. And it would be better soon.

The next morning, Bette awoke to find Curt gone from the little cottage. A note said he'd be home later. She'd tried not to take it as a rebuff, though it had felt like one—a cold slap to her face. No doubt this was part of putting their life back together, this remembering to share plans with one another. She would have to be patient and persistent. This was the man she'd loved for a decade. She had time. She had their long love on her side.

But he hadn't called all day and only returned home in time for dinner. When he entered the dining room at Ivy Manor, apologizing for being late, Bette already sat at the table. He took his chair beside her. Surrounded by her parents and brothers, she tried to keep reproach from her expression. She held her tongue between her teeth as her stepfather asked the blessing.

"I went grocery shopping today," she said in a cheery tone she didn't feel. She passed the bowl of fresh green salad to Curt. "Now that I'm a wife, I'll have to start learning how to cook."

Curt looked up, but made no comment.

"Well, what kept you busy today?" her stepfather asked Curt.

Bette was grateful her stepfather had posed this question. It was good to have her family around her, helping her. And she wanted to know what had been important enough to take Curt away from her on his first day home?

"I went looking for a job." Curt served himself and passed the glass bowl of salad to Thompson, now an awkward fifteen.

"You want to work already?" Rory, now a gangly sixteen, demanded. "If I'd just got home from war, I'd spend some time having fun. Hey, I heard that veterans get first pick of the first new cars out of Detroit this year. If you get a job, you could probably buy one."

"Wow," Thompson agreed, sounding awed. "A new car."

Curt chuckled in a dispirited way. "New cars cost money."

Bette looked up, suddenly alert. Maybe she could give Curt something to be excited about. "We have enough money if you want one, Curt," she offered. "With all the rationing, I didn't have anything to spend my pay on, so the money's just been piling up in the bank. Why don't we get a new car?"

"You mean *your* money has just been piling up." His voice was wry, but with an undercurrent. "Your pay as a mail censor beat my GI pay, didn't it?"

His scolding made her feel funny. Was he still mad about

her not staying in Maryland during the war? Was that what was causing trouble between them? "But, Curt. My money, your money. It's our money."

"You know I didn't want you working in Bermuda during the war." For the first time since yesterday's reunion, Curt sounded vitally present and very angry.

Bette blinked away tears. Curt hadn't recognized that by suggesting a new car, she'd only wanted to please him. Why did Bermuda matter so much? Or was it just an excuse for something else? Why was he acting the way he was?

"No doubt Curt would like a new auto," Chloe commented smoothly, "but I'm sure he's more concerned about settling down at a job and making use of his good education."

Bette still reeled from Curt's touchiness. It felt as though she were standing on a cliff and a bit of pebbles and earth had slid from under her feet, giving her a breathless fearful tug at her heart. Hiding her hurt, she concentrated on eating her salad. *This is hard, so hard.* She tried to tell herself that this was just part of working things out after so many years apart. But it didn't ring true. Again, she was glad for her family's rallying around at this time. It made it easier to face Curt. *I'm not alone in wanting to make things work out.*

Curt looked down at his food, willing Bette to drop the subject of money. He didn't want to talk about it.

"What kind of work were you looking for?" Bette's stepfather asked in a neutral tone. "I could use someone at the bank—"

"No, thanks," Curt said quickly, glad his father-in-law had broached this topic. "Last week, my dad got a call from a principal over the line in Baltimore County. I'd interviewed there before the draft. They need substitutes to finish out the school year. I went over to apply today."

He didn't look at Bette, couldn't look at her. He couldn't tell her why he had to earn some money fast. He knew his show of irritation had hurt her. She didn't deserve this kind of treatment, but he couldn't find a way to tell her. He'd known that being honest with Bette would be the hardest thing he'd ever had to do. *What will she say? What will she do when I tell her the truth?*

CHAPTER FOURTEEN

*T*wo days later, in the warm evening gloaming, Curt and Bette sat on the small porch in front of their cottage. Today, Curt had interviewed again for an end-of-the-year teaching job in Baltimore County. A woman teacher had resigned when she found herself pregnant; her GI husband had come home in March. "So the second interview went well." Bette groped for something Curt might open up and talk about. "You think you'll be offered the job in Baltimore?"

"I don't see why not." He stared off in the distance as if she weren't even present.

She fought the urge to shake him out of his reticence. *I must be patient. He'll come around in time.* She went inside and brought out the magazine she'd bought in town that afternoon. Staring into the distance, Curt didn't even act as if he noticed she'd moved. She cleared her throat. "I picked this up today in Croftown. I thought you'd be interested in this article about new postwar housing." She flipped open the magazine to the beginning of the article about new home styles. "I was thinking that this might be similar to what we always talked about building." She turned a page and offered it to him. "See?"

He glanced down—for a fraction of a second. "It's too early to be talking about building. I don't even know if I have a job. I don't know if I'll be offered a contract for the fall." Excuses seemed to flow from his mouth.

"I know that." She clung to her patience. "But, Curt, why can't we just talk about it? We always used to like to plan for our future together and our future is now. And we have the money to build right now. But—"

"I've told you. I don't *want* your money. It's yours, not mine." He shoved away the magazine.

His gruff words hit her right between the eyes. "What's wrong with you?" She heard the forbidden words pop from her lips. "Why are you acting like this?"

Curt surged to his feet. He stalked down the two steps and headed for his father's car, which his parents had loaned them. He got in and backed the car down to the turnaround.

Bette stood, dumbfounded, the magazine dangling from her hand. *Something's wrong. Something's terribly, terribly wrong here.*

Hours later in their darkened bedroom, Bette feigned sleep as Curt undressed and got into bed beside her. She couldn't think of anything to say. No words that would bridge the puzzling gap that stretched between them. No words that would bring him closer, not send him farther away. Who was this man and why was he treating her like this?

Still, he had come home finally. She'd half-expected him not to return. She hugged this fact close and tried to keep her weeping silent, unnoticed. She experienced the standing-on-the-cliff sensation again and she was losing more ground. Every time she tried to reach out to him, precious earth slipped from beneath her feet. *If he doesn't come around soon, what am I going to do? How do I get him to open up and tell me what's wrong?*

Maybe you *are what's wrong,* an inner voice taunted. Bette squeezed her eyes shut, refusing to listen. *God help me, help us.*

Over a week later, home from grocery shopping, Bette walked into the small kitchen of the cottage and halted, brought up short. "Curt? What happened? I didn't expect to see you home yet."

"I quit." Curt didn't look up. He sat with his elbows propped on his knees and his chin on his folded hands. "I couldn't take it anymore."

Bette stood there with the paper sack of groceries in her arms, not knowing what to say. Curt had sounded relieved when he'd gotten the Baltimore job so soon. Now he'd already quit. Should she say something to him about his quitting or stay silent? What could she say? In a carefully controlled voice, she said, "I see."

"Stop handling me like I'm a live grenade!" Suddenly he was on his feet, in her face.

She gasped and drew back. But his attack released the floodgates. "I'd be glad to if I knew how. What do you want from me? Where are you? You came home but you're never really with me. In bed, you are only a body, not my husband—not the man who loved me, whom I loved. Tell me what's going on!"

Curt made no reply, but his chest heaved as if he'd just run a long, hard race. "I can't do this." He shoved past her and practically ran out the door.

Bette threw the bag of groceries to the floor and charged after him. "Don't you dare run away from me again! I won't have it!" Her long suppressed anger broke through—blazing, crackling, roaring in her head. "Don't you dare!"

She caught up with him and grabbed the shoulder of his suit jacket. He tried to pull away but her grip held. He swung around and shoved her. Shocked beyond belief, she stumbled and nearly fell. But her grip on him saved her. She only skimmed one knee over the ground.

"Let me go," he growled, his face twisted with rage.

"No!" She clung to him. "We're going to have this out once and for all!"

"No." He yanked her hand from his shoulder, ripping the seam.

She then seized both his hands in hers, hanging onto them, not giving an inch. Curt cursed and squeezed her hands painfully, then tried to pull away.

Ted had taught her a few self-defense moves. She slid her foot between Curt's. Then suddenly, instead of countering his force, she shoved forward. It threw him off balance and she tripped him with her foot. They went down together on the new grass. Both panting. Curt cursed again.

Bette pushed herself up onto her knees, rubbing her bumped elbows. "What's wrong, Curt? Why can't we talk? Why do you close your eyes when we make love? Why aren't you ever here with me?"

He turned his head away and wouldn't answer her.

She grabbed his lapels and twisted them, shaking him.

"We've got to work this out. Good heavens, we've been sweethearts for ten years and married for five now. Do you realize that? We waited and waited for each other and then the war came and now, finally, we have a chance to begin our life. But you won't let us. Why?"

"I can't do this." He averted his face.

His continued intransigence enflamed her. "Well, you'd better decide to." Her voice was a lash and she couldn't stop it. "I went to the doctor before I went shopping today. We're expecting a child in February."

"No. Oh, no." Curt wrenched free of her hold and raced toward his car.

Too stunned to move, Bette watched him drive away. Her heart thudded against her breastbone. She bent over, feeling nauseated, and wretched in dry heaves. *This can't be happening. What am I missing? What do I do now?*

After the nausea passed, Bette staggered back into the cottage, feeling weak—dazed. Had she and Curt just had what amounted to a physical fight? *How did this happen? How did we get here? What's responsible for this?*

She stood in the tiny kitchen, wringing her bruised hands. "What should I do?" she whispered to the empty room. Tears began to leak from her eyes, flowing down, dripping to the floor. Finally, she bent down and gathered up the canned goods and bread that had spilled out of the bag and had rolled over the wood floor. Putting the items away in the small pantry, a homey chore, soothed her frazzled nerves and she was able to think.

Something had changed Curt. Something had happened to him in Europe, in the war. She shoved her mussed hair back from her face. Over the past month, she'd repeatedly tried to draw him out and he had rebuffed her each time—often walking out on her and not coming home for hours. He didn't want her to know some . . . secret.

At this thought, her jaw firmed. She knew all about how to keep *and* how to uncover secrets. She marched into their bedroom and reached under the double bed. Just yesterday, she'd surprised Curt as he was pushing his Army duffle back under the bed. At the time, she'd thought it was just a reflex— a residual jitteriness leftover from combat.

Now, without any qualms, she yanked the heavy cotton-khaki duffle bag out and tossed it up onto the neatly made bed. She unzipped the bag. Inside were Curt's service revolver and three letters. She lifted out the secreted letters. Shock buzzed in her head.

But then her training took over. She studied the front of the three envelopes, reading the mailing address—a post office box in a nearby town—and the return addresses—a town in France. She looked at the postmarks for dates. The three letters had all been received during the past two weeks. Then, methodically, as if she were routinely investigating for British or American intelligence, she arranged the letters on the bed, according to postmark. Then she sat down and began to read them, one by one.

The first began: *"Mon cher, Curtis."* Bette read each letter in order, and as she deciphered the broken and misspelled English, anger sparked and burned in the pit of her stomach. A small photograph with scalloped edges fell out of the third and most recent letter. When she'd finished this letter—which Curt had received only a day ago, she looked down once more at the duffle at her feet. His service revolver lay there, just within reach.

*   *   *

Night had fallen before Bette heard Curt's car ease up the lane behind Ivy Manor. She sat at the little kitchen table, waiting for him, ready for him.

He let himself in through the door and halted just inside. The bellowing and croaking of frogs at the nearby creek sounded loud in the silence between them. He stared at her and shut the door behind him. He still wore his suit, but he'd loosened his tie, opened his shirt.

She'd neatly laid the letters and the revolver out on the kitchen table with its red-and-white printed cloth. Curt's face paled as he took this in. "You went through my things."

"She's very pretty," Bette said in a lethally soft, assessing tone. "I'd say about ten years younger than I am—about the age I was when you took me to the prom." She held up the photo and read the name off the back. "Maurielle—such a pretty name, too."

Curt swallowed. "I didn't mean it to happen—"

"That's probably true," Bette went on in her cool, impersonal voice. She felt encased in ice while she roiled with hot lava inside. "But *she* meant it to happen—"

"She's not like that," he fired up.

"Does she know you're a married man?" Bette's eyes narrowed and her jaw was so tight it was painful.

"Well, yes, but—"

"Then she planned it," Bette snapped. She offered Curt a pen and paper, snapping them sharply down on the table in front of him. "Here. It's time you wrote her the truth—that you're a married man about to become a father and you're sorry if this hurts her—"

"No." He drew himself up. "I want a divorce."

Bette had thought she was already as angry as she could

be and survive. But the force of her reaction to this horrified her. Now she knew why she'd carefully loaded the revolver and brought it to the table. She saw herself picking up the revolver and pointing it at Curt. She closed her eyes and drew in breath to steady herself. *No, I won't do that.*

She surged to her feet, stalking over to him. *"Divorce?"* She drew back and slapped his face as hard as she could. Pain shot up her arm, but it was a good pain, a satisfying pain. Curt looked stunned. He rubbed his cheek and split lip with the back of his hand. A fleck of blood smeared his cheek.

"Divorce is out of the question." She flexed her fingers, itching to slap him again. How dare he insult her, how dare he play her false? "I've invested ten years of my life in you. I am carrying your child. We took vows. Lifetime vows."

"I love Maurielle." Curt's face took on that look she knew so well—that stubbornness of his. "I'm going to marry her."

"You love me," Bette growled into his sanctimonious face. "You are infatuated with *her.*" She spat out the final word as if it were sour milk.

"No, I'm not." Curt drew himself up even straighter. "I want a divorce. I know this is difficult—"

"Difficult? Try impossible. Let me make this very clear." She lifted her chin with defiance. "I will never agree to a divorce. And no judge in Anne Arundel County or anywhere in America will ever grant you a divorce. You have no grounds."

"You can't mean that." He pulled back as if she'd slapped him again. "It isn't reasonable."

"Reasonable? You're the one who's being unreasonable. I refuse to let you disgrace me with a divorce. I am a Carlyle of Ivy Manor." She folded her arms over her breasts. "No Carlyle has ever been divorced and I will *not* be the first. You will write this cheap little French . . . home-breaker, tell her you've changed your mind, and then you will live up to the vows you made to me."

"I don't love you anymore." He stood ramrod stiff now.

His words didn't even graze her. "And I don't love you either. But I'm expecting your child and you will remain my husband—till death do us part."

"I'm leaving you. You can't make me stay," he said stiffly.

"That's right, but I can prevent you from divorcing me. Let's see if Maurielle wants you if she can only be your mistress. Write and ask her." Bette flipped a hand in his face and let her sarcasm flow—unrestrained. "Let's just see what she has to say. And tell me how many school districts will hire a teacher who's still married with a child but who keeps a French mistress?"

Bette ripped the photo of Maurielle in two and threw the pieces into his face. "If you're going, get out. The sight of you makes me sick."

That warm evening—a precursor of summer heat to come—Bette navigated the shadowy, empty back roads so she wouldn't see or be seen by anyone. After her two confrontations with Curt, she felt hollow, drained. And somehow shamed. Though she'd had no part in Curt's infidelity, she felt smeared with its indelible stain, which seemed as crimson and sticky as fresh blood.

Without knocking on the back door, she entered the quiet McCaslin house. It was Wednesday night and Bette knew the housekeeper and her husband would be at the Wednesday night prayer meeting at their church and the house would be empty. She needed to talk to someone without being overheard and this was the one place she could have privacy. And there was only one person she felt could understand her situation, even though he wouldn't be able to help her.

She dialed the operator on the old-fashioned phone in the front hall and then paced, receiver in hand, waiting for the long distance call to go through. Finally, the voice she'd hoped to hear came over the phone line, faint but still familiar. Weak with relief, Bette plumped down on the chair beside the phone table. "Jamie, I had to talk to someone."

For a moment standing at the window of his apartment on the Naval Base at Pearl Harbor, Jamie couldn't believe his ears. This was one of his rare weekdays off. He hadn't expected to hear from Bette. And worse, she sounded desperate. "Bette? Is that you? What's wrong?" The thought that something might have happened to Uncle Roarke shook him like angry hands. *I should have gone home on leave.*

Bette burst into loud sobs.

"Oh, no, something is wrong." He clutched the phone. "Is it Uncle Roarke or Aunt Chloe?" His voice rose. "Are they sick?" *Not dead, please. Please.*

"No, no." Bette's voice trembled. "It's not like that. I didn't mean to worry you. It's Curt." She stopped to gasp for air.

Jamie's tension loosed. "What's wrong with Curt? Is he sick?"

"He just moved back to his parents' house."

Jamie doubted his hearing. "He what?"

"He wants a divorce," Bette announced in a harsh, flat voice. "Curt says he's in love with a French girl and wants a divorce."

"He's nuts," Jamie muttered gruffly. "Doesn't he know how lucky he was to come back from the war? And have a good woman waiting for him?"

Bette continued between fresh sobs. "He says . . . he doesn't . . . love me any . . . more."

Jamie shook his head. The blue outside his window shone so brilliantly that it almost hurt his eyes. "What are you going to do?"

"That's why I called you. I can't bring myself to tell my mother and stepfather about Curt, about what he's done. But everyone will know. People will see that he's back with his parents. Gossip will start. I can't face it. What do I do, Jamie? I don't know how to bring him to his senses."

Jamie clenched his fist and wished he had something convenient to punch. The tropical beauty just outside his window mocked Bette's disastrous news. He'd chosen to stay away from family. The war was still too real to him to go back to Maryland and live as if it had never happened. "I should be there. Maybe I could talk to him."

Bette gave something that sounded like a painful laugh. "I don't think that will do any good. He's so blasted stubborn. When are you coming home, Jamie?"

He didn't want to answer. "If you need me, I'll get leave."

She'd stopped weeping but sounded drained of emotion, strength. "No, you couldn't do anything. It's just that you were the only one I could tell, maybe because you're so far away." She drew in a deep breath. "I've told him I'll never give him a divorce. If he brings her to the States, she'll never be accepted."

"I should think not. No one would receive her. What a rotten thing to do to you. Someone ought to take him out and horsewhip him."

"There's more. I'm pregnant." Bette's voice was muted by fresh tears. "He got me pregnant knowing he wasn't going to stay. I feel like I could kill him."

Jamie shook his head. He rubbed his hand against the back of his neck. Words failed him.

"I think I'll go crazy if I stay here and have to face the gossip." Bette's voice was suddenly infused with an edge of panic. "I've waited ten years for Curt and me to be together and start our family. Now he wants someone else."

"What are you going to do, Bette?" he asked, feeling guilty, but knowing it wasn't in his power to help her.

"Something drastic." Bette's voice rose. "Something soon."

CHAPTER FIFTEEN

Washington, D.C., June 1946

*A*rriving in D.C.'s large, bustling station on a bright June morning, Bette felt smaller, more insignificant, than she already did. But at least in this place crowded with strangers she was anonymous. Here, no one would shake a finger in her face and scold her for being a bad wife or gossip behind hands that her husband loved another woman. Shopping in Croftown had become purgatory. Why did everyone assume that Curt's leaving was her fault?

Shaking off these depressing thoughts, she hailed a taxi and rode to Georgetown—and found herself gawking like a tourist. Where had the pre-war lazy, small-town Washington, D.C., gone? Evidently while she'd spent her war years away in Bermuda, the capital had exploded with new buildings and neighborhoods. Would her plan work out? Would she fit into this modern, bustling city? Did she have any other choice?

With a strange sense of coming home, she arrived at the Lovelady townhouse and paid off the cabbie. When she'd called Drake earlier in the week, he'd graciously but somberly told her to treat the townhouse like home for as long she needed it. Busy in New York City, he wouldn't be using it any time soon and he hadn't delved into her reason for needing it. She'd been grateful. Putting Curt's betrayal into words was something else she couldn't bear doing again. Telling Jamie and finally her parents had been wrenching. She still hadn't been able to tell her parents she was expecting.

She unlocked the townhouse door and recalled the first time she'd arrived in Washington. But those memories included Curt and were sharp, slicing, bittersweet. Curt had loved her then. *I was so young and naïve. I never thought . . .*

She stopped that line of thought. From her days in Bermuda, she recalled how some women she'd worked with had behaved when affairs had ended badly. Self-pity and clinging were negative and unattractive. She wasn't going to wear her heart on her sleeve for Curt or any man. Her marriage had failed, but she still had to live. And that was what she was here to start doing.

She let herself inside the silent, stuffy townhouse and walked upstairs. After Curt left—even before he'd moved out—the little cottage behind Ivy Manor had become a silent, haunting mausoleum, the final resting place of her bright hopes for a life with Curt.

But that was back at Ivy Manor, she reminded herself, and she'd left it all behind. So she opened the windows in her bedroom, letting in fresh air, and unpacked the few pieces of clothing she'd brought with her. For a time, she stood in the middle of the room, frozen with self-doubt. And she knew why. Memories of Curt and her pre-war life in this city, when she'd slept in this room, kept intruding, rolling over her—hot and imperative. She squeezed her eyes shut and clenched her fists. *This isn't like me. Snap out of it, Bette.*

Critically, she checked her appearance in the wall mirror—it was important that none of her doubt show—and then headed downstairs. Ignoring the persistent tug of misery, she donned her hat, forced herself outside, and hailed another yellow taxi. A trip to Garfinckel's, her favorite department store, to buy some suitable clothing could only help and was absolutely necessary. She had to do something, had to keep occupied, had to figure out what she was going to do for the rest of her life—without Curt, and raising a child alone.

And surely in this large, busy city, she wouldn't run into many people who knew her from before. There was one person above all others she never wanted to know about Curt preferring another woman. But they wouldn't be moving in the same circles this time around. She'd make sure of that.

After a day of filling out applications at various governmental agencies and another day of interviews, Bette had a new job at the State Department. She'd started as a receptionist with the promise that she could work her way up to personal secretary. Now at the end of her first day, she finally arrived home after six. As soon as she closed the townhouse door behind her, she slipped off her pumps. She hadn't spent such a boring day since she'd filed and typed and filed at the War Department.

A shadow moved in the doorway from the kitchen at the rear—a blond man. Bette blinked. "Drake?"

"No. Ted." Ted Gaston stepped out of the shadows into the hall.

Shock riddled Bette, taking her breath. "How did you get in?" she finally blurted out.

"Really, Bette, that's not worthy of you." Ted gave her one of his lazy smiles and advanced toward her.

She realized then that she was in her stocking feet and for some silly reason that upset her. She shuffled hurriedly back into her shoes and then took a step back. "What are you doing here?" Her heart pounded so hard that she felt nauseated. Images, sensations from the past surged through her mind and rocked her emotions. Ted was the one person she'd hoped to avoid.

"And what are you doing getting a job as a receptionist of all things?" He smirked at her. "What is this world coming to?" He clicked his tongue like an old woman.

She still couldn't grasp that he was there standing in front of her. "How did you find out I was here?"

"Let's go into the kitchen. I made iced coffee. I figured you'd need a lift after a hard day of answering the phone and smiling at every idiot passing through the State Department." He took her hand and led her to the rear, to the small kitchen. "You must be bored with a capital B."

Her mind couldn't take it all in. Questions clogged her throat, so dumbly she let him lead her to the white wooden table. But his touch still had the power to affect her and she pulled her hand from his grasp. Staring up at him, she sat down. With a flourish, he served her a tall glass of creamy iced coffee and then settled across from her and sipped from his own frosty glass.

She leaned her head into her hand and closed her eyes against the piercing pain of imminent disclosure. Ted must know about what had happened between her and Curt. And oddly, seeing Ted only forced Curt back into her mind. How many times had Ted taunted her to forget Curt? How had Ted known that Curt would betray her in the end? Or did he know? These questions were all land mines. She stuck to the mundane. "How did you find out I was here?"

"You know how."

"Tell me," she murmured and took a creamy-sweet, icy sip. Ted's presence lapped against her, enticing her to forget Curt, to remember, to imagine many things . . .

Ted let out a long-suffering, very theatrical sigh. "Mr. Lovelady told his mother *who* happened to call Mrs. Hoover *who* then mentioned it to her son *who* called me and said to find you."

Had Mrs. Lovelady included the pertinent information of why she'd left Ivy Manor? Feeling her face blaze, she gazed down into her drink. *I didn't want anyone*—she amended, *I didn't want Ted to know that*. Why? Because Ted had been right all along? Because she'd put her trust in a man with clay feet? Because she'd been played for a fool?

Yes, that and much more she'd sincerely hoped Ted Gaston would never find out. He would have to bring it up. She couldn't. Then she remembered Bermuda—Ted kissing her under that purple bougainvillea and proposing they have an affair. Then the photo of Maurielle flashed in front of her— invisible, but very real. It stung and added a waspish overtone to her next question. "Why does Mr. Hoover care about my working at the State Department?"

"A good question—to which you know the answer. You're too valuable an agent to sit at the State Department answering phones. What were you thinking, Bette?"

Embarrassing tears popped into her eyes. *I couldn't face*

you, face anyone who knew me before. At least the gossips in Croftown had spread the news, saving her the necessity of saying, "Curt has asked for a divorce." She continued looking down, hoping he wouldn't notice her reaction. Hoping if he did, he wouldn't mention it. "Has the agency started hiring female agents?"

"No, sorry." He paused. "And I mean that; I'd love working with you again. But no, not the FBI. On the other hand, Mr. Hoover and I know someone else who'd be thrilled to meet you."

This made Bette glance up. Some knot deep inside her loosened a fraction. Someone would be thrilled by her? "Who?"

He ignored her question. "Things have really begun to heat up again—internationally."

"You mean Truman's fight against communists in Greece and Turkey?" Bette swirled the ice in her coffee, trying not to notice how much she wanted to look at Ted, study him.

"The woman reads the newspapers." Ted made a gesture as if he were awarding her a prize.

"I can still read between the lines, too." Why hadn't the war put an end to strife? Hadn't enough thousands, millions died? She cautiously lifted her eyes to his, wishing she could be as cool as he. "We're fighting Stalin's agents now, not Hitler's *Abwehr.*" She tingled with the approving look he gave her in response.

Sitting alone and close to Ted was sensitizing her to him in the same old way. He had such an expressive face, so unlike Curt, who always tried to appear the cool academic. *Stop comparing them. You have no future with any man—whether Curt finally succeeds in getting the divorce or not. If I let Curt divorce me, I won't be welcome in my own church. I won't be able to remarry. And there will be a child.* Without thinking, she pressed a hand to her abdomen.

"Would you be interested in helping your country again?" Ted asked, shaking her loose from her misery.

Should she have anticipated this? Of course Ted hadn't looked her up for any personal reason. Against her will, the disappointment crushed her. She stared into the creamy-tan coffee as if it held the answer.

"Well?"

"What are we talking about?" She dragged her mind back to the present. "The new Central Intelligence Agency?"

"You can take the girl out of espionage, but you can't take the espionage out of the girl," Ted quipped. "That's exactly what I'm talking about. Interested?"

Say no. A baby's on the way. This part of your life is over. She looked into Ted's blue eyes. He hadn't asked about Curt. Did that mean he knew or not, cared or not? Did it matter? Why did she care?

"Well?" Ted goaded her.

Three days after arriving in Washington, D.C, Bette entered the restaurant at the Willard Hotel. She wore a carefully chosen two-piece suit in severe black. She offered her gloved hand to Rear Admiral Souers, the man appointed by President Truman to head the new CIA. Once again she experienced the jolt that such a powerful man would be interested in meeting her. Somehow Curt's rejection had led her to believe no man would want her or respect her. So she was surprised, but heartened.

"So nice to meet you, sir." The net veil of her new ebony hat concealed her face, as she had planned it to. She gave him a polite smile, holding back her inner uncertainty. Had she let her hopes get too high? She might still be asked to become nothing more than a glorified but very trustworthy secretary. The war was over and the anti-female career bias had settled back in place. Rosy the Riveter was supposed to return to the kitchen and smile about it. That had been her plan, too—until Curt had made it ludicrous.

"An honor to meet you, ma'am." The Rear Admiral stood across from her in his impressive Navy reserve uniform adorned with ribbons and medals.

At that moment, Ted appeared beside Bette. She sensed his arrival with a visceral reaction. Ted had come to stand with her. It gave her daunted spirit a small measure of confidence. And caution.

Souers shook Ted's hand. "I didn't know you'd be here, Gaston."

Ted smiled. "Bette's my protégé and I like to witness any and all progress in her career." When she sat, both men took their seats. A waiter appeared with a silver pot of coffee and a pitcher of water.

Bette tried to suppress her marked reaction to Ted's appearance. She had no doubt Ted was quite capable of proposing another affair. Would he? She shuddered at the thought. After Curt's betrayal, she felt stripped, vulnerable. Why did she feel like Curt's defection was her fault? Why did people look at her as if she were to blame? As if she, not Curt, had done something disgraceful?

Souers's steady gaze focused on Bette. "Your dossier is quite impressive. But I thought you had retired."

Bette took a deep breath, suppressing the rush of unwelcome emotion this reminder unleashed. "Things didn't turn out as I expected."

Ted sipped his coffee. But she could feel his attention. He hadn't asked her any personal questions about her marriage before this meeting. Did he know about Curt? Would he ask her when they were alone again?

"I can't say that I'm sorry to hear that you have come out of retirement." A corner of Souers's stern mouth lifted. "After I finished reading your record, I think you're just the kind of agent we need. Things are happening so fast in Europe espionage-wise that we need to hit the ground running. We need someone with a sharp eye, and you have that. You seem to notice things that other operatives overlook. In this new struggle, we need that kind of talent. I have something in mind that would start immediately with a sharp learning curve. Are you interested?"

Bette felt something inside her ease. Curt didn't want her but her country still did. She looked down at her black-gloved hands primly folded in her lap. *But I'm going to have a baby. Spies don't have babies.*

Chapter Sixteen

Ivy Manor, July 1946

Her eyes gritty with lack of sleep, Chloe rose, careful not to disturb Roarke. In her rose-sprigged nightgown, she walked softly to the window that looked out over Ivy Manor, its darkened back lawn, its distant tobacco fields and grove of buttonwood and scrub pine. She rubbed the back of her tight neck as she looked out on the moonlit scene. Home—her home.

Tonight, here alone, she admitted to herself the truth that she was in her middle years—something she usually tried to ignore. No matter her care to keep her complexion protected from the sun, little telltale lines had begun forming around her eyes and mouth. So far she'd resisted dressing in the black or navy colors matrons over thirty were supposed to wear. But dressing in young colors hadn't held the clock back. Or the spiteful gossip about her losing her looks—payback for her unconventional ways. But that wasn't what she was losing sleep over.

"Can't you sleep?" Roarke asked behind her.

"I'm sorry," she said over her shoulder. "Did I wake you?"

"No, I was trying not to disturb you." In well-worn blue pajamas, her husband rose from the bed and came to stand behind her. He settled his arm around her front just below her neck and leaned his face into her nape. "I never tire of feeling you close to me."

"I hope you never do." Just his nearness comforted her; Roarke loved her and he was here.

"It's the children, isn't it?" He rubbed his face into the back of her hair.

His touch soothed her even as it heightened her desire to be closer to him. She relaxed against him, luxuriating in the firmness of his chest. "How did everything unravel?" She pressed a kiss to the top of his hand. "I was so happy—so grateful that Curt and Jamie survived the war. But after all that, new problems came."

Roarke pulled her even closer against his warmth. "War has a way of mixing things up." His voice rumbled beside her ear. "Curt wouldn't have met that French girl. And Jamie would have come home to Maryland."

His breath on her neck made her respond to him like fingers strumming guitar strings. She reached back with both hands and slid her fingers into his thick hair.

"I wonder what is keeping Jamie in Hawaii in the Air Force."

"I don't have any idea." He softly kissed the side of her neck.

She felt the stubble of his new beard against the sensitive skin of her nape. She lowered her hands and put them over his as she prepared to reveal the deep guilt that had kept her from sleep. "I keep thinking that I should have been a better mother," she whispered, soft against the night sounds from the open window. "What if I hadn't spent the first ten years of Bette's life away from her?" The old guilt still had the power to grind and shred her. *Regret* was the saddest word she knew.

"This is not your fault." Roarke shook her just enough to show his objection. "You did the best you could. So did I. Life didn't play softball with us either. Remember what my mother said on her deathbed? That she must have been a bad mother to lose both her children? Well, that wasn't true of her then and it's not true of you now."

"I know it wasn't true of your mother." Chloe closed her eyes and pictured Miss Estelle lying on her deathbed with Bette and Jamie—just children—on either side of her. It was an image she would never forget. "She was wonderful and so was your father. But—you're right—they couldn't stop history any more than we can."

Roarke nodded against the back of her head, ruffling her hair, rasping her scalp. "I do regret that we wasted the 1920s. We could have been together, but I was so stubborn."

Chloe rotated in his arms and kissed him—putting all her love for him into the warm touch of her lips on his. Then she drew breath. "We were together for the 1930s and we have our boys and we finished raising Bette and Jamie together. You're right—we will not play these blame games."

Roarke took his time kissing her back. He let his lips roam over her soft skin, breathing in her subtle fragrance— roses and Chloe. "We're going to do something special for our twentieth anniversary. Just think—1950 is coming up fast. I was thinking Paris or—"

"Maybe Hawaii?" Chloe suggested, tracing his stubbly jaw with her forefinger.

"Yes, let's hope we'll be visiting Jamie and maybe he'll have a family by then."

Chloe straightened. "We can only wait and pray. Bette and Curt, and Jamie will have to sort everything out for themselves."

"I know." Roarke pulled her back for another lingering kiss.

"Mmmm. I can't believe I'll be fifty when we celebrate our twentieth," she murmured against his mouth. "I'll be an old woman."

"Never." Roarke chuckled. His mouth explored the tender skin of her throat and she sighed her pleasure. When she feared her knees would melt, she moaned his name softly.

Then he lifted her and carried her toward their bed. When she tried to object, he chided, "You're still as slender as you were when we married. And don't tell me to be careful of my back. That day hasn't come yet."

She chuckled and kissed him lightly on the cheek. "Roarke, you are the love of my life."

"And you're mine." He kissed her eyes.

I love this man. Please, dear Lord, give us many more years together.

On a July Saturday morning, in a linen suit that was already wrinkling in the heat, Curt stood at the door of the Lovelady townhouse. He held his hat in his hands and shifted from one foot to the other. He tapped the knocker again. Standing here at this familiar door brought a wave of unexpected nostalgia. He recalled all those pre-war Sundays he'd stopped here to escort Bette to church and then brought her back here in the twilight for a good-night kiss—two kids together. He felt his emotions rising so fast he couldn't stem the flow or sort them all.

The door opened. Bette, looking lovely though slightly disheveled in a white-satin robe, stood before him. "You."

The one syllable held a wealth of meaning—all negative. He ignored the underlying message, "Go away." They stared at one another—inches between them. In a rush, he recalled the nights he'd spent with her in the little cottage behind Ivy Manor. He stopped himself. "Good morning, Bette," he said in a tight voice. "I was wondering if we could talk."

"About what?" She challenged him with a lift of her chin.

He wasn't going to say, "About us." "We . . . I need to discuss some things with you."

With a grimace, Bette stepped back and waved him inside. She led him to the parlor. "I slept late this morning," she said, looking down at her robe. "Sit down. What do you want?"

He perched on the edge of the blue wingback chair, his hat in his hand. "I want to know if you've reconsidered giving me a divorce."

"Why would you wonder that?" She brushed her lush, dark hair back from her face.

And Curt remembered suddenly how beautiful she'd looked on their wedding day. Guilt clanged inside him—a deep, scolding knell. "I'm quite aware that the failure of our marriage is my fault," he said stiffly. "I didn't plan on falling in love with . . . I didn't plan it."

He'd fallen in love with Maurielle in the midst of a skirmish near her village. He'd been separated from his squad. A bullet had grazed his shoulder. She cleaned and dressed his wound and they'd ended by making love. Guilt choked Curt.

Bette eased down into a languid pose in complete opposition to his stiff posture. He didn't like seeing her sit that way—like a woman replete with worldly knowledge. It wasn't like her. He cleared his throat, starting to point this out, and then stopped. What he thought no longer mattered to her.

"So you want to know if I'll give you a divorce." Bette crossed her legs, letting one foot dangle at him.

He nodded, not liking his role in this conversation. He'd betrayed Bette by making love with Maurielle and then he'd betrayed Maurielle by resuming relations with Bette. Somehow he had to make things right with one of them. And Maurielle needed him more. He hated the words he was saying, but he'd made promises to Maurielle, and Maurielle had suffered so through the awful Nazi occupation. He couldn't break his word to Maurielle—so frail, so lovely. Bette was the stronger of the two. "I'm leaving for France on Tuesday. I'd like to file for divorce and get the ball rolling before I leave."

Bette played with the thin satin tie of her robe. "Have you given any thought to our child?" She wouldn't look at him.

His shame blazed full now. "Yes." He cleared his throat. "I will of course pay alimony and child support. And I'd like to live close enough so that I can have the child on weekends."

"And just how will you manage to support two families on a teacher's pay?" Bette's tone taunted him.

Curt had wondered this himself, but what could he say?

"Have you written about my pregnancy to . . . *her*?"

It felt as though someone were setting fire to his stomach. "No," he forced himself to speak the distasteful words, "but she'll do what's right for . . . our child. She has a gentle heart."

Bette made a subtle sound of disbelief. "I had one, once

230

upon a time." She dropped the satin strings. "When you came home from the war," Bette's voice hardened, "why didn't you tell me you were going to leave me? Why did you get me pregnant knowing you would be deserting me?"

He stared at his hands, hating the fact that her accusations were justified. "I know it sounds inadequate, but how could I tell you? 'Pardon me, but I'd like a divorce?' My parents, your parents, everyone was rallying around so happy we were back together. I just couldn't—"

"You could have sent me a Dear Joan letter," Bette said with sarcasm. "Then this child wouldn't have been conceived."

"I know, but I thought I should tell you face to face."

Bette gave a deep, weary sigh.

It dragged through him, tearing through his pretension of honor.

"I regret that you were not more honest with me," she said at last. "And I regret that I didn't realize that after waiting a decade to be together, we'd waited too long. I'm not the sweet little thing you fell in love with at Croftown High."

Was she trying to tell him that she was involved with someone else? He couldn't believe that Bette had been unfaithful to him. That kind of behavior wasn't in her. But then, he'd never imagined falling in love with Maurielle. What might his unfaithfulness have caused Bette to do? "Is there someone else?" he tried to stop the words but it was impossible.

Bette gave him a narrowed look. "I don't think that's any of your business. This child, however, is. And I won't have him or her slighted just because you decided to break the vows we took."

His face burned, but she had the right of it. "I won't. I

promise you. I want this child to be in my life, too. I won't let the child down." *The way I let you down.*

"I still can't think of divorce. I can't." Abruptly Bette stood up to dismiss him.

"What are your plans, then?" he asked, rising politely, but hating her dismissal and hating himself more.

"I've been offered an interesting position. And I may be traveling soon."

He paused, trying to figure out what she was going to do about their child. "Shouldn't you be getting ready to have the baby? Won't you want to be near home?"

Her stiff back to him, Bette marched him out of the room. "I'll just take maternity leave. After the child's born, I'll hire a nanny or leave the baby with my mother until she's a bit older. I don't know." She sounded ruffled, irritated. "I can't do the traditional mothering with you gone."

"Why not? I'll be near. My parents and your parents will help out. You should be home at Ivy—"

"Curt," she snapped, "you don't get to commit adultery, ask for a divorce, *and* tell me how to live my life. You made your choice. I'm making mine. Good day."

CHAPTER SEVENTEEN

Nuremberg, Germany, September 1946

Near the rear of the press section, Bette sat on a hard wooden bench in the grim, dark-paneled, very crowded courtroom. In a dark-red suit with black gloves, she wore a press badge, identifying her as a reporter for a newspaper that had not sent a reporter to Germany, but who would claim her if her credentials were challenged. They hadn't been.

Then Bette saw her.

She blinked her eyes, unable to believe who she'd just recognized—or thought she had—among the bank of numerous translators. Nearly lifting the black net veil on her hat, she quickly sat forward on the edge of her seat, trying to catch another glimpse.

The witness on the stand muttered on. Bette would be heartily glad when she could leave this dismal place. After a few days spent here with eyes and ears open, she would visit occupied Berlin and then try to get into Soviet-occupied

Czechoslovakia and anywhere else she could weasel herself in. This was a fishing trip. Bette was to gather any and all information about what was happening—names and faces and places.

The chessboard was still being set up for the struggle between the free nations and the Communists. Her orders were to travel wherever she could and to notice people and things. She had a few old Resistance contacts to meet in various capitals. Stalin was consolidating his grip over Middle Europe and had his own minions out doing just what she was.

Realizing suddenly that by sitting forward, she was calling attention to herself, she slid back in her seat. Had her eyes deceived her? Bette stretched her neck as if it were stiff—all the while trying to get a better view of the translators. But she wasn't able to. So to fit her role, she jotted down a few meaningless notes on her pad of paper. She couldn't concentrate. Her heart pounded with the possibility that she was right—that her eyes hadn't played tricks on her.

Before this trip, in a quick two weeks in Washington, D.C., Bette had been trained in new spy techniques: bugging rooms, taking photographs without being seen, and learning how to develop her own film. She'd also been primed with a large assortment of faces to memorize—faces of suspected KGB agents from the USSR and Eastern Europe, faces of Nazis who were still on the loose, some *Abwehr* agents that had slipped through the Allied net, and more.

Now in the stuffy, oppressive courtroom, she only half listened to the horrifying testimony from a witness being cross-examined by US Prosecutor Robert Jackson. The man answering questions had witnessed atrocities in Poland, where he'd been a concentration camp prisoner. The main defendants in the Nuremberg War Crimes Tribunal were Hermann Goering, Rudolf Hess, Albert Speer, and other Nazis.

Not just because she was distracted, she had trouble listening to the witness's graphic account of the disposal of corpses. Of course, she'd known of Hitler's "final solution to the Jews," genocide, because even before the war she had moved in espionage circles where the truth was known. She now thought of Breckenridge Long in the State Department who'd worked so hard before and even after Pearl Harbor to block Jewish refugees from reaching America. How many had been gassed because of him? Shouldn't he be here, too, standing trial?

One of the many black-robed judges announced the lunch recess and gaveled the session to an end. Set free, Bette rose and with practiced ease cut through the crowd surging toward the nearest open doors. She knew just where she must stand to be sure to catch the person she'd seen. *If* she'd really seen her. Her pulse raced with the possibility. Maybe this was just a trick of the mind, bringing up a treasured dream.

Bette reached the door and waited, blocking everything from her mind but the face she sought. People streaming past her buffeted her, but she held her place, but craning her neck, trying to glimpse . . . Finally, she saw the back of the woman's head and caught her arm. The woman swung around and . . . after nearly a decade apart, Bette stood face to face with Gretel. Her friend was a lovely blond woman now, but she had a fine white scar over her right eyebrow and she was very thin. Otherwise, this was Gretel.

After a visible double take, Gretel stared at her as if she couldn't believe her eyes. Bette clung to Gretel's arm, suddenly unable to speak. Shock raced up her arms like electrical charges. People pushed Gretel and Bette closer and moved around them, flowing away. Finally, it was just the two of them and two strangers who stood behind Gretel. "Gretel?" one of them asked her a question in German. Gretel waved them away with a brief answer. Reluctantly, they walked away with several backward glances.

"Gretel," Bette was finally able to speak in the deserted hallway, which had gone so quiet.

"How are you here? Why?" Gretel rubbed her forehead. "It's like a dream."

Bette couldn't answer Gretel honestly so she went on, "I saw you out of the corner of my eye. I couldn't believe it was you, really you. Why are you here?"

"I'm a translator, of course." Gretel let go of Bette's hand and pressed her hands to her face. "Seeing you . . . It takes me back. How are your mother and father? Your brothers?"

"Fine. All fine. Did you . . . did you find your parents?" Bette held her breath.

"No. I lost everyone."

The words were cold and bleak. Bette folded Gretel into her arms. "I'm so sorry, so sorry."

Gretel accepted the first few moments of comfort and then pushed away. "Why are you here?" she repeated.

Thinking fast, Bette studied Gretel. "We must find some place private to talk." *Where we won't be overheard.* Bette had been sworn to secrecy again and she would have to let Gretel think she was really a journalist. But somehow she had to heal the rift between them. She might never get another chance. Meeting Gretel like this—it almost felt like a miracle.

Gretel nodded. "Come." She led Bette outside into the cool autumn sunshine and down the street to a park, surrounded by the shells of bombed-out buildings. Shabby street vendors were selling sandwiches and the peeling park benches were filled with people from the court snacking and chatting. Gretel and Bette bought sausages in buns and black coffee and then sat down on the grass with their legs folded under their skirts, far from the benches.

"I can't believe we're here together." Bette held her sandwich and gazed around, making sure no one was taking any interest in the two young women having an impromptu picnic. She was still awestruck. *Gretel's here, right in front of me.*

"Eat your sandwich and tell me why you are here." Gretel unwrapped her egg salad on dark rye. "When did you become a journalist?"

Bette bit into her sandwich, trying to think of what to tell Gretel. What could she tell her? She remembered with aching poignancy the last time she'd seen Gretel—in Philadelphia at the 1940 GOP Convention. Bette had been with Lundeen. She had to make that right—no matter what. "Gretel, first I'm going to tell you something that I've never told anyone else," Bette said recklessly, but in an under tone. "And it must remain secret."

Gretel's eyes narrowed. She nodded. "I will not repeat anything you tell me."

Bette nodded once and then said in a lower voice, "I worked in espionage before and during the war."

Gretel's mouth opened. "You? A spy? How? I can't . . . *You?*"

Bette smiled grimly. "You just pointed out a big part of my success. I don't look or act the part of spy, do I?" She sobered. "That day you saw me in Philadelphia—I was working for the FBI trying to keep tabs on Senator Lundeen and the *Abwehr* agent he was so chummy with. The man didn't have a clue who he was working with and the harm he was doing with all his isolationist propaganda. That's the best I can say of him."

"I thought . . . I thought—"

"That I would work for a skunk like Lundeen?" The old wound rankled. Still, her eyes roamed the park. Were there any faces she should recognize? Was there anyone close enough to overhear them?

Gretel looked pained. "It was . . . it never made sense. I couldn't figure it out."

"Why didn't you write me, call me?" Then the foolishness of this hit Bette. She put her sandwich down on the brown paper it had been wrapped in. Not all of that was Gretel's fault. "I couldn't have told you. I couldn't tell anyone. I've never told anyone." *Not even Curt.*

"I understand that." Gretel worried her lower lip. "I had my own secret reason for not coming to your wedding. Soon after that day, I returned to Europe."

Bette stared at her friend, astounded. Gretel had risked returning to Nazi Europe. It boggled the mind. "To find your parents?" she finally asked.

Gretel put her sandwich in her lap, too. "That was at the back of my mind, of course. But I came to do whatever I could to fight the Nazis. From a southern port, I was smuggled into unoccupied France and then made my way east into Germany and then Czechoslovakia. I worked with the Resistance all through the war."

Bette put her hand over Gretel's. She knew others who'd done this dangerous work. "You were brave."

Gretel looked away. "I survived. Most didn't." Gretel

shook her head as though shaking off memories. "Where did you go after Lundeen?"

"I was sent to Bermuda to work at the mail censorship center at Hamilton there." She picked at her crust. "I read mail and looked for coded messages, secrets being sent to Germany."

"I bet you were good." Gretel grinned.

Bette caught Gretel's eye. "Why do you say that?"

"Because you don't do things by half measure. You always give everything." Before Bette could react to this, Gretel continued, sober now. "Where's Curt? Did he make it through the war?" She began nibbling again, not meeting Bette's eyes.

Bette took the question like a punch to her mid-section. She hadn't thought about Curt since she'd arrived in court this morning. But now, seeing Gretel brought it all back—starting with the burning cross on the very morning when Curt had asked her to the senior dance. Events that were inextricably linked with Gretel. She dropped her sandwich back onto its paper. "Curt wants a divorce."

"I can't believe that." Gretel looked aghast. "Curt—a divorce. Never."

"That's what I thought." Her mouth felt filled with sawdust. Bette leaned back, resting on her palms, trying to look nonchalant.

"But why?" Gretel watched her closely.

Bette looked away into the distance to the few trees that had survived Allied bombing raids, at the ragged people who hurried past on the bleak city street. "He's leaving me for a pretty little French war . . . mistress." Each lightly said word chipped away her peace.

Gretel cursed in German—or that's what it sounded like. "What is he thinking? You are a . . . special, so special."

Bette smiled sadly, soaking in Gretel's sympathy. Then she halted that. She couldn't give into emotion. "Curt and I waited too long." Her tone was brisk. "We should have married after I finished secretarial school. We would have had a few years then before the war separated us." Should have—should have . . . Meaningless.

Gretel shrugged. "Maybe. Maybe not. Who can know these things?"

Bette nodded and picked up her sandwich, though her appetite had died. She sighed. "I feel a million years old sometimes."

Gretel nodded soberly and swallowed. "I also."

No doubt. But Bette knew better than to ask Gretel for specifics about her part in the war. Those who'd lived on the edge didn't want to put the horror into words. Too many close calls, too many friends and comrades killed—hadn't Gretel said so? Bette tore off a piece of her bun and tossed it to cooing pigeons that milled nearby. "We can never get back those years, lost years."

"Well, we are alive," Gretel pointed out pragmatically. "And you will meet someone else and make a new life."

Bette shook her head. "I can't even think of divorce. In any case, I won't marry again. I'm pregnant."

"What?" Gretel's eyes widened, stunned.

"Curt got me pregnant before he told me he wasn't staying around."

Gretel cursed in German again.

Bette took comfort from Gretel's anger on her behalf. She'd wanted to curse Curt, too.

"Why would he do something so low as that? It's unconscionable."

Bette shrugged. "He said, how could he come home with everyone celebrating our being together again and say, 'By the way, I want a divorce'?"

"He could have taken precautions. Is the man an idiot?"

Bette had wondered this also. "I might have wondered about his doing that, too. Why *shouldn't* we try to conceive after all those years apart?"

Gretel made a sound of disgust and tossed pieces of crust to the pigeons, scattering them. "Don't make excuses for him."

"I'm not." Telling Gretel—telling her best friend—had somehow lightened Bette's load. She was able to draw a deep breath. "I'm just telling you what happened, what he said."

"Did Jamie survive the war?" Gretel looked away this time.

Did she still have feelings for Jamie? "Yes, he is a decorated Navy pilot. He's still in the service stationed in Hawaii."

"I'm glad he made it through the war," Gretel murmured.

Bette nodded in agreement, pursing her lips tightly.

"Have you seen Ilsa?" Gretel asked in a suddenly uncertain voice.

Bette paused, remembering all those times Ilsa had wished for Gretel to be near her. "Yes, they had two more children after Sarah, a son and then another daughter. She and Drake seem very happy together, Gretel."

"I'm happy for Ilsa." Gretel looked directly into Bette's eyes. "I was young—too young—to understand all Ilsa had suffered."

"Why don't you call them . . ." Bette asked impulsively, "tonight?"

"No, I couldn't put you to that expense."

Bette decided she'd ignore Gretel in this.

A few little girls with tight golden braids ran through the park, giggling like little children everywhere. Their carefree sound contrasted with a serious subject in this somber, ravaged city of judgment.

Bette had a sudden thought. But she'd have to okay it with Souers before she said anything.

Gretel stood up. "I must get back to court on time and get ready to interpret. We will get together after court today, yes? I want you to meet my friends."

"Good." Bette stood up also. First, she'd go back to her hotel, make an important phone call and then send a telegram—a coded one to Souers. Meeting Gretel might be helpful, very helpful.

After sharing an evening meal with Gretel and some of her fellow translators, Bette invited Gretel back to her hotel room for the surprise she'd planned. She'd put through more than one call to the US today. They entered the neat but sparsely furnished hotel room together. Gretel looked around. "Very nice. Your paper must pay well. I share one room with three other translators." Then she paused, looking to Bette.

Bette glanced at her watch. "I hope you won't mind but I set up a kind of date for tonight."

Gretel looked shocked. "What? You want me to date someone?"

"Not that kind of date." Bette went to the phone and dialed the operator and started the process of placing a long distance call to Drake and Ilsa's number. "I called Drake at work today and we calculated the time difference and he promised he and Ilsa would be at home awaiting your call."

"Bette." Gretel held up a hand. "You shouldn't do this. It will cost the moon and stars."

"Nonsense," Bette replied. "And besides, the call might not go through. You want to talk to them, don't you?"

Gretel gazed at Bette, but Bette could see she wasn't really seeing her. Gretel took a few paces and then halted. "Yes, after all this time. Yes."

The placing of a transatlantic call took a few more minutes of operators talking back and forth. Gretel began pacing again, rubbing her arms as if she were cold. Then Bette heard Drake's voice over the line. "Drake, here's Gretel."

With regret and hope, Gretel took the phone from her friend and forced herself to gather her nerve to face her cousin—the cousin she'd scorned and wounded. "Drake, hello." A shiver shook her.

"Gretel, we thought me might never hear from you again." Drake's voice was thick. "Here, here's Ilsa."

"Gretel?" Ilsa's voice quavered.

"Ilsa," Gretel gasped. Then it hit her. One member of her family still drew breath. "Ilsa, I've missed you so." Then tears clogged her throat. "Can't talk," she gasped, wiping her face wet with tears.

"Neither can Ilsa," Drake said, coming on the line again. "But just stay on the line. I'll have Sarah say hello."

"Hello," a little voice said. "Hi, I'm Sarah."

"Hi," Gretel said. She began shaking all over. "Hello, Sarah, this is Gretel."

"I've got a brother and a sister and we went to the park today," Sarah explained. "Are you sad? You sound like you're crying."

"I'm happy. Sarah, please . . . ask your mother to take the phone again." Gretel waited, longing to hear her cousin's voice again.

"It's me again," Ilsa said. "*Ich liebe dich*, Gretel."

"I love you, too, Ilsa. Always."

The operator came on the line. "We are sorry, but a higher priority call must be allowed. Please say good-bye and disconnect. Thank you."

"Good-bye," Ilsa said, weeping. "Write soon."

"I will. Love you." And Gretel hung up. She embraced Bette, glad to have someone to share this moment with, someone who loved her.

"I knew they'd be thrilled to hear from you," Bette said at last. "Drake called my parents today and they'll be writing you, too."

"I've been without family for so long." Gretel hugged herself and continued weeping. "I regret cutting off communication with Ilsa, with you. But the war . . .

"Why don't you fly home with me after the trials are over?" Bette invited.

Gretel tried to grin, wiping her tears with a handkerchief. "You Americans, you think money grows on trees."

Bette shrugged. "If you don't think Drake would gladly pay your fare—"

Gretel held up both hands. "Stop. I can't."

"Why not? Wouldn't you like to visit them?"

"I don't think I will ever go back to America." Gretel was

able to take a deep breath once more. "My life is moving in a different direction."

"What direction?" Bette asked.

"Palestine."

Bette couldn't speak for a few seconds. This was one answer she had never expected. "Palestine?"

"Yes, I want to walk where the prophets walked. I want to see the land of milk and honey."

"Can you get a visa?"

Gretel shrugged. "I didn't get a visa when I came back to Europe. I don't intend to ask anyone's permission for this trip either," she added with an imperious lift of her chin. "I'm a Jew and I'm going to live or die in Palestine. I didn't come back to Germany to stay. Frankly, I can't stomach the people." Gretel's lip curled in disdain. "I remember how they screamed for *Der Fuehrer*."

Gretel's loathing came through clearly and it struck a chord in Bette. How could Hitler—one man—destroy so many lives? "But what kind of future can you have in Palestine? The Arabs won't welcome you with open arms. You might even be deported."

Gretel shrugged again. "Nazis didn't stop me. Arabs won't either."

The next evening after a call from Souers in which he gave her his coded reply to her telegram, Bette waited in the same spot for Gretel to come out among the other interpreters. Gretel appeared and came directly to her. "Come with us," she invited again. "We're going to a small café for supper."

Bette nodded and walked beside her friend. Listening to the strangers all chatting in a mixture of English and German, Bette tried to keep calm. Inwardly, though, she hopped from one foot to the other like a child awaiting a treat. Souers's reply to her coded cable had come swiftly and she knew what she needed to do. Would Gretel agree?

After supper, Bette invited Gretel back to her hotel again. Gretel had obviously recognized the urgency in Bette's eyes and agreed. In the room, Bette did something different than she had last night, but very necessary tonight. She went over the room with her eyes and then in places with her hands, feeling under lampshades and behind the lone picture frame. Perhaps she was being too careful. But in her work, could one be too cautious? She turned to Gretel. "We need to talk."

"What were you doing just now?" Gretel asked, staring at her, her brows drawn together.

"Before I broach a certain topic, I needed to know that no one had planted any listening devices."

Understanding smoothed Gretel's forehead. She grinned. "I thought you said that you were a spy 'before and during' the war." Gretel lifted a quizzical eyebrow.

Bette grinned and then became serious. "I thought I retired, but then Curt asked for a divorce. The OSS was dissolved after the war. Now I've been recruited by the new Central Intelligence Agency." She sank down on the end of the bed and folded one leg under her self-consciously. Gretel was the first person from her "real" life she'd ever told about her secret life. "I was sent to Europe to observe and make contacts." Barely taking a breath, she went on, "You hated Hitler. Do you hate Stalin?"

Gretel's reply came instantly. "Yes."

"Because of your Resistance days, you have contacts in Europe, which may be useful to me and to the CIA. Souers checked with some reputable Resistance contacts and you were known to them. And of course, I vouched for you. Now, Gretel, would you be willing to give me names, places, and passwords that will introduce me to your friends in the former Resistance? I believe the people who fought Hitler may also fight Stalin. And my boss agrees."

Gretel walked to the window and peered out into the twilight. "I will—for a price."

This surprised and interested Bette. What would Gretel want? "What is your price?"

"Safe passage to Palestine after this trial is over."

Bette considered it. Smuggling Gretel into Palestine and providing her with forged documents would be child's play for Souers. "I don't think that would be a problem."

"Then we have a deal." Gretel walked to her and offered her hand.

Exhilarated, Bette shook it firmly and then leaped up to embrace Gretel. It felt so good to have someone she loved know the truth, one who understood what she did. Both of them had forged lives that neither could have predicted. "It's hard to believe that we were those two young girls who used to sleep in the small bedroom upstairs at Ivy Manor, isn't it?"

Gretel squeezed her close. "We were always different, yes, but together in spirit. Let us begin."

Bette stepped back, surprised. "Tonight?"

"Yes." Gretel's hands became fists. "What if I am hit by a car on the way home tonight? One thing I learned in the Resistance: never leave anything until tomorrow because tomorrow may never come."

Nodding soberly, Bette went to the small, scarred desk and sat down. "You'll have to speak slowly because as you give it, I'm going to take down your information in a shorthand that only I know."

Gretel followed Bette and pulled up the chair and sat. "I will give you names, places, and passwords—everything. And I will send word for my friends to expect you."

Bette's hand cramped. Gretel had kept her busy scribbling for almost an hour and a half. Bette tapped the sheaf of ten pages of coded notes on the desktop. Gretel rose. "I must get home and sleep. If I stay out any longer, my roommates will be suspicious."

Tired but still elated at her progress, Bette followed her to the door. Gretel's information would give her a place to start, access to a great many eyes and ears that the CIA would put to work. "I'll see you tomorrow at the lunch recess."

A brisk knock came at the door. Both Gretel and Bette froze. Bette shook off the feeling that something awful was waiting for her on the other side of the door. Still, she went to her bag and pulled out a small, cold pistol, which she slipped into her pocket. *I am a journalist here, reporting on the Nuremberg trials and I have papers to prove it. And Gretel has a new German passport and is an interpreter.* Bette opened the door.

Ted Gaston sauntered in and took her into his arms.

She was so shocked that he kissed her before she could push against his arms, stopping him. "Ted!"

"*Guten Abend, mein Herr,*" Gretel said, watching everything with an interested eye.

Unabashed, Ted looked up and smiled. "Same to you, *Fräulein.*"

Bette pulled free of Ted's arms. "Gretel, this is my friend Ted."

Grinning, Gretel offered her hand to Ted. He shook it and smiled. "*Fräulein,* you were just going, I take it?"

"Ted," Bette objected, flushing with embarrassment.

Gretel chuckled. "I will see you tomorrow, Bette." With a broad smile, she picked up her purse and walked out and closed the door behind her.

Bette scanned Ted. He was tan and lean and grinning—nothing like the dour or wasted men she'd watched in court today.

Ted gathered Bette into his arms once more. She couldn't take it all in—his appearing out of the blue. A rush of pleasure made it impossible for her to form words. She knew she should tell him no. And yet, being in his arms felt so . . . wonderful. "Why are you here?" Her mind scrambled for a logical reason for his being here. "Is the FBI operating in Germany now?"

Ted grinned. "Of course not. I had some vacation time and decided to tour Europe."

An unwelcome thought: he must know about Curt leaving her. Did he think she'd have an affair with him now that they were a continent away from prying eyes? Bette shook her head at him, leaning back from him. "That makes perfect sense. Europe's so scenic now after a world war."

Ted chuckled. Before she knew what he was doing, he was kissing her again. Her mind went back—all those years ago—to that evening in New York City when he'd first kissed her. The passing of time had no effect. Ted's kisses and touch were just as enticing now as they had been then. Her pulse raced and she thrilled as he lowered his lips to her neck.

But she had to remember that though Curt had betrayed her, she was still married. And pregnant. She stiffened her resolve. "Why have you come?" she asked in a cool voice turning away her face.

"I would think that was patently obvious."

Stung, she shoved against his shoulders. "I still don't do affairs." Hovering near, he looked into her eyes. She stilled.

"I don't remember asking you to have an affair with me today." His voice was casual.

"I don't—"

"What is wrong with the few kisses between very good friends?"

His kisses meant more than friendship; she knew that much. It was hard to be strong. He felt so good, holding her. And she had been alone for so long. For a few moments, she'd allowed herself to relish the texture of his lips, the scent of his lime aftershave, his desire for her. Curt had rejected her, but this man wanted her. But now she blurted out the first thought that came to mind. "Curt wants a divorce."

He murmured into her ear, "I know all about Curt."

She waited for him to toss back into her face all his prewar warnings about Curt. But instead, he went on holding her. Ted's touch was a seductive balm to her aching heart, wounded pride. She wanted to close her eyes and let him begin kissing her again, just let it happen. But she made herself push him away. "Tell me why you've really come."

*　　*　　*

At the end of the next day of the trial, Ted in another well-cut suit waited outside the courtroom for her. Knowing that Ted would seek her out, Bette had dressed with special care in a stylish royal-blue outfit with the new longer postwar skirt. And she couldn't stop the thrill that went through her when she caught sight of him. Was it just because she was so bruised from Curt's betrayal? Was she that shallow?

"I see your boyfriend is here again," Gretel whispered slyly into Bette's ear. "Maybe he will take you out somewhere for dinner?"

Bette hadn't been successful in convincing Gretel that Ted was not her boyfriend, that she didn't want one. And then Ted sauntered over and leaned down to kiss her hello. She turned her face, but his lips still grazed her cheek. Then he glanced up at Gretel. "Will you join us for dinner?"

Before Bette could add her approval to this, Gretel was already moving away.

"No, I don't want to be a fifth wheel. I'll see you tomorrow, Bette." Gretel waved and hurried to catch up with the other interpreters heading for the exit.

Ted tucked Bette's hand into his arm. "Are the trials interesting?"

Being close to this handsome man unleashed all the lush, very dangerous sensations he'd reawakened the night before. She could resist him, but why couldn't she prevent her response to him? "*Grueling* is the word." Bette took refuge in talking about life on the surface. "It's very hard to listen to these people try to justify their actions."

"Then let's talk about something more pleasant." He led her down the marble steps through the milling crowd. Voices rumbled, echoing around them under the lofty cathedral ceiling.

"What's that?" She thought she knew what he'd say, but prayed she was wrong. She couldn't bear it if he proposed an affair. Though as a rejected wife, she should probably get used to men viewing her as an easy target. Before she'd left, a few in Croftown had already begun giving her lewd glances and suggestive whistles. Again, she wondered why Curt's betrayal had somehow smeared her reputation, too.

"I think we ought to go to Berlin together," he said as they shuffled down the stone steps outside the gloomy building. "You're not enjoying these trials and you've probably seen as much as you need to of the people involved and the observers. Why don't we get train tickets and leave tomorrow?"

His words were totally unexpected. "Why?" At street level, cars honked and people vied for shabby taxis.

"Because I'd like to help you with your fact-finding mission." He navigated them through the crush and down the street.

"Why do you want to help me?" Even as she hurried to keep abreast of him, she searched his clear-blue eyes for his reason.

"Because I stayed home fighting the bad guys all through the war. Now I'd like a little foreign intrigue."

"And that's your idea of a vacation?" she asked in a voice laced liberally with disbelief.

"Well, yes, as long as you're at my side." He firmly tucked her blue-gloved hand into the crook of his elbow.

A ragged little blond girl slipped up to them, her grimy open hand held out. *"Bitte, mein Herr."*

Ted pressed a coin into her hand and moved Bette on. As the child called, *"Danke! Danke,"* he went on as if they hadn't been interrupted. "I'd like to continue the discussions that we started in your room."

She lifted one eyebrow. "What discussions?"

Ted tucked her closer. "Oh, I think our lips were doing a lot of conversing last night, don't you?"

Bette felt her face warm and she wouldn't look him in the eye. She should have been stronger last night and stopped him after the first kiss.

They entered the same park where she and Gretel had lunched that first day they'd been reunited; pigeons fluttered out of their way. She had to let him know everything. She couldn't let him go on thinking that they shared anything but a common profession and friendship. "Ted, I'm pregnant."

He stopped to look at her again. He looked disgusted and his expression wounded her. What had she expected? Ted wouldn't want Curt's child. She'd already told herself that. Holding in the pain of his rejection, she pulled free from him. *This isn't Ted's fault.*

He halted her with a hand on her sleeve. Guiding her back under his arm, he kissed her cheek, then he rested his cheek against her forehead. "Don't be ridiculous." He lightly laid his palm on her abdomen and said, "Hey, kid, I'm Ted." Ted moved as if he were going to kiss her.

Shocked, Bette stepped back, ashamed and aware of people looking at them. "Ted, remember where we are, who we are."

"Okay." Grinning, he took her hand into his arm again and began to lead her away. "I asked at the hotel and have found a good little café—"

"Ted," she interrupted in an under voice, "do you understand why I told you about the baby? I'm not . . . available. Curt wants a divorce, but I can't face that. And I'm pregnant." She fell silent, unwilling, unable to put into words her feeling of being mired in hopelessness.

"I get that. I just think that your life isn't over. Curt's a fool, but I'm not. Do you really think I came here to take advantage of you?" This time his voice held an edge.

Bette wished she'd kept her mouth closed. "No. I don't. But I'm sorry about how I behaved last night." Speaking of these private topics in public made her cringe inside. "I let things get out of hand at first. I was weak. But I'm still a married woman. Even if my husband has dishonored me—our vows—that doesn't mean that I am dishonorable."

Ted tightened his grip on her. "You are the most honorable woman I know." He sounded angry, truly angry. "And I've made it my job to know."

Her eyes flew to his. "What do you mean? Did you keep tabs on me?"

"Yes." He began marching her at a brisker rate.

"Why?"

"Do I have to tell you?"

She tugged at his sleeve. "Ted, I can't let you think . . . It isn't fair to involve you in my troubles."

He paused. "Just let it go, Bette. I'm not here to seduce you. Let's just concentrate on the work you came to do. And let the future take care of itself—for now."

Bette didn't know what to say to this. Ted couldn't be in love with her; he never took anything seriously—not even war. But she'd been honest with him. One thing she'd already decided: she wasn't going to make things worse by becoming involved with any man, not now and not for the foreseeable future. And if Ted didn't believe that he was as blind as Curt.

After court the next day, Gretel and Bette stood facing each other at the train station. "I don't want to leave you," Bette said.

"I hate to see you go." Gretel glanced at Ted, who was getting a porter to take care of their luggage. "He's very handsome," Gretel murmured into Bette's ear.

Bette gave her friend a sharp shake of her head. "You won't break our connection again? You know you can always reach me through the Ivy Manor address."

Gretel wrapped her arms around Bette. "Don't worry. I only have you and Ilsa for family in this world. I won't run away again."

Gretel calling her family meant everything to Bette. Ted came up behind her. "Time to board."

Gretel released her. "Go on." And then she gave Ted a look. "Take good care of her."

Ted saluted Gretel and swept Bette up the steps onto the train. The charging of the engines roared and all voices were overwhelmed. Bette waved and then let Ted lead her to their seats. A feeling of loss, of being left behind, surged through her, but she made herself smile as she waved through the window to Gretel until she'd left her friend far behind.

As if sensing her mood, Ted took her hand and held it. She let him because leaving Gretel had been almost too hard to bear. But she had Gretel's promise, and if she knew Souers, he would have someone keeping tabs on Gretel when she headed for Palestine.

God go with you, Gretel, my dear friend, my sister.

Chapter Eighteen

France, October 1946

*C*urt stood at the graveside. All around him, mourners wept. But he only felt cold and distant, remembering how he'd met Maurielle. His squad had entered the village and had immediately been pinned down by Nazi snipers on the village church's high roof. His men had scattered. He'd tried to edge closer to take out the sniper and instead his right shoulder had been grazed. Seeking shelter, he burst into an empty barn—more like a lean-to. The snipers maintained their post, picking off anyone who tried to come out and take them. Curt hoped someone still had the shortwave set and was calling for backup. Minutes had passed and then he'd realized he wasn't alone.

A very young, very thin, brunette had emerged from a loft and murmured to him in French and broken English. He'd never forget that moment. She was so beautiful, so ethereal. For a second he thought he was imagining her. Surely this lovely vision didn't fit the rough setting. Then she brought out a bucket of water and broke off pieces from a salt lick and bathed his bleeding shoulder with the stinging salt water.

Her touch had sparked his desire.

All the lonely years spent in the company of men over-whelmed him. Other men in his squad had picked up willing women when short leaves came. He had not. But now he gave into temptation and kissed her. When he began to apologize, she kissed him in return, a long passionate kiss filled with a desperate longing that matched his own. And before he knew what he was doing, he was holding her and then making love to her in the fresh straw in a stall.

Afterward, he was appalled with himself. How could he have let himself be unfaithful to Bette? But recalling his wife hadn't helped. The attraction to Maurielle had only grown stronger as the long night of the snipers passed. She told him of Nazis and what they had done to her and her family. Just after dawn the next day, backup had rolled in with tanks and taken out the snipers. Curt and his squad had been ordered to secure the village and hold it and its bridge until the next wave of troops caught up with them.

That evening he'd shared his rations with Maurielle and her father and had ended up spending the night with her. Her father had turned a blind eye. That had shocked him, too. But he hadn't been able to resist being with her again. It was as if all his suppressed passion had burst its bounds and he couldn't put the genie back in the bottle.

Two days later, he'd left the village, but he'd given Mau-rielle his home address and promised he'd come back for her. When the other guys made vulgar remarks about his good luck, he defended Maurielle. But they just hooted at him—

saying that being conquering heroes had its benefits and why shouldn't he enjoy them. They had insulted Maurielle by saying she'd been on the prowl to snag an American. That had hardened his resolve to keep his promise. He wasn't the kind of man who compromised a young woman and then deserted her. That would have put him on the par with the Nazis who'd occupied her village. And Maurielle had needed him so. She'd begged him not to forget her. She'd suffered so under Nazi occupation—horrors he didn't want to think about.

And in the end, he'd come to the resolve that she needed him more than Bette did.

Now, Maurielle's father touched his arm, yanking him back to the present. "Come."

Curt let himself be persuaded. He walked down the narrow lane back into the little village. Everyone knew about him—Maurielle's American—and everyone along the way offered him sympathetic glances and words. It was as real as a nightmare and just as incredible. In the end, he hadn't been able to save Maurielle. His life had become a cruel joke. *What do I do now?*

A small, lazy Italian wharf, October 1946

Gretel held her passport and ticket in hand as she waited to board the seedy-looking ship that would take her to Cyprus and then to Palestine. Her name was no longer Gretel Sachs. She'd practiced leaving her German accent behind but she tried to speak as little as possible.

She'd tired of the trials and when her new passport and money had been delivered to her by a nameless agent, she'd quit before the next round of cases had started. Every mile she'd put between her and Germany had been liberating.

On the gangway, her turn came. With a nonchalance that was completely fabricated, she presented her passport and her ticket for approval. The ship's officer glanced at them, at her, and waved her aboard.

She felt a silent sigh of relief echo through her. *Thank you, CIA.* Free. She was finally free of the past and heading toward the land of her fathers. And mothers. A land of milk and honey where no one would ever tell her she wasn't welcome. She was through wandering and if the authorities in Palestine didn't like that—too bad.

Maryland, February 1947

It was over. Exhausted and in pain, Bette Leigh lay in her bed in a private room at the hospital near Ivy Manor. Old Dr. Benning stood at her bedside. "Well, for a first baby, that went very well." He patted her shoulder and then walked from the room. Bette couldn't reply aloud. *My first baby . . . and my last. I always wanted at least four children.* Silently, she mourned for all the children she would never have. The fairy tale she'd longed to live—a home with children and a husband who loved her—had disintegrated. All because Curt had broken faith with her.

Nearby, her mother and Jerusha were "helping" the nurse bathe the baby in a basin of warm water. Bette watched them and tried not to think about Curt. He hadn't written or called in the months since she had returned from Europe. Ted's face came to mind. Their work in Europe had been exciting and risky—as had been his continued but more subtle pursuit of her. She'd easily refused his light-hearted advances, of course. But underneath all his teasing, she'd recognized that he hadn't given up. And deep down she knew she didn't want him to give up. Was it fair for her to be condemned to a lonely life because of Curt's unfaithfulness?

The thought of divorce still struck terror into her heart. And she couldn't help wondering if she'd broken her engagement with Curt and married Ted instead things would have turned out just the same. Would Ted have been any more faithful to her than Curt? Was it her—was she the kind of woman men left behind?

After Europe, she'd told her boss at the CIA about the baby. He had been surprised but pleased when, instead of resigning, she'd asked for a maternity leave. He'd agreed without any objection. Obviously he had expected her to quit. So she'd continued her work at the CIA offices until Christmas and then she'd come home to have her baby. She would return in a month or two, unless Souers changed his mind about her. Ted had said she was too valuable for Souers to let go. She hoped that would continue to be true. She had savings, but they wouldn't last indefinitely. She couldn't depend financially on Curt, didn't want to live off her family. When she returned to Washington, D.C., she'd have to find an apartment and a nanny before she could resume her work.

Jerusha propped Bette up with pillows as her mother carried her little daughter, wrapped in a soft yellow baby blanket, to her. "Here she is, dear, your own little daughter, Linda Leigh."

Bette accepted the warm bundle and looked down at her child. Linda Leigh was very much Curt's daughter. All newborns had blue eyes but Bette doubted Linda's eyes would turn brown or gray like hers. And her daughter's sparse hair was a baby-fine blond.

Again she thought of Ted. After their heated conversation in Nuremberg, Ted had never proposed an affair or anything else. But in D.C. he'd bought her little presents for the baby and teased her about becoming a mother. What did Ted want? Did he think she'd finally divorce Curt and then—as a divorcee—start up an affair with him? She couldn't believe he knew her so little. But he'd never spoken of marriage.

Forget all that. You're on your own. Whatever she wanted or Ted wanted was not as important as this little girl in her arms. *Dearest Linda, I won't let you pay for your father's sins. You'll come first. You won't have the family life I had hoped my children would have, but I'll make sure you're well cared for.*

"Mother, would you please call Curt's parents?" Bette's words caught in her throat. "I'm sure . . . they want to know that their granddaughter is born—healthy and very pretty."

Curt opened the cablegram and read: "You have a daughter. Come home and make things right. Mom and Dad." Curt sat down and reread the telegram over and over. He'd promised Bette that he would not ignore their child, not make this child pay for his sins. But facing Bette would be the hardest thing he ever did.

Ivy Manor, March 1947

Bette walked slowly down the stairs at Ivy Manor and picked up the receiver waiting on the hall table. "Hello?"

"Bette, according to Souers, you're a mother," Ted said. "Why didn't you call me?"

His voice affected her, loosening the tight grip she'd maintained on her rampant sadness, but she tried to keep that from her voice. "I haven't been feeling very peppy. How are you, Ted?"

"I miss you. Can I come and see you and the baby?"

The truth of how much she wanted to see Ted arced through her like an electrical current. She closed her eyes and clung to the receiver. But she couldn't lead him on. "I'll be back in Washington in a month or so—"

"Bette, I don't want to wait that long. I miss you."

She tightened her lips, afraid words might break loose on their own. "I'm not myself, Ted," she managed.

"You would be if I were kissing you."

She'd dreamed of kissing Ted—vivid dreams. His golden hair shining in sunlight, his lips full on hers. "Ted," she said, her voice cracking, "I'm nearly thirty years old, married to a man who's asked for a divorce, and I have a baby—"

"What has that got to do with the fact that I want to kiss you?"

I can't give in. "Ted, be serious."

"Bette, I am very serious."

She rubbed her taut forehead, her self control lagging. "Ted, what am I going to do with you?"

"That is the question. Now we need to come up with the right answer."

Suddenly she felt too weary to hold the receiver. She sighed. "Ted, you're not making this easy on me. I don't intend on divorcing Curt. I can't even bear to think about it."

"Bette, don't tell me you're going to be one of those clinging women who hold onto a man when he's moved on to another woman. You have more self-respect than that." His voice was even and slightly mocking.

"Ted, it isn't that easy. Maurielle died. Curt's in Maryland again. He wants to get back together."

There was a very long silence at the other end of the line. Bette began to bite her nails, a nasty new habit she'd just developed the past week. Tears lodged in her throat.

"I can't," Ted finally spoke, "believe that you'd do anything that stupid." His voice rasped low. "The man has been a jerk since the beginning and you're planning to reconcile with him?"

"He's the father of my child," she muttered.

Another silence stretched out. The baby began crying overhead. "Ted, I need to hang up."

"Bette, let me make this very clear. I am not the kind of man who clings to a woman who will never be his. Do you know how long I've loved you? Do you have any idea how many times I told myself to murder any idea that we might eventually get together?"

"Ted, I—"

"And after Curt commits adultery, makes a fool of you . . ." He fell silent—a very thick silence. "If you go back to him, that's it. I'm out of your life for good. There are other women in this world, you know. I won't have trouble finding someone else."

His words sent fine shards of ice right through her heart. She gasped silently at the pain. Losing Ted would be like losing the sunlight, like losing her right hand. She clutched the phone tighter, remembering that day in Bermuda under the purple bougainvillea when Ted had proposed to her. *I was a fool to stay with Curt.*

But maybe not. How could she trust any man after Curt's betrayal? Ted might not prove any truer than Curt. And little Linda was more important than her own happiness, more important than Ted to her. And Curt was Linda's father. Bette had always loved her stepfather, but he hadn't been her real father—the father who'd died before she was born. How could she keep Linda from having her own father in her home?

"I'm sorry, Ted. Forgive me," Bette murmured and hung up.

Curt had refused his parents when they'd wanted to accompany him to see his daughter for the first time. He knocked on the door and Bette opened it. He stepped inside as she shut the door against the cold. He didn't know what to say to her.

She folded her arms. "The baby is in the parlor." She turned and marched away. He followed obediently, his hat in hand.

There was an antique bassinet near the fire. He walked over and looked down at his daughter. "You named her Linda Leigh?"

Bette sat down. "Yes."

No discussion, no explanation. The child was his, but he had no rights. He didn't blame Bette. How could either one of them behave as they should? And this was all his fault.

"I hear that Maurielle passed away," she challenged him.

Curt sank into a chair opposite her. The dead feeling that had begun with Maurielle's death weighed him down—mercilessly. Even seeing his baby girl didn't lift his spirit. "Yes."

"And you think that will change matters between us?" Her chin jutted out, daring him.

He dragged in air. "Don't you think that there's a chance that we could get back together?"

Bette stared at the fire on the hearth. "Why would you want to get back together? You said you didn't love me anymore. Is it just because of the child?"

Bette's bitter tone lashed him. "I must admit that Linda Leigh is my main reason to ask for a reconciliation. Don't you think we should try?"

"I don't relish playing second best." She turned her face from him, her hurt tone flaying his tender conscience.

He'd unforgivably wounded this woman who'd loved him. "You were never second best," he said and he meant it.

She looked at him, her eyes flashing. "If you had not gone back to France, I would have tried to put your infidelity behind me. But you went to France." Looking down, she adjusted the hem of her skirt. "I know you're right. We owe it to Linda to see if we can get back together. But how can I trust you not to play me false again? How can I?"

"If I were you, I'd feel the same way."

"But that doesn't tell me how to forget, how to put this behind me." She sounded suddenly exhausted.

He fell silent, rotating his hat brim with his fingers. He had no answers. "May I hold my daughter?"

Bette stood up and gathered the sleeping baby in her arms. She brought Linda to him and waited.

He formed his arms into a cradle and Bette laid his

daughter there. He gazed down at the white skin, the blue eyes, the fine blond hair. "She's so tiny."

"I'll leave you two alone." And she walked out the door.

Curt stroked the baby's cheek. "I failed your mother, failed you, failed everyone." A cold tear slid down his face. "I've got to find a way to change that. There must be a way."

In the early hours of an April Monday morning, Curt stood in the front hall of the McCaslin house, holding two-month-old Linda Leigh and watching Bette don a stylish hat and gloves. Bette had finally agreed to a trial reconciliation for the sake of their daughter. During the preceding week, they'd moved into the McCaslin house that had stood empty when Jamie didn't return. The week had been tense. He'd weighed every word before he uttered it, and he was exhausted. And now he couldn't stop himself from saying in an irritable tone, "I wish you didn't have to leave us. We just moved back together."

In front of the wall mirror, Bette straightened her hat. "We knew getting back together wouldn't be easy." Her voice was overly calm, as though she were talking to a cranky child. "You know I'd rather stay here with the baby, but we agreed that until you get a job, I need to continue at my job three days a week. We don't want to live off my parents or yours."

Everything she said was true, but each word shredded, stung his pride as a man. He was living in his wife's family home and she was supporting them. *This is all wrong.* "I know," he agreed, hating every syllable he spoke. "It's just . . . I should be going off to work."

"I will be back Wednesday evening on the 7:00 p.m.

train," she replied, dismissing his feelings. "It's only three days a week. I'm grateful my employer agreed to this part-time position. I'll quit just as soon as we're able to make it without my working." She did not look or sound happy about that prospect.

Tell the truth. You can't wait to get away from me. Then he felt guilty for these feelings. Bette had been so generous to him. *No matter how I feel, I have to hold up my end of the bargain.*

"Curt, we need to get going." Bette called for the house-keeper, who bustled in and took the baby after Bette had kissed and cooed over her once more.

Grudgingly, he put on his hat and overcoat and went out to get his father's car. He picked Bette up at the front door. He didn't want to say anything to upset things before she left for three days. He clamped his jaw shut so tightly it began to ache and in an awkward silence drove her to the train stop; he noticed a headache coming on. When he parked, Curt felt the eyes of everyone there turn to observe Bette getting out of the car with her briefcase.

At the small station, he was the only man driving his wife to leave for work. The condemnation and sneers he detected around him said he was a lesser man, living off his wife and her family. Each one pierced him like hot needles. He didn't try to kiss Bette good-bye and she didn't act like she'd welcome it anyway. He'd been unable to bring himself to show her any affection or passion. Guilt overpowered him . . . because of his adultery.

Bette took her place beside the railroad tracks among the suited men and Curt drove away as quickly as he could. The migraine took possession of the right side of his forehead in a tourniquet of blinding light and pain. Bette's forbearance and her agreeing to reconcile were further debts that were nearly impossible for him to swallow. *I brought this on myself. I have no one else to blame.* What he wouldn't have given to see Bette look at him the way she used to. But the chances of that were slim, less than slim.

Chapter Nineteen

A month later just as the eleven o'clock radio news was about to start in the Lovelady townhouse where she stayed nights during the work week, Bette stood phone in hand, unable to speak. She couldn't believe the words she'd just heard. Suddenly hollow, she clung to the receiver and stared down at her black pumps.

"Bette, did you hear me?" her mother asked.

"Curt tried to commit suicide?" Bette repeated the impossible words.

"Yes, he left Linda with your housekeeper and went to his family's garage, supposedly looking for some tool. His mother left him there while she went into town, but she forgot something and came back. She found him."

Mrs. Sinclair had always been so sweet. How awful for her. The earth seemed to shift under Bette's feet. She leaned back against the staircase for support. "How?"

"He shot himself in the chest with his service revolver." Bette tried to blot out the picture this brought to mind. "But it didn't kill him outright," her mother continued. "He might die at any moment. He's asking for you. You must come."

Bette wanted to argue with her mother, wanted to say anything to keep from going home. "Isn't there any hope that he'll pull through," she began. She couldn't put it all together. She and Curt had been having a rough time. She'd expected that. She hadn't expected this.

"No. He's asking for you. You must hurry."

Bette knew this was only right, but she wished she could do anything to make this not real. "How is Linda?"

"She's fine. Curt's parents are just holding her and holding her. All this has hit them . . . very hard."

Bette's heart clenched, thinking of what they were suffering. Curt was their only son. "Tell them I'm coming. I'll borrow a friend's car."

"I will. I love you, Bette. I know you will do what is right."

Bette did not like the last sentence. She wanted to run out of this house—run far away and never come back.

It was nearly midnight when Bette walked into the hospital. The familiar hospital, where years before her brother Rory had had his right arm set and where Linda Leigh had recently been born, was dim and quiet in the night with that peculiar hospital odor hanging over all. Bette stopped at the nurse's station and in murmurs was directed to Curt's room. When she stepped inside, she found the small, silent room filled with people—her parents, Curt's parents and sister, and Dr. Benning. Linda Leigh—innocently untouched by what was happening around her—slept in her Grandmother Sinclair's arms. She glimpsed Curt between the people grouped around his bed.

Her mother rose and came to Bette and put her arms around her. "You're in time."

Bette couldn't reply, couldn't draw breath.

Dr. Benning gave her a doleful look. "We took X-rays. A bullet's lodged in his heart. We tapped his chest fluid. He's filling up with blood." He shook his gray head. "I can't fix it. He's slowly bleeding to death internally." Each word battered her, one after the other, like powerful fists. Lights danced before her eyes and her knees weakened. She reached out. Dr. Benning gripped her arms. "I don't know how long he has."

With a glance to his parents, Curt said with obvious effort, "Please, may Bette and I be alone?"

His parents looked as if they wanted to lie down on the gray-speckled linoleum and die. They didn't want to leave; that was obvious from their expressions. But they moved toward the door. Each of them patted her shoulder as they passed her—a silent appeal for mercy. Her parents and Dr. Benning followed them out and Bette moved to Curt's side. It felt as if the air in the room had thickened, become difficult to move through. She reached for the back of the bedside chair to steady herself. She could only remember feeling this shaken on the night she'd gone with Drake to rescue Ilsa.

This shouldn't be happening. The man before her had been her first love, her husband, the father of her child. And he'd put a bullet into his heart.

She forced herself to sit in the bedside chair and to look into his face. He was pale, almost waxen. His lips were blue and sweat dotted his brow. How long did they have? An hour? Minutes? Only Curt mattered now. She took his trembling hand in hers. She shivered at his touch—so cold, so weak.

"Why did you do this, Curt?" She didn't like that her words chided him, but she had to know. "I thought we were making—"

"The principal of the school in south Baltimore called me," he interrupted her as if he couldn't waste time. "His board had rejected me for the job. He said I should have mentioned our—I mean *my*—marital difficulties when we met. The board had heard some unsavory facts."

"Unsavory facts?" Bette couldn't stop herself from asking, even though she knew what she'd hear.

"Somehow they'd heard about Maurielle."

The news stunned her. How did gossip fly that far?

"I realized then that it was hopeless." His voice became thin, but words came fast. "The truth would always follow me. And I didn't blame them." Curt's voice rose. "Any man capable of that type of behavior would be a poor example to students."

"Stop, Curt." She squeezed his arm. "Stop."

"I had no right to teach," he went on anyway, "and I couldn't face— It would be like this every time I interviewed. I'd never be able to support my wife and child. I saw myself— a man reduced to living off my wife, who despised me for my weakness."

Then there was silence between them as Bette absorbed this. How could he do this to them? Hadn't she suffered enough from his bad choices already? *This isn't fair.* But he lay before her utterly defenseless, visibly fighting a fierce agony. Inside her, anger and pity vied equally. But time was passing—passing too quickly for her to vent all her feelings at this moment. Later, she would walk from this room. The man in the bed wouldn't.

"I wish you hadn't done this, Curt. It might not have worked out between us." *I should have told him I forgave him, should have tried harder.* Huge hands of regret dragged at her heart. She had trouble taking a breath. "But there was still your daughter. Somehow we would have managed together for her sake."

"I know." He gazed at her hungrily, his face haggard and aging with each moment. "This isn't your fault. As soon as I pulled the trigger, I knew I had done wrong—*again*. I just keep hurting you. But the guilt and loss . . . I tried to deny it, but they were crushing the life from me. I started to think that our daughter would be better off without me."

He gasped for breath between phrases. Sweat trickled down the side of his face. "When you were at work . . . I'd sit and think about all the guys . . . the good ones who'd died in France. I'd managed to get out . . . alive only to make a mess of everything. I should have died . . . and one of them should have lived. I didn't deserve to live." He shivered sharply and then gasped with the exertion.

She pressed his hand. *Dear God, help him, us.* "Lie still."

"You did the best you could under the circumstances," he continued in a hollow voice. "I'm the one who broke our vows, our trust, destroyed my reputation. I shouldn't . . . have even asked you to try again. If our roles had been reversed . . . I would have felt just as you did."

She wanted to tell him to save his strength. Instead, she clung to his hands. Why was everything between them so clear now? She stroked his cool cheek. She'd thought he killed all her love for him. But all her warm feelings for this man that had lain dormant over the past year came welling up. It took her back to their beginning. She rubbed her cheek against his hand. "I remember the first time we spoke—that day in the chemistry lab. How embarrassed I was to have you overhear those girls. How I hurt for Gretel."

"I know. You were wonderful." He implored her with his eyes. "So pretty and such a faithful friend to Gretel, so brave. I couldn't . . . understand how anyone could say bad things about you."

It was painful to watch him force out the words. Each one appeared to cost him the same effort he would have used to heave a large stone. "Don't talk, Curt."

"Must speak now. Our time . . . short. I'll never see Linda Leigh grow up." He shuddered with pain. "I hope she will . . . never know that I did this."

"I won't tell her and I won't let anyone else." Tears began to gather in Bette's eyes. "You just had an accident with a gun."

"Please don't tell her about Maurielle. I understand now. Dying brings everything into focus. You see . . . I saw you in Maurielle. She was beautiful and so brave. And she had suffered so. She was so frail. She needed me. I wanted to save her . . . Stupid."

Bette found that hearing the name *Maurielle* did not bring that sharp jab of pain followed by trickling acid, as it had over the previous months. And she understood what Curt had said. Yes, it was just like him. After all, he'd been her champion. She squeezed his hand, rocking back and forth in the chair with the tension of the moment.

"When Maurielle died, I saw everything so clearly then."

Curt was hoarse and trembling with the effort of speaking. "But I was a coward. I stayed in France . . . couldn't face you or our child. If Maurielle had lived, I would have . . . married her. But would it have worked out? There would have been the shame of divorce . . . There would have been a stepdaughter." His voice thin, his words poured forth, unstaunched as if he'd been saving them up for a long time. "Money would have been tight. She wouldn't have been welcome here . . . And I would have wanted to live near Linda Leigh." He began wheezing, straining for air. "So in the end, I couldn't face my own stupid mistake—my own failures . . . Not yours."

Bette turned to call for the doctor. Curt stopped her, clawed for her hand. "Please forgive me."

She leaned down and kissed him. It was like kissing one already dead. She recoiled. *No, no.* "All is forgiven. Linda Leigh will never know. I'm sorry if I've done anything that may have caused you to do this."

"Not you." He gasped for air. "Not you. Me." He drew her hand to his lips and kissed it.

She leaned over, again forcing herself to kiss his pale, cool cheek. "No more talking. All that needed to be said has been said."

He nodded and then grimaced as a pain-drenched moan escaped his lips. It hurt her to see him die like this, in so much agony and remorse. She searched for something comforting to say to him, something to give him hope. Then that day from long ago when they'd been young and so in love, attending church together came to her mind—as clear as if it had been that morning. She stroked Curt's hand and then pressed it between hers. "Do you remember all those Sundays in D.C.? How we'd go to church and then spend the day walking around and when the tourists would give us a moment, you would kiss me and hold me close?"

Curt smiled through his pain. "Yes, I was so proud . . . you were mine."

She went on recalling event after event they'd shared and she took comfort in the strained smiles that she drew from him. She could only imagine the pain that riddled his body. Then she noted he was faltering more and more. She stood and called softly, "Mother and Father, everyone, come back in."

Curt looked up at her and understood. His time was short and his parents needed to say farewell. She leaned down and whispered, "I always loved you and I always will." She took Linda from his mother and laid their baby in his arms. Then she stepped back into the shadows, letting his parents and sister hold him and weep.

Her mother and stepfather stood one on each side of her, bolstering her, showing their love. She gave them each a hand to hold and they waited, waited to hear Curt draw his last breath. Her understanding of what had happened between her and Curt had cleared. *Why is it that sometimes life only comes clear when death puffs away the mist?*

Tears flowed from her eyes. As she watched her first love pass away, it was more than flesh and blood could bear. Her heart cried out to God for strength. She had none left of her own.

Curt was buried in the churchyard two days later. To avoid the stigma of suicide, Dr. Benning cited heart failure as the cause of death. After all, he said, that was what had killed Curt. Who needed to know *why* Curt's heart had failed? And he'd sworn the medical staff to secrecy. The story was that Curt had been cleaning his service revolver and had an accident.

The funeral was well attended—a soldier had come home and then died. Others who had lost sons in the war came to comfort Curt's family and also to talk of their sons who'd been buried far from home. Curt's love affair with a French girl was forgotten.

Bette's mother held a buffet luncheon afterward at Ivy Manor. The downstairs of the old house echoed with voices as Jerusha, in uniform for the occasion, kept the buffet dishes filled, retrieved used plates, and ferried them to the kitchen. Rory and Thompson were unnaturally quiet. Curt's mother sat in the parlor, holding Linda Leigh and trying not to weep. Bette felt powerless to comfort or be comforted.

Two months later on a warm July Saturday afternoon, Bette opened the door of her white bungalow with a wide front porch and well-tended lawn in Arlington and there stood Ted, as handsome as ever. Her heart jerked and then cantered a moment, before complete shock overran her. A very pretty redhead was on Ted's arm.

Going against her pride and better judgment, Bette had gambled and invited Ted to come over. But he hadn't come alone. That thought had never even entered her mind. "Hello, Ted," she said, trying not to faint.

"Hello, yourself." He stepped inside, pulling off his fedora and dropping it on the small entryway table. "This is Julia, a secretary at Headquarters and my fiancée."

Remembering to draw breath, Bette forced her frozen face to bend into a smile. "Julia, best wishes." Her throat was so dry she nearly gagged on the words.

Julia thanked her and managed to flash her tasteful diamond engagement ring.

"So this is your new house?" Ted said, looking around.

"Yes, I just moved in this week." Bette wished there was some polite way to end this now. But of course, there wasn't. She'd invited him. He'd brought along his . . . fiancée. It was over between them. She'd lost Ted.

And I have no one to blame but myself. I was a fool and evidently I still am or I've would have taken him at his word.

She couldn't think of another thing to say aloud. Or rather she couldn't think of a thing she'd be allowed to say. She longed to say, "Ted, I love you. I know that now. Please give me another chance."

"I was—I'm sorry to hear about Curt passing." Ted didn't look at her as he said this phrase she'd heard too many times already.

"Yes," Julia added, holding Ted's arm casually but possessively. "Ted told me about you losing your husband. And you've got a little girl, too. It must be awful."

Bette tried to look appropriately appreciative of their sympathy. Evidently, Julia was the kind of woman Ted wanted. Julia certainly looked like the type most men wanted. And Julia would be no trouble to Ted.

Not like me. Ted's words came back to her: *"Do you know how long I've loved you?"*

It's too late. He said so and I should have accepted that.

Ted sauntered into the dining-living room of the bunga-low. "Where's your little girl? I want to meet her."

Bette led them to the small nursery next to her bedroom. In a pink romper, Linda was just making baby wake-up noises and kicking the slats of her oak crib as she stared at the bunny decals on the headboard.

"She's cute," Ted said. He gathered up the yawning baby and held her close. "Hello, Linda Leigh. I'm Ted."

Bette was suddenly transfixed by the sight of Ted grinning at her daughter and then trailing a finger under the round baby chin. She nearly reached out to brush her fingers over his golden hair. She jerked herself back to reality. "I better take her. She'll need changing. My nanny has the weekend off."

"I'm an uncle," Ted said. "You never knew that, did you?"

"No, I didn't," Bette said.

"Oh, Ted, I didn't know you liked babies," Julia cooed, looking over his shoulder. "I want us to have at least four."

Bette felt defeat overtaking her. She'd gambled and lost. The rest of the brief visit passed in a haze of yearning and de-spair. Then she was smiling painfully and closing the door as Julia called back, "Thanks for inviting us. You have a lovely little baby. 'Bye!"

Holding Linda close, Bette walked to the rocking chair beside the small fireplace and sat down. "Well, it's just you and me, kid."

Using the word *kid* unleashed a rush of memories of Ted. Bette sucked in tears and rocked Linda. She began humming softly to comfort her baby—or was it for herself?

Arlington, Virginia, September 1947

Bette stepped into the elevator at the CIA offices and nearly choked with shock. Ted stood nonchalantly inside. The door closed, sealing them inside, alone and together, going down. A sudden hope that he'd come to see her blossomed. "Hi," she managed to say. "What brings you here?"

Ted looked her over thoroughly, giving away nothing. "Running an errand for the Chief. We picked up some information we thought Souers should know." He paused, then shrugged. "How's the baby?"

"Fine," she forced out the single word. *Why did you think he'd come looking for you?* "How's Julia?"

"Fine."

They lapsed into silence. The elevator descended, taking Bette's mood down with it. Staring at the closed elevator doors, she was hit with a desperate ache to tell this man that she loved him. But he remained detached, obviously unwilling to treat this meeting as anything more than casual. Miserable, afraid she might blurt out her feelings, she clamped her jaw shut. Her heart was rioting inside her. Words bounced around her head, wanting to get out, to speak the truth.

It was impossible to contain them. As the elevator reached ground floor, Bette gave in to the yearning she'd fought for too long. Her heart overflowing with feeling, she turned to Ted. The doors hushed open and he started to leave her. She whispered, "Ted, I love you."

He showed no sign he'd heard her. Bette's hope died as he lifted a hand and waved good-bye, strolling away without looking back.

She remained frozen in place as strangers entered the elevator. She rode back up with them, standing stiff and straight, concealing her utter desolation. When she finally reached the haven of her office, she stood and gazed at the patch of blue sky outside her window. *Just keep breathing*, she told herself. *Just go on living. And someday each breath won't slice your heart.*

She'd told Ted she loved him. And he hadn't cared.

CHAPTER TWENTY

Virginia, December 1947

*O*n Saturday afternoon, Bette heard the doorbell peal and walked through the living room to answer it. Knee-high, Linda staggered after her, still unsteady in her newest skill: walking. Bette opened the door to a Christmas tree. "What?" she exclaimed, trying to see who was holding it.

"It's me." Ted's face peered around the deep green boughs.

Shock jolted through Bette. "Ted?" She hadn't seen him since that September day in the elevator. "What are you doing here?"

"I would think you'd figure that out for yourself. I brought your little girl a Christmas tree."

"Oh," was all she could think to say. But of course this was something she could see Ted doing—for a friend. She forced down the thickening in her throat. *Just be pleasant. He doesn't know you still cry every night over losing him. And he doesn't need to know.*

"Let me in." He pushed through the doorway. "It's chilly out here." He had taken her by surprise—just as he'd planned.

She fell back and the prickly needles grazed her bare arms. Linda squealed.

Ted led her into the living room, where he paused and looked around. The cozy room beckoned him, calling him to sit in the wingback chair by the fire and kick off his shoes. "Where do you want it set up?"

"Ted, this is really sweet of you," she began, quelling the urge to burst into tears. "But I wasn't going to have a Christmas tree. I'll be going home to Ivy Manor for Christmas."

"No, this little sweetheart"—Ted glanced down at Linda, who was gazing up at him as if he were Santa Claus himself—"deserves a tree of her own."

"Ted, I—"

"No arguments." He leaned the tree against the wall. "Decide where you want it set up. I'll be right back in." He left her staring around trying to get a grip on her runaway emotions and trying to figure out how to make space for the large tree in the small room. This was so sweet of him, but she wished he hadn't.

Ted came in with boxes piled up in his arms. "A tree stand and lights and a few ornaments." He set the tower of boxes on the sofa. "I didn't get a lot because I thought you would want to buy some of your own." He bent down and scooped the baby up into his arms.

"Where's Julia?" Bette forced herself to ask. "Couldn't she come with you?"

"I don't know where Julia is. I don't know why I proposed to her, but the engagement didn't last three months."

Bette couldn't help herself. She burst into tears and ran to her bedroom.

Within seconds, Ted was there with Linda riding high in his arms. The baby had accepted him immediately. Such a beautiful little girl. He'd love hearing her call him Daddy.

Bette sat up on her bed, digging into her pocket for a hankie. "I'm sorry. It's just..." She didn't know what she could ascribe her outbreak of tears to that he'd buy.

"Thanks." Sitting down beside her, Ted laid the baby on her other side. And then he pulled Bette into his arms. "I hoped you wouldn't be difficult about this."

"About what?" she said to his shoulder.

"The tree is a package deal. It includes me for the rest of your life."

Bette stopped breathing and just stared at him.

"But I must stress—it's a one-time offer. We're going to put the tree in water and then drive to Maryland where we can get a license and marry all in the same day. Then we'll come back and decorate the tree to celebrate our wedding. But this is strictly a one-day offer. I'm not going to jump through any more hoops for you—"

Bette stopped his words with her lips. She let her kiss tell him her answer. And he gathered her even closer, kissing her in return. "Yes," she whispered finally. "Yes, please marry me today."

Ted gazed down at her. "You mean it? You know I would have cheerfully killed Curt for what he did to you. But all I could do was stand there and watch it happen, watch him torture you."

She hadn't realized that Ted had suffered, too. He was always so upbeat. Was it true? She pressed herself to him, craving his touch. Tears of hope, of letting go of the past, hovered only a breath away. "I might have known that you'd come up with a very strange way of proposing," she said, trying to lighten her voice.

He let himself shout a laugh of triumph and wrapped his arms tightly around her. The baby girl beside them watched him with her innocent blue eyes. *You're going to be my little girl, sweetheart.* He slid his fingers into the hair above Bette's nape and pulled her face close and kissed her. "You and I don't do things the way other people do," he whispered against her soft lips. "We're different. We're spies."

Though his lips were as persuasive as ever, Bette leaned away. His words brought her a measure of regret. Her work at the CIA had become very important to her and so crucial, she felt, to the US's future. "But I won't be a spy after we marry."

"Why not?"

He'd astounded her again. "How can that work? You'll be at the FBI in Washington. And I'll be wherever Mr. Souers sends me. And what will we do with the baby?"

"I'll work at the FBI. You'll work at the CIA." Linda fussed and he picked her up, soothing her. He held her tiny hands as she stood, swaying on his lap. "Sometimes we'll work in the field. Sometimes we'll be at base working in the office. You've already hired a good nanny for Linda Leigh, and in a pinch our girl has two—make that three—grandmothers. My mom will want a turn with her, too."

His saying "our girl" moved Bette to tears once more. She closed her eyes and thought of the past, what she had envisioned for her life. "I wanted to be a wife and mother. I dreamed of taking care of my children myself. I wanted to clip recipes and cook delicious healthy meals."

"We're not like other people," Ted interrupted. "You could have done that with Curt before 1939. But this is 1947 and you are an excellent operative. So am I. Cooking and cleaning are highly overrated."

Blinking away tears, Bette tried to put this all together in her mind. Marry and still work. It sounded too good to be true. "But will it be good for Linda Leigh?" She stroked her daughter's fine hair. "I want her to have everything."

"No one gets everything. It isn't good for them." Leaning forward around Linda, Ted kissed Bette again and again, taking his time. He'd waited so long to claim this woman and now this child. He breathed in their mingled scents—Chanel No. 5 and baby powder. He pulled away from her lips and finished, "But finally, I will get you. And you will get me. And Linda Leigh will get both of us."

Bette stared at the man who was right when he said he knew her better than any man ever had. She'd never have to lie to Ted. He'd never ask her to break a vow of secrecy. The dry, thirsty years—the war, Curt's betrayal, and almost losing Ted—were over. "I love you," she whispered.

"I love you, Bette Leigh." He slipped a ring box out of his pocket. "To seal our deal." He grinned his usual cocky grin.

Without opening it, she slipped it into her pocket. All the loneliness of the past months, past years, shivered through her like an arctic front and then shattered into ice crystals. "Kiss me, Ted." *Warm me. Love me.*

And he did.

HISTORICAL NOTE

*B*ette lived in a special time in American and world history. The rise of Hitler in Germany, Tojo in Japan, and Mussolini in Italy threatened the world's peace and freedom in a very real way. I did a great deal of research on both the plight of Jews trying to flee Germany and Nazi espionage in the 1930s in America. America was not a world power in the true sense in the 1930s and so had no previous reason to have a strong espionage for defense. FDR early recognized the Nazi threat and authorized J. Edgar Hoover and the FBI to take charge of defeating Nazi espionage. Though Hoover's reputation, later in life and history, has suffered some tarnishing, his understanding and efforts in this area were superb. Without Hoover and his FBI agents, the US would have entered the war with its enemy knowing all its military secrets. Very scary.

I dipped into history for some of my story. The plot to undermine War Department officials with a Georgetown brothel that Bette discovered actually happened. (I made up Bette and the dots.) Nazi agents with flirty blonds did travel around to defense factories and army bases and were given guided tours—until the FBI put a stop to it. A Nazi agent was killed in a Manhattan traffic accident. An American woman did uncover new ways to make invisible ink at the very real Bermuda Mail Censorship Center.

And unfortunately, the FBI didn't accept women until 1972. Susan Lynn Raley and Joanne E. Pierce were the first women FBI agents. However, the OSS, which took over espionage from the FBI during WWII, used women such as Betty MacDonald McIntosh and Virginia Hall, and so did the CIA. So while Bette had to work unofficially for the FBI, she could have been recruited by the CIA just as I described.

And though it may be hard to believe, Bette's visit to Mrs. Hoover was accurate to the period. Washington, D.C., was just a small provincial town in the 1930s. And there were no spy schools. People who showed an aptitude for espionage like Bette were recruited informally and did "on the job" training.

I also tried to portray Ilsa and Gretel's experiences accurately. It's hard to believe that someone like Senator Lundeen could abet Nazi agents with his isolationism or Breckenridge Long would actively block Jewish immigrants from coming to America in the years before Nazi Germany decided that the "final solution" to the Jews was extermination. But he did. Eleanor Roosevelt was often the one who swayed her husband not to listen to Long, who maintained that spies would be planted among the immigrants. Mrs. Roosevelt saved at least one shipload of Jews on the SS *Quanza*. Unfortunately, the SS *St. Louis* and many other ships full of immigrants were turned back to Europe and then to the death camps. Gretel's desire to immigrate to Palestine after the war was the fruition of years of Zionist fervor and the result of the Jewish frustration over the fact that no nation wanted the German Jewish immigrants—as Ilsa found out as she hunted for a visa to freedom and life.

If you'd like to read more on this exciting era, I suggest William Breuer's *Hitler's Undercover War: Nazi Espionage Invasion of the USA* and Henry L. Feingold's *The Politics of Rescue: The Roosevelt Administration and the Holocaust.*

Reading Group Guide

1. Do you have any family members who served in WWII?
   What stories have they related to you in the past? Are
   there any questions you wish you had already asked
   them? (If so, do it; their time remaining with us is short.)
   What are they?

2. Divorce is an ugly fact of our time. Contrast how it was
   handled in Bette's time and ours. Do we treat divorced
   women the same now as then? Think before you answer.

3. What was Curt's fatal or tragic flaw? How do you feel
   about his feelings for Bette and then Maurielle? What
   about his views of the perfect wife?

4. Bette was greatly influenced by both Curt and Ted. In
   what ways? Was she the better for those influences?

5. Have you ever been in a situation like Bette's, where you

had to keep secrets about your life from those you love? How did that affect you and your relationships?

6. Drake and Ilsa married in spite of their religious and cultural differences. What are the pitfalls of such a marriage and how may they be overcome—or can they be? Do you know anyone in such a marriage? How have they handled it?

7. How would America be different today if Rosie the Riveter had not gone back to the kitchen after the war?

⌐THE WOMEN OF IVY MANOR⌐

Meet the women of Ivy Manor—four
strong and independent ladies who live
and love throughout the decades of the
twentieth century. Each has experiences
unique to herself; each must learn to
grow and succeed on her own terms.

Chloe
Born in the early
days of the new century, she gives up
her old life for a new one—before
realizing that perhaps what she's
always wanted was right in front of her.

Bette
Coming into her own during World
War II, Bette learns that dreams and
expectations often change, hopefully for the better. Can
she give up her childish hopes and
embrace real life?

Leigh
A child of the civil rights movement,
Leigh lives and breathes the exploration of
new ideas and thoughts. But independence
isn't always easy, and mistakes are made.
Can she learn to accept who she is before
it's too late?

Carly
Carly longs for independence, and finds it in the
military. But when all that is stripped away, will she
realize that her sense of identity comes from within, not
from anything and anyone else?